Welcome Me to
the Kingdom

Welcome Me
to the
Kingdom

STORIES

MAI NARDONE

atlantic·*fiction*

First published in the United States of America in 2023 by Random House, an imprint and division of Penguin Random House LLC, New York.

Published in hardback in Great Britain in 2023 by Atlantic Books, an imprint of Atlantic Books Ltd.

Some stories are previously published: 'Stomping Ground' in *American Short Fiction*, 'Like Us for a Whiter You' in *Apogee*, 'English!' in *The Bridport Prize Anthology 2013*, 'Easy' (as 'Only You Farang Are So Easy to Come and Leave') in *Catapult*, 'Exit Father' in *Granta*, 'Captain Q is Dead' in *Guernica*, 'What You Bargained For' in *Kenyon Review Online*, 'The Tum-boon Brigade' in *McSweeney's Quarterly*, 'Welcome Me to the Kingdom' in *Ploughshares*, and 'Goodbye, Big E Bar' in *Vol. 1 Brooklyn*.

1 2 3 4 5 6 7 8 9

A CIP catalogue record for this book is available from the British Library.

Hardback ISBN: 9781838958299
EBook ISBN: 9781838958305

Printed and bound by CPI (UK) Ltd, Croydon CR0 4YY

Atlantic Books
An Imprint of Atlantic Books Ltd
Ormond House
26–27 Boswell Street
London
WC1N 3JZ

www.atlantic-books.co.uk

Contents

PROLOGUE   *3*

LABOR   *5*
Pea & Nam (1980)

WHAT YOU BARGAINED FOR   *22*
Rick, Nam & Pea (1980)

PINK YOUTH   *35*
Hasmah & Nam (1982)

EXIT FATHER   *51*
Ping (1985–)

PARADE   *68*
Lara, Nam & Rick (1991)

STOMPING GROUND   *88*
Benz, Tintin & Pradit (1993)

GOODBYE, BIG E BAR   *107*
Pinky & Pradit (1996)

EASY   *119*
Lara, Nam & Rick (1997)

FEASTS 132
Ping, Pinky & Pradit (1999)

CAPTAIN Q IS DEAD 147
Benz & Tintin (2000)

MAKE-BELIEVE 164
Pinky (2010)

LIKE US FOR A WHITER YOU 167
Lara & Nam (2010)

HANDSOME RED 183
Tintin (2011)

WELCOME ME TO THE KINGDOM 199
Lara & Benz (2013)

CITY OF BRASS 217
Jimmy & Ping (2016)

ENGLISH! 240
Pea & Nam (1974)

THE TUM-BOON BRIGADE 253
Benz, Tintin & Lara (2014)

Acknowledgments 275

Welcome Me to the Kingdom

Prologue

We came with the drought. From the window of the train, the rich brown of the Chao Phraya River marked the turn from the northeast into the central plains. We came for Bangkok on the delta. The thin tributaries that laced the provinces found full current at the capital. And in the city, we'd heard, the wealth was wide and deep.

The train arrived alongside trucks hauling into the outskirts, flames painted on their fenders, bumpers lined with Michelin Man dolls. The fanfare of a conquering army. And the city received us with familiar faces, celebrities we knew from Channel 7 smiling from the gauntlet of signs, promising the best in soda, soap, and gold.

We came with our own talismans—jade, bronze—protections against a city that didn't live up to our expectation: just this? In the station, no one seemed to be boarding the trains. They sat waiting, surrounded by the tourism banners. *Take Home a Thousand Smiles.* This, too, we read as a promise.

Labor

PEA & NAM (1980)

The coins Pea wouldn't spend had worried a hole through his pocket, so he was jingling them in his fist as he passed the pawn shop that sold foreign liquor by the shot. The bottles were dusty, proof of another life in some formerly rich man's cabinet.

"Always the last to go, the liquor," the old pawnbroker said to Pea. "You know when they bring the whiskey they've hit the bottom. Sell their wives first, most of them."

"This is the real stuff, right?" Pea asked. "You're not just reusing the bottles? I know the taste of Mekhong."

"You tell me."

Pea drank. "Fucking gasoline."

"It's from Kentucky, USA," the old man said, holding the indecipherable label out to Pea.

"Well, in Kentucky, USA, they must use this to run cars." Pea spread the rest of his money on the glass cabinet. "Another?"

NAM HAD GIVEN him a deadline: thirty days. That was how long he had to make them a living. Tucked in Pea's breast pocket was a page from a free Chinese calendar, the numbers smudged by sweat. Sixteen inky days already blued away by his thumb. Sixteen days since he and Nam had come down on the train together, down from the northeast to Bangkok. Since then, Nam had been staying with her last living kin, a cousin, while Pea roomed at a boardinghouse apartment with other men from the provinces, what counted to him now as family. They worked security, gardening, driving—all of it better than the wet suck of the rice paddies in the northeast, the shining white flats of the salt pans along the coast, the hot pools of the shrimp farms across the central plains. The men had traded that work for slow days and shade, for nights sharing food on the plastic mat, talking women and money, pooling their daydreams. Pea contributed what he could, except his worry for Nam. He needed her to himself. Sixteen days spent.

"Nothing, kid?" the other men asked daily of Pea, the newest among the six that shared the main room. The landlord had the bedroom, which was air-conditioned, and standing at the door Pea could feel the cool air gracing his toes. He had never seen the room, but in two weeks had come to know the life of its sounds, the frequent *ding!* of the microwave and enduring patter of a TV, which during the day ran Chinese soaps and at night porn that kept the other men awake with longing.

"He updates the video monthly," one boarder had told Pea. "But this month it's a squealer."

Pea could hear it wasn't Thai.

"French," the man said. "He likes the *farang* women." His hands cupped imaginary breasts. "Bigger, you know?"

For two weeks Pea had listened nightly to the same movie, counting down the VHS's two-hour capacity. And when he couldn't bear another performance, he forced himself outside.

Which is how he found himself, on night sixteen, hovering by a flower market, drawn there by its fluorescent sting, by the ant line of laborers shuttling huge cane baskets. There was a buyer, too, marked by his good shoes, the way he skirted puddles. Pea looked for a foreman. He was looking for work.

The market was busiest after sundown, without the daytime heat on those neat flowers in foam boxes, petals spritzed, glistening like first-world candy. Not the thorny, twisted sentinels of the up-country temple where Pea was fostered, here was something imported from a lush planet.

"China," a laborer told him. He said the blue *anchan* and white jasmine buds were local, but the roses and orchids came from abroad.

Pea said he needed work. Anything.

The man gestured. "That's the boss in the blue."

Soon after, Pea began a hard night lugging flowers by the kilo and basket from truck bed to stalls, bearing supplies for the wreath-makers—two lines of women with pincers for fingers threading jasmine buds onto long needles. When he finished that, the foreman had him packing ice. He was the only worker without a cart to trundle the weight, so Pea managed on his back alone.

At the end of the night he stood at attention before the boss, heels together. He wanted to look tidy, fresh, but his hands were blue from the iceboxes, left shoulder soaked where it had borne the ice sacks. The man counted out Pea's pay twice, rubbed each bill between his fingers and splayed them on the table.

Pea picked up the bills and made a show of looking around the room. "How much are you paying these men?" he asked, gesturing.

"Don't worry, boy. You're all paid the same."

Pea divided his money and laid half of it back on the table. "Yeah, well, I'll work twice as hard as them for half the pay if you'll hire me full-time."

"How old are you?"

"Twenty," Pea lied. He could barely pass for the eighteen he actually was, but the man gave him the work anyway.

On his way out of the warehouse Pea saluted the laborer who had first ushered him in. Then he tucked a vine of bougainvillea under his shirt for Nam. Only, by the time he got them to her, the papery flowers had turned to pulp in his palms. She liked them, she assured him.

"Let's have breakfast at that stall you like," he said. "My treat."

The sun had risen by now, but the city buildings, wreathed in smog, eclipsed the show. He paid extra for one egg each to stir into the murk of their porridge. "Flowers like you've never seen before," he told Nam. "The expensive ones they keep in refrigerators, like food."

She twined the bougainvillea in her fingers and picked at her porridge.

Pea shook white pepper into his, then vinegar and soy sauce. He offered her the condiments. "No? You want it plain like that?"

She wasn't hungry.

"But eat the egg at least." He didn't want to remind her of the price of food. Three weeks into the monsoon season and still no rain. Even in Bangkok people looked hopefully at the clear skies.

"You look tired," he said.

She had been dragging this mood around ever since they arrived, by turn worried or distant. She asked about his fellow boarders and he passed her details, never mentioning the landlord. Not that Nam wasn't used to him relaying sex talk. The lives of temple boys back in the northeast *was* sex talk. Nightly the boys paraded past the one sex bar on their side of town, a karaoke place with tinted windows and an English sign: *Happy 2 You*. Thumping and hooting, the boys would romp by, tripping one another in front of the door, hoping it might swing in as they passed. But that was different. Those women were locals. The landlord's taped women were white, and Pea couldn't say why, but the videos were to him somehow a violation.

"Is it your cousin?" Pea asked. "You staying up to watch TV with him?"

"There's a job he wants me to take. It's good money."

Pea swallowed. He pulled the calendar page from his pocket. "You promised thirty days." He circled the number with his finger. "I can take care of us."

"It's not enough, though, is it? It's not enough to live in this city."

"It *will* be. See how fast this place is changing?"

He took Nam's bowl from her and stacked it over his empty one. "If you're just going to waste this, *I'll* eat it. Look, just give me time with the job. Who knows what kind of work that cousin wants to find you."

"I know," she said.

"Except you don't. You don't understand." His job was a beginning for them, and he wanted her to see that it was good.

That night he brought her to the flower market.

"Hey!" Pea gestured over to his coworker. "This is my girlfriend."

Nam was distant; she wouldn't enter the warehouse.

"I don't know." She held his arm but pulled away. "I'll get you in trouble."

"I'm not even on duty yet. Look at these." They were flanked by the red eyes of a hundred roses. "Just buds, see, but soon they'll bloom." He pulled one free of its newspaper bunch. "Here. For you! Oh, watch the thorns, ha ha!"

"Are these from China?"

"I think so. Take it home. Or take a whole bunch for your cousin. Here—"

"No, don't waste the money."

"It's free. Don't worry. The boss likes me and he lets me take things home. These will wilt soon, anyway. And then they'll just throw them away. Isn't that funny? They come all this way just to live a few days."

Every morning that week, returning from the warehouse at sunrise, Pea brought Nam stolen flowers. Like a bird adding strips of cotton, foam, twigs, and newspaper to a nest, Pea made his best effort to construct their new life.

Every morning he counted his pay and turned the number in his head, waiting for Nam's cousin to leave for work. The man didn't know about Pea. The cousin was unmarried, but the young maid Nam shared the back room with was loyal, and she reported everything back to him.

The next day Pea brought the maid an attar of roses to perfume her clothes. She liked that, this maid who didn't seem to work but spent her days reclined on her bunk. She was gone most nights.

"A boyfriend?" Pea had asked Nam once, but she didn't say.

Pea cut the noses from plastic soda bottles to make suitable vases for his gifts: hibiscus, gardenia, a jasmine wreath. "Aren't they beauti-ful?" he asked, and the maid said yes, beautiful. Nam said nothing. She picked at the Pepsi label.

Didn't she like them?

"*I* think it's romantic," the maid said.

Nam let the plants accumulate and then decay, as if to prove a point. What point, though? Soon the bedroom was looking like a carnival, twisted creatures crusting across the dresser, curling on shelves and, in the warped and cracked mirror, multiplying into a kaleidoscope of faded, darkened color. The vase water thickened aw-fully. The room was behind the kitchen, and in the heat the scent invaded the cooking area, infusing the food. The steam rising from the rice cooker had the fragrance of decayed vanilla orchids, and the smell of old needle flowers clung to the dishware like a dank nectar.

Nam's cousin complained. But Pea did not need to be told to stop. By the end of the week, on their twenty-second day in Bang-kok, he was out of work.

So, Pea, what have you done now? Nam would say. *It's your attitude,* she would tell him.

"That boy's temper," the elders back home had bemoaned again and again. "He'd better grow out of it." The temple's older foster boys had even tried to beat it out of him.

"How about we fill that big mouth of yours." They scooped ma-nure from the mounds of fertilizer and came after him.

Or they would pin him at the shower bucket and take turns hold-ing him under, saying, "All you have to do is cry 'Bingo!' Got, it? *What's* that? Want us to *stop*? Bingo!" Pea writhed and coughed, but never pleaded. One night they came at him while he toyed with his new cigarette lighter, an American Zippo. Before they could grab his wrists, Pea used the hot metal to brand a boy's cheek.

"Who the fuck *does* that?" They backed away.

"Bingo," Pea said.

The head monk laughed when he heard about it. "Too much *Die Hard*."

The monk beat the boy but let him keep the lighter. Pea had seen the wrong lesson in his prize: fight.

THE OTHER MEN were asleep when Pea returned to the shared room the night he lost his job. He drummed his fingers on the water kettle, thirsty, wanting a clean drink now.

His inky fingerprints seemed to collect everywhere these days. Blue on the bathroom tap, blue on the hem of his shirt. An absent stain on his lip. When one boarder complained, Pea held himself back from marring that man's face, too. Now he had marked the kettle.

The apartment window faced a narrow *soi* where the dawn vendors were already setting up. Below, a woman was preparing the first batch of fried dough, and the sound of the batter striking the hot oil carried up to Pea, reminding him of eating at the stalls back home. Why had he even come to this city?

The foreman's words echoed in his head. "I don't think we have room for you, after all." He said he didn't need a boy who couldn't keep his mouth shut. There were others waiting for work, still coming off the trains and buses, brought in by the drought. But Pea hadn't come because of the drought; he'd come for Nam.

He hadn't hesitated in following her to the city after her father, her only immediate family, had died. Both Pea and Nam came from small families. A house was never meant to be held up by a single pillar, and when Nam's father died, everything had quickly come down.

He went to find her, walking by way of a fresh market. It wasn't quite dawn. Men were unloading the day's produce: fish in green baskets that leaked over the sidewalk, sagging pork already being sliced for the first customers. He bought a bag of soy milk and approached the flower vendor.

"You have any old stuff?" he asked.

The woman didn't seem to understand him. He often had to repeat himself with these Bangkok people, their bland way of speaking utterly unlike his own.

"Anything? Any scraps?"

She didn't.

"Well, how about this bunch?" He gestured to a small display of flowers. "These are local, right?" Not that he could afford them. When he said it was his aunt's funeral, that he wouldn't show up empty-handed, she relented and gave him a pair of lilies.

Pea was on the sidewalk of Nam's *soi,* deciding whether to sneak up to her room, when he saw the maid stumble off a bus. She braced a hand on the shophouse's curtained gate as she removed her heels with two violent kicks.

"Hey." He touched her shoulder.

"Shit!" She stepped back against the gate, her shock rattling the metal. "Pea? *Scared* me there. The fuck. Coming at me out of the dark like that?"

Pea didn't speak. The maid's dress was short and black, the bottom crumpled and flaring unevenly. She looked down and flattened the fabric against her thighs.

"So, uh, you waiting for Nam?"

"You're dressed like a whore," he said plainly. "Is this how your boyfriend likes to see you?"

She blinked for a moment. Then she raised her hand and, with her pinkie, carefully edged back her eyelashes.

"Right." She bent to loop her wrist through her heel straps before turning to the padlock on the gate. The dress revealed her back all the way down to the dimples of her spine. Pea brushed his knuckles down the naked skin.

The maid hesitated with the key. She turned to face him. "I'll tell her you're out here, but you can't wait in front of the shophouse."

He knew already what Nam's reaction would be: *What have you done, Pea?*

"No. Here, take this." The nodding lilies. "Tell her I was here with the flowers. Tell her I'm working a double shift."

HE MISSED THE open country. Back home you could see where you were going. Here, the city led the way, forcing turns onto streets flanked by, it seemed, the same shophouses he had already passed. Every pawn shop was built like a prison and every gold store had paid a policeman to stand nearby. Inside, the gold chains seemed to cascade from the walls where they hung. He asked about security guard jobs. He was a good worker. He even knew some English, and said as much to a travel agency hiring a receptionist. They laughed, though, when he demonstrated; they said country boys can't even speak Thai properly. Said he had a way of standing too close. Back up.

That was his problem with the whole city. It was too close to see all of it. He wanted to reach out and grasp it, just . . . hold it still for a moment.

A Chinese neighborhood. The buildings wore the familiar wooden shutters he hadn't seen much here in Bangkok. Another way the city wasn't quite right. He tried to think about perspective, think like a city person, what the monks back home had drilled into him through countless iterations of their precious few lessons. Pea remembered the routine: a monk would improvise with recent headlines, saying, "What accounts for those ten-wheelers colliding head-to-head on the Khon Kaen ring road? Lack of perspective."

"I hear it's because the drivers are all on *ya ba*," some smart-ass would say from the back. "And then when they come down they fall asleep at the wheel."

Ignoring the boy, the monk would walk the novices to a window looking out to the rows of rubber trees behind the old dorm. The four glass squares made a neat grid, except each pane was warped.

A question that was actually a statement: "Which pane shows us reality."

Surely, there was a moral to this. After the others had been absorbed back into their temple duties, Pea returned to the window. He brought his eye to each pane, trying to divine an answer for himself.

Eventually he took to skipping the temple's homegrown education. He searched out his own learning by walking. He told himself stories. Spy games, war tales, Chinese epics. He looked with envy into shop fronts and found his mood mirrored in the faces of idle servers, barbers who, like him, could do nothing but wait.

When Nam returned from school, Pea would meet her at her house. She often shared her notes from school, but he grew impatient, frustrated by his own stalled education. And so he always interrupted her.

"But you wouldn't believe what I've seen today," he'd say.

And when she said, "What've you seen, Pea?" he would tell her his stories, invite her to visit his otherworld.

Their favorite place that he'd discovered was the swimming pool. It was the only finished structure in a sports club that had been recently abandoned. The pool was deep and bare, tiled over in a winking blue. They climbed down the ladder and dropped into the deep end. When the rainy season came the pool would be lost to them, turned forever into a reservoir, making its welcoming, dry depths more precious now.

Sitting against the pool wall in the late afternoon, they were shaded to their ankles, all the way to Nam's modest school socks that were folded over three times. Always three—Pea had watched her don them.

They played a game. Nam made the rules, but never seemed to follow them herself. They threw stones and removed clothes. It never went further, though, than Pea's underwear and Nam's skirt, which was fine. It was her naked back he coveted—the slight contortion of her shoulder blades as she pulled off her blouse.

Afterwards, as they dressed, Nam would count the items of clothing removed. "Five."

And when he took her home, they sometimes stopped to a buy a lottery ticket. "Something ending in five," she advised.

———

Pᴇᴀ ᴘᴀᴜsᴇᴅ ᴛᴏ scan the lottery tickets on a street-side vendor's tray, but he didn't like the numbers. He walked through boys playing soccer on a side *soi,* kicking the ball off cars to complete their passes. He cataloged everything he saw so as to try and convey these impressions to Nam, over dinner, as he made his usual assessment of the food.

"Old fish paste, crumbly rice, clumped sugar. Everything's a little off. It's the whole city." They were in a shophouse near her cousin's house. Pea laid down his spoon with finality and washed his mouth out. "And the water tastes like salt." He held the cup out to her.

"You're imagining it."

He sucked his lips. "Yup, salt."

"I didn't see you this morning," she said.

The day was over and he still hadn't found work. "Yeah, they had me take an extra shift."

"Wait, let me pay this time," Nam said. "I have the money."

"Money from where?"

"My cousin gave it to me."

He turned away while the vendor made change.

"Why's he giving you money?"

"I helped clean the upstairs." She had spread her fried rice across the plate. Now she ran her spoon through it, turning it up like turf.

"You're not a maid. I hope your cousin knows." Pea grasped her hand, stilling the spoon's progress. "Okay? You're not a maid."

She put down the spoon and clasped his hand.

He cupped her cheek in his other palm and she leaned into it. Then he ran his thumb in a line beneath her eye, inadvertently pulling the skin and making her flinch. His nail came away shaded with charcoal.

"Who asked you to put makeup on?"

She jerked back. "Stop."

"*You* stop. I saw the maid this morning, all dolled up."

She dipped a napkin into her glass and wiped the color from her eyes. She folded over the stain, then wiped again with a clean side.

"It's nothing. I'm just trying it out."

"Don't lie to me."

Nam looked directly at him, the charcoal around her eyes smudged.

"I can't talk to you when you're like this." She rose from the table and dropped the napkin into her glass.

He didn't follow her, but remained where he was, watching the paper napkin bloom in the water.

A MONSOON WAS rolling in from the Philippines. In the corner-store TV the storm was a red wound over the belly of the globe. At least it would break the heat that had the migrants churning—nobody at the apartment was getting sleep.

"And this new porn actually has a story," one of them was saying as Pea returned. "Which is somehow even worse. All talk."

"Where've you been, kid?" another said to Pea.

"Don't touch me." Pea shrugged off the man's hand. He felt surrounded. The apartment was like a mousetrap.

"Hey! That's all right. It's no problem."

"Hush now." Two of the men were huddled outside the landlord's door. "Kid, you came back for the right night. Quiet now or we'll miss it."

Pea went to stand over them. "What is it?" He heard the woman's throaty, steady gasps, a repetitive smacking.

He was about to retreat when the sound suddenly cut as the speakers exploded into the national anthem, a swelling chorus of singers, a sound that returned the boarders to boyhoods spent lined up on the cracked concrete of schoolyards. It returned them to schoolboy grins and a muffled laughter that broke their cluster, had them shaking as the TV was abruptly switched off.

One man held Pea by the shoulder, barely holding back his laughter. "I recorded over the tape this morning. How about that? You'll

sleep tonight, huh? Now don't tell me we don't take care of one another."

It was this man who sent Pea, the following evening, in the direction of a job.

"Old man Gui's generous," Pea was told. "He's been helping kids
a long time."

The man turned out to be a fried-chicken vendor, work-worn, his
body chewed to the bone. His shirt was unbuttoned, and whatever
weak substance a tattooist had used on the man's chest had gone faint
now, appearing gangrenous, like a sickness laying its roots in the
man's ribs.

"I'm looking for work."

Seeming to recognize Pea as one of his own, an Isaan boy, the man
perched on the motorbike attached to his cart. Pea could smell the
chicken that was spitting in the deep fryer.

"You and everyone else who came in from the country." The man
lifted a drumstick from his tray and offered it to Pea. "Go on."

It was still hot. The rich oil filled Pea's mouth, but the texture was
wrong.

"Mix the rice flour with baking soda to lighten it up. It'll make it
crispier."

The man studied Pea. "You think so?"

"And your cuts?" Pea turned the drumstick to display the gouges.
"They're too deep. The meat loses its bite."

The man held out a bag for the bone. "How long you been here?"

Pea swallowed and unfolded his calendar page. The oil from his
finger made a clear circle of the number. "Twenty-five days."

"You look sturdy enough."

The man said Pea could work as a night guard. He led Pea to the
warehouse where he would keep watch over street carts, which at
day's end were wheeled in by the vendors.

"You line the carts facing that wall, in rows. Morning carts go in
last. The vendors will tell you."

"Doesn't seem that hard."

"It's not," the old man snapped. "You think people want to steal food carts? You're here in case it floods when the rain finally comes. It's happened before, so don't wander."

Midday sun cut into the space through a hole in the ceiling as Pea walked along the wall.

"What is this place?"

"A movie theater. Can't you see that?"

The room was all decay. Termites had chewed through everything, even the sound insulation. Pea ran his nail up the laced wood, imagining he could hear it, the insects' crunching, the sound of a city feeding upon itself.

"But what happened to it?"

"It closed." The man looked at Pea closely. "Can't you see that?"

"Must've been sad when it happened."

"This isn't the only one. If you don't find a way in this city, you're gone. Doesn't matter if you're rich, either. I've seen rich go poor." He led Pea back up the ramp. "You find them everywhere. Those dancing clubs. Some of them barely opened a year. Now? A parking lot. Soon, a mall. Or McDonald's. That man's buying everywhere."

WHEN PEA RANG the bell this time it was Nam's cousin who approached. Pea realized he had never called on her in the evening. He had come to tell her about the job.

The cousin was tall and thick with shoe-polish-black hair. Even his eyebrows seemed to have been unnaturally inked. He parted the metal gate.

"Who are you?"

"I'm looking for Nam."

"And what do you want with her?"

"Just to talk to her." Pea looked beyond the man.

"She left already. She's working."

"Working where?"

"And who are you?" Her cousin came forward now, filling the opening he had made. He stood over Pea, the padlock heavy in his fist. "Hey? You looking for trouble?"

Before the cousin could advance again, Pea shoved him back against the gate, which slid aside as the man tried to catch himself but fell to the ground. Pea came forward, putting his weight on the man's wrist. He felt it crack underfoot.

Pea took the padlock and hefted it. He considered its weight.

Pea stepped back, releasing the spongy wrist. He slid shut the gate but kept hold of the padlock, never looking away from the man now cradling his arm.

THE DRINK CARTS were the heaviest, the jangling bottles of syrup all stocked full, making a deadweight of this thing on wheels. When he lost his grip on the ramp, Pea nearly ran himself over. The men he worked with were polite but weary. When they finished their work they didn't linger, and soon Pea was alone. Wasn't this what he'd wanted?

Only now that he was alone, the question was unavoidable: Was Nam's cousin lying about her working? Pea was afraid he might not be. Finished with the cigarette he had salvaged from a food cart, he drifted off to sleep thinking about those four windowpanes from his boyhood, and the glass-warped trees beyond them.

He woke with his fingers still clipped around the cigarette stub, from which emanated a sticky, black dread. It was finally raining outside. He could hear it on the roof of the theater and there was a dark puddle at the entrance. But that wasn't what woke him.

Nam looked stark under the one fluorescent tube he had on, a bulb webbed to a cart by its own wires.

"Your roommates sent me here."

He pictured her at the apartment, the clustered migrants, a woman's moan looping behind the landlord's bedroom door.

Nam could read him. "They were polite."

"This is where I work now." He felt the need to explain this, but she walked away from him to the back where some seats were still bolted to the floor in ranks. She let her fingers brush the brass number on one of the arms.

Pea stood up and followed her, pointing up at the movie posters high on the walls. "These are actually hand-painted."

"*Battle of the Bulge,*" Nam read. "*Cleopatra.* I can't make out this name, though. *Doctor . . .*" She trailed off.

She looked at him again. "The rivers are so low, my cousin told me, the seawater's backing up into the delta, into the pipes. That's why the hose water is salty. They're using it to wash dishes and cups. You were right," she said. "I know that's important to you."

"Your cousin . . ."

"His wrist is broken."

Pea sat down again. "You know why."

"*What* do I know?"

"What work has he forced you into?"

She moved to stand before him. She took his face in her hands, gingerly, as if laying her palms on a hot surface, and turned his chin up to her.

"What work?" she asked.

"You know."

"You won't even say it. So how can I try and talk to you about it? And it wasn't my cousin, either. He doesn't even know. It's his maid."

The maid's naked back. Her dress. Pea remained silent. Then he pulled out his calendar page.

Nam took it from him. "I can take care of us, Pea. Okay? I can do this."

She laid his head against her chest then. He clutched her, fingers plucking unconsciously at her blouse, then working the back zipper down an inch. "The old, swimming pool days," he said. "Remember? I want to go back."

Pea hadn't acknowledged this to himself until he heard his own voice speak the words. It sounded weak, and when Nam didn't respond he wanted to reclaim them. But what could he tell her in their place? He had prepared his stories.

"You know what I've seen today . . ." he began.

"What've you seen, Pea?"

His first aerial view of Bangkok from a futsal pitch on a dormitory roof. The owner of the herbal remedies store doing lunges behind her store counter. A bleached-blond woman on a bicycle, hair lit up by oncoming headlights.

He couldn't tell her. He knew she had prepared her story, too, and didn't want her to tell him yet. So he stared up at a movie poster. A woman in gold reclined between two men.

"Tell me about this film," he said. "What's it about?"

She saw what he couldn't.

"Power."

What You Bargained For

RICK, NAM & PEA (1980)

Women are meant to be Thai. That's what your buddy Phil told you before you flew over from the States and became the man you'd sworn you'd never be, sitting at this bar with a woman—no, a girl—you want to describe as a flower. Not because she's pretty—she isn't really—but because of the way she leans toward you with an open face as painted up as a false rose, glistening under a sheen of moisture, a red mouth widening in a way that reminds you of what's between her legs.

"Her" being your wife. You haven't slept with anyone but Mary since you were seventeen. Twenty-five years. That's fidelity, you told yourself during the divorce last year, when you were peeking down the shirt of your daughter's friend as the girls did push-ups in the garage. Her breasts hung down in points. You toyed with the idea of them over you, over your lips.

"Juicy," Phil says on your left, eyeing a girl in a green Heineken minidress.

"Steaks are juicy, Phil. Not people."

Phil puts a hand on your shoulder and kneads his thumb into your collarbone.

"Rick, look where we are. Why'd we come to Bangkok?"

He's right. This is exactly what you came for. This bar-lined street. Its drinking holes extending right out onto the sidewalk, so that you're sharing your space with passing motorbikes and drunks stumbling in the gutter. A fluorescent palm blazes above you. The metal stool between your legs scrapes the pavement as you shift, and you keep shifting because Nam—the flower beside you, now fingering the ice in her drink—has her knees pressed into your leg. Is *this* what you came here for? You notice the splotches beneath her eyes. She looks up at you and smiles.

"*That's* what you came for," Phil coaxes with a grin. "My friend here's a little quiet," he tells Nam. He takes her hand and slaps it down on your leg. "So you'll have to do the talking, sweetheart, *khao chai*? It's his first night."

But this is all it takes—just this. A year from now, at your wedding, Phil will drunkenly recount this night. "So there's our damsel, Rick, getting his lights punched out by some Thai kid when this beauty here steps in to save him. She even taught him to dance. I remember the moves. Awful," he'll say, resurrecting your heel-shuffling for the wedding reception. You'll insist on the church, even though those God-granted bonds hardly held for your first marriage.

"You like dancing?" Nam's hand is still planted on your leg.

"I can't. You'd laugh."

"Like him?" She indicates a man larger than you who is keeling from side to side like a rowboat. Nam mimics his gait on her barstool, rocking her head between her shoulders. She laughs. "Come on, dance with me."

You shake your head, make excuses. You say you don't even know the tune—something thumping out of Nam's generation. *Christ, Rick, she's nineteen. Your daughter's age.* That's if she's telling you the truth. And nobody's telling you the truth. Not your daughter, Sam, who had known about the other man, and certainly not your wife. What did you expect? That's what Mary told you—"What did you expect?"—when you found the condom floating in the toilet, pink and still slimy in your fingers when, in your shock, you picked it up. *Not my dick,* you thought, sizing up your competition. Had she put it on for him, you wondered.

"You like Bangkok?" Nam says.

What do you even know about Bangkok? So far, you've seen the inside of a mall and this street. You're jet-lagged. It's morning on the East Coast, completely and utterly the wrong time to be out. You pick up Nam's hand and lay it gently on the bar.

"Is this where you're from?" You make a twirling motion with your finger. "Well, not *here*, this street, but, you know, Bangkok?"

Nam smiles.

Try again. "Bangkok. Are you from Bangkok?"

"No," she says. "My home in Udon Thani."

"Right." Though, where is that? You've heard of Phuket, the beach you're headed to next week. You turn to Phil, but he's trying to explain the plot of some movie to the girl in his lap—"And he's a real slugger, know what I mean?"—so instead you sip your whiskey.

Nam takes your hand. Unexpected. Raises it like you're about to make a vow.

"Bangkok," she says, pressing her finger into the meat of your palm, somewhere near the bottom where hand joins wrist. "In Thai called Krung Thep."

You repeat this.

She traces her finger up the palm, racing northeast, across the callused expanse from your rowing days. You're ticklish. The skin flinches. She moves up the pinkie of your splayed fingers.

"Udon Thani. My home." She pinches the finger at its tip.

"How about Phuket? I'm going next week."

Back down the length of the country, through Bangkok, south, southwest, onto your wrist, lower, tracing the blue rivers below the skin. She stops halfway down your forearm.

"*Koh* Phuket. Island." She looks at you. Coyly, "I go with you?"

Swell idea. Or . . . not. Reclaim your hand.

"Maybe." You're drunk. "My daughter's your age, you know."

"What her name?"

"Nineteen this year. Samantha."

Nam tilts her head. "If I go America, I be friend with Samantha?"

God, no.

Nam puts your hand on her bare knee. Her legs have these tiny hairs, and when your hand moves against them it feels like someone's breathing on your palm. When was the last time you touched something that smooth? Mary's belly? At eighteen maybe, and in the last months of her pregnancy with Sam, the taut flesh like a great tent roof.

Beneath the skin, you think you can sense Nam's pulse. You're remembering what Mr. Jobson told you back in high school biology, about where you can feel the body's beat: wrist, neck, elbow crook, the fold behind the knee, the warm place between the legs. So you start touching with your fingers, not a stroke, softer, the way you used to touch Sam in her crib after she'd screamed herself to sleep, laying two fingers across the cushion of her cheek, a curl of spit drying around your fingertips.

You always saw more of Mary in Sam—Mary's boxy teeth, the way she slept with an eye peeking open, a white crescent that watched you through the night. She's got Mary's rolling temper, too. You were reminded of that last Christmas when she shut the front door on you, as if the divorce had been *your* fault. She didn't even take the present—an Arthur Conan Doyle collection from your childhood along with a tuition check, so she could reenroll at college—which was the only reason you were even there. You certainly hadn't planned to stay. Of course not. Just far enough into the foyer to see the tree all lit. You hesitated, thinking how stupid it was to knock on what was, after all, your own door.

Your hand has stopped at the hem of Nam's skirt. You're poised to go farther, to breach the door, but also to take your hand back, heft the Christmas gift under your arm and return to the car. You teeter on the brink.

Nam scoots forward until you're under her skirt without even trying.

Oh.

She picks up her glass and takes the straw in her mouth.

"You like Thai woman?" Her knees squeeze together, pinching your wrist, an encouragement to get closer. Go on. Her knee against your arm. You think about those knees around your back. Young, strong, embracing your waist. The tendons tight against your side. You'll feel those legs tonight, in your hotel room, when you'll also discover that she's never had sex.

In your head: What kind of bar girl—no, never mind. How will you know? Not the blood—she was forced to pop that herself, as she'll tell you much later, squatting in a black toilet reaching up inside. It'll be her eyes: afraid of you. It will make you think about your size, the swell of your stomach looming over her like a pale moon.

You'll recall the first time with Mary, and how afterwards you sat on the car hood watching the moon rise, the soft pink glow on the ocean's horizon ballooning in your memory. Mary was right beside you, sitting up against the car windshield wearing your t-shirt. Your jeans piled on boots nearby, and, farther off, your belt, in the bush where Mary had tossed it. Her body stretched into the view: the dimpled muscle of her legs, the gloss on her toenails. You fell in love with her languid confidence, the sense that she was strutting even while just lying still. That evening, it had been enough to make you come out with some stale line about her, the sun, you in orbit. Only, Mary shook her head. "No, nothing so cosmic," she said. "We could be anybody, really."

When you remember this you'll stop. Your knees will sink into the hotel bed. You'll stare at Nam's dark face below you, like a stain on the sheets. Her curry sweat. The slight sour between her legs. What are you doing? You'll say it aloud, to yourself; only, Nam will think it's her. She'll blink, then apologize. She'll shift beneath you and fold her legs so you slip out. She'll hide her face from you.

"I'm sorry." You slip off your barstool. You're going back to the hotel. To the States.

Nam stands, too. She's worried. She looks over her shoulder.

"Please." She catches your hand. "Where you go?"

"Home."

You see Phil dancing inside the bar. He's laughing, lifting a girl against his chest as if he means to make off with her, dance her into the horizon for the fairy-tale finish that you have twice been promised. Once by your wife on the day you were married, and again by Phil when he invited you out here.

"Why Bangkok?" you had asked when you met up to celebrate the divorce.

"Life is cheap. We could live like kings."

But it was too far from Sam.

"Oh, you love your fucking women so much," Phil said. "Look, you want women? We'll find you some."

And that's what Phil's found, all right, that girl with her swollen look, like bleeding fruit heavy on its branch. Phil saw Sam only once, a couple of years after she was born. "Kids are anchors, you know? Around your feet. You're up here right now," he said, drawing a line at his neck, "but for the rest of your life you can expect to sink." You and Mary laughed about it afterwards. You never invited him back to the house, only meeting him out at bars every couple weeks.

"I just keep him around to remind me what I would be without you," you told Mary, when she asked why you wasted time on that creep.

Phil's still dancing. He doesn't hear you shout his name.

"Why you go?" Nam asks. On her feet she's smaller. The dress loosens around her, pulls at her shoulders so that she looks like one of those Japanese cartoon characters made up of all lengths and no girth.

"Stay with me."

You know it's a production-line comment, just another gear in the works of what these girls are taught. It's also what you said to Mary after you found the condom. Unlike your wife, you've never had the conviction to walk away.

You sit back down, making sure there's an entire barstool between

the two of you. And maybe it's worked. She's lost that confident ve-
neer, that pin-on twinkle.

"A year ago my wife found another man," you say as Nam pours
your drink. "Right in time for our big anniversary, too, you know?
Twenty-five years. Can you believe it? Empires have crumbled in less."

"Yes," Nam says.

"Enough time to pay off a goddamn mortgage. And what do I
have to show for it?" You empty the glass. "A lying, college dropout
of a daughter." You wave away at the air in front of Nam. "No, actually, that's not fair. It's not Sam's fault. I was the one who told her if
she moved in with her mom I'd cut her college funding. So then she
left school. Look how *that* turned out."

Nam's eyes are fixed on your extended hand.

"You don't even understand me, do you?"

In a small voice: "I understand."

"No you don't."

You have to stretch across the empty seat between you. A jagged
kiss. Half lip, half cheek. Their mouths are so damn small, these Thai
women.

Their hips, too, thankfully. You'll always be able to wrap Nam's
waist in the crook of your arm. Not like Mary. One Thanksgiving
you made a joke about Mary easing off the pumpkin pie. "You all
should have seen the woman I actually married. I mean, wow."

Mary had turned to the table with that bizarre smile of hers—
teeth that didn't meet, more like a grimace. She gave a small laugh as
if to say, *What can you do?*

"Jesus, Dad," Sam said. "Why do you have to be such an asshole?"

That Thanksgiving night, as Mary changed by the bed, you
pressed your chest into her back and bunched her stomach in your
fist.

"Some things that stretch don't go back," Mary said, referring to
the difficulties she had with Sam's birth. You told her that she wasn't
being fair, that it was a joke.

"That's the thing, Rick." She unclasped your hand and stepped out of reach, but red fingerprints clung to her rumpled skin. "You're always making jokes."

YOUR MOUTH IS still on Nam when it comes: the cheap shot, the punch that knocks you out of your seat. At first you think you've just slipped off your stool. That the ground itself gave in. But no, you realize, palm against the thumping of your temple. You stare up at the Thai boy who has punched you. Young, Nam's age. His eyes are bloated and red. Teeth clenched. Teeth that you can smell, suddenly, as he throws his weight on you and jams an arm under your chin, forcing you back to the ground. Another strike to your ear, which you hear now as though you're under water, a muted ring dulling all sound. You fumble at his face. But he's out of reach, in Nam's arms. She's facing the boy, blocking him. And he won't touch her.

Phil steps around Nam and takes an elbow to the boy's head. He follows with a heel when the boy curls onto the ground. *"Huy, huy, huy,"* some Thai men are yelling, pulling Phil away. Two of them lead the boy across the street. Nam follows them.

You stare across the street. A yellow sign for Teen Love Massage Parlor winks at you. The bar girls lean in. *Alive?* their faces seem to say. *Awake?* They twitter in Thai. One's in a cowboy hat. Another in tassels and a bra. You tell them you're not really hurt. You lift yourself onto your elbows.

"Fuckin' junkie kids," Phil says.

A bag of ice is dropped beside you. When you lift it dirt has crusted on the plastic, but you press your head against it anyway. The bar girls laugh, as if you've just knocked yourself out.

"No, keep it there," Phil says, when you let the bag drop. He curls his hand and looks at the knuckles. "Fuck *me*. He went right at you. You see that?"

"No."

"Man, sorry about that. Some crazy kid or something. I mean, it's not like that here. These people don't fight. Trust me, I know."

"All right," you say.

"Get you a drink?"

The bag's dripping a thin spool of mud down onto your shirt. Nam comes back, stepping around the motorbikes in the street. She kneels beside you and wipes at her red eyes. She smiles: no teeth bared, just the pinch of a dimple in her cheek.

"Kho thot." She raises her arms, hands pressed together, fingertips brushing her lips, lashes down. She looks so sincere that you clumsily lift your own arms in response. You fall onto your back.

"Sorry, *kha,*" Nam says, a hand on your cheek, where she seems to imagine the blow connected, though it's actually higher, closer to your eye. Her thumb rubs the grit from your face. "Hurt?"

"Who *was* that?"

She shakes her head, touches her chest. "My brother, Pea."

"Oh, God." You begin to laugh hysterically. "But—what the hell is he doing here?"

"Come to see."

"See? I mean, I'd be pissed, too. Actually, bring him back here," you say. "I'll meet him properly." But you won't ever see that boy again. "Too far," Nam will claim when you ask about her absent brother, even though you'll be living right here in Bangkok. And then, gently, "He don't like *farang* men."

"Too far." That's what Sam will tell you as well after you decide to stay in Thailand.

"Not if you come to stay," you tell her. "There's work here for English speakers. And everything's cheap, you know? You could move out here."

"*You* moved there," Sam will say. "*You* picked the other side of the world, Dad. There's nothing for me in Thailand. You just want to, like, keep me—to isolate me like you did with Mom."

Only, it's your wedding. And you want your daughter there.

"Dad, *stop,*" Sam will say. "I'm not going, okay?"

Try again. "Please just come."

Nam helps you to your feet and guides you through the bar all the way back toward the bathroom. Everyone watches you pass now, the injured player, the tipped pawn led from the board. You can't shake the feeling that it's all a show. They're thirsting for a spectacle, these people, their stares fixed on your nose, your eyebrows, your gut.

Your emotions: inflated. In the corner Nam's panderer has probably got an eye on you, on Nam. A matronly woman wearing—God knows why—an apron. A pimp in an apron. Chuckle sheepishly. Who are you kidding, anyway? The bar is packed with your type: foreign men in loafers and breezy shirts; and hers: young girls. It's like Mary said way back when—you could be anybody.

You pass Phil, gesturing at the state of your belly.

"Look at this mess. And the shit on my face."

Nam leaves you with him and the girl on his arm.

"My first night here's looking a lot like my last," you say. "I'm going home."

Phil hands you a beer. "That's why I always come back to the same woman, see? She's no trouble. This is Bee." Phil tugs the zipper of Bee's leather vest down to her navel, then back up. With a buzzing sound, he takes his mouth to her shoulder and stings her with a kiss. Bee laughs.

"No brothers?" you ask her.

"No family!" She takes the beer from you and drinks. "All here. All no parents. Orphans."

Phil turns away and lights a cigarette.

"What about Nam?"

"Same same," Bee says, nodding.

"That explains the protective brother," you say.

"Brother? No, Nam have no brother. No family."

"He just punched me," you tell her.

"It was her *brother* who punched you?" Phil asks.

You both look at Bee.

"Nam strong woman. She like you. Fight for you!" Bee mimics kangaroos boxing, bouncing on her feet and rolling her arms.

"No, no," Nam says, returning for the end of Bee's act. She wipes your face with a cloth. You flinch. "Oh, oh," she says.

"Your brother?"

She waves her arm loosely. "He go home."

"Me, too, I think."

"Please come," Nam says.

"No, time for me to be leaving."

"Okay but clean first." Nam loops her arm through yours and pulls you toward the bathrooms. Looking back, you'll know this point as the pivot. It was so easy, you'll think, like slipping back into a warm bed.

THE LAST TIME you slept with Mary was near the end, months after you found out about the other man. She had hired a divorce lawyer and was sleeping in Sam's room, empty now since Sam left for college. Only in the middle of the night Mary crept in, and you woke to find her back against you, burrowing into you, furiously, as if she meant it to hurt. Your lips against her neck—how long had it been?—and behind her ear where the flesh was twisted.

You lifted yourself above her. Her eyes were shut tight, the crescent of white gone—she was awake.

"You aren't just anybody, you know."

"I know," she said.

You looked for it, the muzzle she had, a mouth made for tearing. Her kiss was fierce, but she let you do the work, moving downward to her chin, the nub of her collarbone. Callused hands catching on the fabric of her shirt, pushing it up. You skirted her breasts. The taste of her skin: salt. Your tongue found the fold between thigh and body. There, you could feel a heartbeat.

Mary kept her eyes closed. Maybe she imagined the other man's mouth, his attention. You lost yourself in another, too—this girl you married before the meat of her waist was enough to fill your hands. You shut your eyes and recalled the feel of her. Eighteen. The firm press of her hips.

But Mary knew what you were doing. She wouldn't let you. She made it unfamiliar. She didn't arch her back for you. She didn't cry out, pull at your skin or your hair. She didn't want you to enjoy it. When you were done she slid away and walked to the bathroom.

THE BATHROOM IS a single black stall. The soot on your face matches the walls. Nam latches the door hook, soaks the cloth under a tap, and dabs at your skin. She hums as she works.

You'll think about the good mother she would make. After your marriage, when she asks you why you don't want to have children, you'll say, "I *have* a child. I left her behind for you." You'll feel as though the unspoken half is justified: So you give up yours. You'll pat her schoolgirl hips beneath the bed sheets. "Why waste this?"

Her voice will flag. "You want me lone."

"Speak English: You want me to be alone."

"Yes," she'll say.

But even during the worst times, when Nam shuts herself in the empty maid's room behind the kitchen, you'll tell yourself that you offered her a better life, away from the floorless homes of the northeast country, not to mention that bar where you found her.

You'll return to this beginning: the sound of cloth brushing around the red sore, softly, the way you used to touch Sam in her crib. This makes you smile. The mud mask cracks along the wrinkles of your face. Nam follows one with her cloth.

"Happy lines," she says.

You kiss her.

Nam giggles, sticks out her tongue and makes a face. You've left a smear of dirt on her mouth and black grains on her tongue. She makes the sound of something wet striking a wall: *pahk*. Then she leans into you, grinning, and licks your chin. Ticklish, you start and both of you fall against the wall, knocking the light switch.

When you kiss her again she's laughing, the ripple of muscle filling your mouth. This time you think only of Nam.

Pink Youth

HASMAH & NAM (1982)

Day work: Hasmah labored with the pregnant women. Then the night work, not quite the labor of an undertaker; at night Hasmah balled the fetuses in black plastic and took them to the temple.

"It's necessary," Hasmah, a Muslim, had said to the Buddhist monks. "You need me. How many orphans can you take at your temples?"

The monks fired the temple's crematory. They understood the work. Or perhaps they didn't, but they understood a fee—call it the toll for passage—for taking the bodies from Hasmah. Not bodies. Smaller. Small enough that they could be tucked under a knee or an arm as the trays were loaded for the furnace. Necessary work.

The monks, to appease the neighborhood, called her a necessary woman.

Still the neighbors prayed for Hasmah to be caught. "She'll get what's coming to her," they said. They stared between the drapes and waylaid women on the walkway, so that when Hasmah found a caller on her threshold ("Your friend Sangkaya sent me"), she made quick decisions.

When she needed time: "What do you want?"

"I'm Nam."

The girl wore sandals, frayed shorts, and a backpack over her front. It was the shorts and that shampoo-ad hair—impossibly long and straight, hanging perfectly still as if apart from her—that gave the girl away as the kind Hasmah knew well. She was from the bars, surely, well-oiled and pliable enough for the foreign men to work her.

"We spoke on the phone?" Nam said.

"I'm not taking anyone now," Hasmah said.

Only a week had passed since the media's latest: a septic tank on temple grounds full of little black bags. It was only a matter of time before journalists exhumed the rest of that story and went digging for other offenders. Already in recent years the papers had accustomed the public to the tabloid version of Hasmah's work—blood smeared on white tile, a doctor bearing a drugged woman, her ankles dragging, her hospital gown blooming red.

"You said on the phone that you would do it," Nam said.

Hasmah straightened her headscarf. She glanced behind her for the phone—hadn't she thrown that thing out? That's why she didn't take calls. She needed to speak to a person's face to remember who they were. And there were always voices on the phone that wanted things from her.

"You gave me your address. You told me when to come."

Maybe it was a setup, but the girl had been too long on the landing. Hasmah let her in before bolting the lock at the top of the doorframe and swinging in the window shutters, solid wood, made to weather monsoons.

Nam slipped her bag off. "Were you talking to somebody? I thought there was somebody else in here."

"It was, uh, the phone." She gestured to the corner. Yes, there it still was. A pearl-white rotary dial. Nam had probably been listening outside the door, trying to appraise Hasmah, decide if today the witch was stable. Well—stable was what Hasmah intended to be, the measure of sanity. She kept her madness in the walls.

"Come forward." Hasmah slid her hands under the girl's waistband. Nam made to step away, but Hasmah's hand on the swell kept her close. "You may as well give birth at this point."

"They told me you could do it."

"Who told you that? No, you're too far along. Go to the hospital."

"Look, I have your money." Nam took an envelope from her backpack. "You're already more than I can afford, really. My husband would notice if I skimmed off more from the household spending. Here, the amount's correct. Go on, count it."

Hasmah didn't take the envelope.

Nam opened it and held it out again. "You don't want to count it?"

"You're married?"

"My husband doesn't want a baby. And . . ." She hesitated, then placed the envelope on the table beside the phone. "And I can't have this baby."

Hasmah unknotted the headscarf and let it slip to her shoulders. What showed was grey. She hadn't colored her hair in months.

"It's not a good time for this," Hasmah said. "Haven't you seen the papers? They're throwing us in prison. I'm next. They're trying to trap me. I've seen it all before." But as she was saying this she could already hear the neighbors picking up the call—*She wouldn't do it? What else is that witch good for?*—their censure parroting along the halls of her ramshackle building, their simmer of resentment given new heat.

They had been against her since her arrival in the neighborhood. The memory of that arrival like a photograph turned in Hasmah's fingers, the picture in black-and-white it seemed that long ago. Who was that person? Hasmah, daughter of Islam, her girlhood spent within calling distance of two mosques in a fading southern town; she came alone to Bangkok, wrapped up in black. The locals had asked her what brought her here.

Hasmah's own daughter was dead, a stillbirth after a round of police violence. Buddhist police, Muslim child. Buddhist rule, Muslim province. Just another story of the country's south. Barely twenty-four at the time, Hasmah refused to live out a barren life. Her husband and the other men were still sitting on the marble steps outside their mosque, sipping tea, telling one another what the Buddhists had coming, as if these Muslims also believed in karmic scales, scales that in the south had been tipped against Islam too long. Balance was coming.

"Retribution for those murdered," the husbands said, hefting the Qur'an for reassurance. Their seething never amounted to anything, though, especially not in Hasmah's husband. And so she had boarded a train for Bangkok, arriving at Hua Lamphong Station with a folded leather kit of long-handled spoons, coming finally into this family profession that she had shunned in her youth.

"What's brought you here?" asked her first landlord.

"Family work."

NAM STOOD AT the window, running her fingers around the frame, which was fitted with metal loops and secured with padlocks. The light switches were webbed in duct tape.

"What are you afraid of?" she asked Hasmah.

"Childproofing." Hasmah pointed at the straw mat. "Sit down. I want to explain something to you."

"You had children? Nobody ever said you had children."

"A family business. We passed it down through the women, see, mother to mother to mother. Only I lost mine. Last of my line, made barren. How absurd."

Hasmah wanted to explain what it was to lose something and still be tethered to the pain of it years later, trussed against the post of what could have been, against those milestones marking the way she had expected to live.

Nam tapped one of the padlocks. "What happened?"

"Those responsible no doubt saw it as an act of justice. It's what goes on in the south."

That's what the police had told Hasmah when she delivered herself into their offices to show them what the body was like a mere month after a woman has lost a child. The police had done this to her. An accident, they called it in their reports. They wrote that she'd fallen by herself.

"What have you done?" she said to them.

The captain explained it to her, the police work, justice.

He told her this was not his fault. If anyone was at fault, it was Hasmah. This was retribution, the karmic wheel turning like a mill with Hasmah in its teeth, punishing her family for their work. Baby for baby.

Perhaps Hasmah herself had believed it. She had wanted to, really, tightening the noose of her headscarf, rubbing her forehead bloody on that prayer mat, asking Allah why. That was what she fixed upon, that there *had* to be a reason.

"Your actions," the police captain said.

Hasmah hadn't seen a choice in it. What choice? What she offered—*that* was choice, the vital calculation: Can we afford to have children now? Yes, no. She midwifed, too; she was a midwife first, actually. Buddhists with their narrow tallying of plus and minus, as if life was a sum. And somewhere the bookkeepers had wronged her. Included her efforts in the wrong column.

For weeks after her stillbirth, Hasmah stood sideways before a full-length mirror, watching the body reverse its swell—a subtraction, perhaps, but not a choice. How could she have expected to take without losing, too? *Does it work in reverse?* she wondered. She would test it, bring the tools to take back what was hers. Their children. Their children for her child, and perhaps, through the toil of a lifetime, her daughter might finally be returned to her.

She had opened her door indiscriminately in those early days, going about the task with a vindictive industriousness. She took all their children. Whatever the girls' stations of life or stages of pregnancy. Gone. Out. She helped them make the choice, of which she envied them. Medical abortion was in its shy days back then, and Hasmah's practice burgeoned.

At first she misunderstood the feeling it gave her—power, she thought. Power over these women. She held their fertility against them, she wanted to take that away from them, too. But if that had been the first purpose of this work, it had become a fistful of mud in water—some current had gotten hold of it.

The work wasn't without cost. The feeling, she came to realize, was fear. Each visit was a seed of fear sowed deep within herself, pitting Hasmah's insides. She was being watched, had traded the police of the south for the police of the city. They knew her work. The feeling soiled her body, manifested on the skin as an odor, the tracking scent of dread. This foul trace made Hasmah check her underarms obsessively. She bathed three times a day until her flesh was raw and mottled from scrubbing. How her hands shook, as if someone gripped her at the wrists, took hold of her.

Rumors came roiling into the slum's corridors to fill mouths at a time when the city was hungry. The trouble in this country, the business, the economy—Hasmah didn't understand it. What she understood: There was no work.

The neighborhood fathers went unemployed. They bent their plastic chairs with restless flexing, idling in canteens, smoking cigarette after cigarette to the stub. Surely, someone was cheating them. The foreigners—well, yes, but who had ever seen a *farang* mucking through their neighborhood? They needed more immediate villains. Hasmah came easily to mind. A Muslim among Buddhists, she could be identified from afar by the banner of her headscarf.

"That veiled woman," Hasmah heard through her window. "What has she done to our daughters? Where are the little girls of our little girls?"

That was not Hasmah's fault. Families had drained back into the countryside and the neighborhood was shrinking. Nearby construction projects had been abandoned, their busy din hushed. Across the city buildings stood vacant.

But the neighborhood's fathers—those former builders and scaffold walkers—grumbled that their place in the world had been usurped.

"Where are the children?" they asked.

"A Muslim's work," they called it.

"She's taken them from us."

In this lull Hasmah could sense them turning their ears up to her window, from which the evening's call to prayer was spitting out of an old radio that picked up more static than song. Hasmah switched it off, rubbing her forehead where the threadbare prayer mat always left a red burn, a reminder that faith is hard. It was hard. What was she doing here in this place with none of her own people, where they could so easily make her the enemy?

After the men it was those people Hasmah knew and spoke to. It was Thaan, the corner vendor Hasmah bought fruit from.

"Prices are up today," Thaan said from behind her heaving counter. "All the way up. I don't have anything for you."

But Hasmah had bought fruit from Thaan every week for over a decade.

"Everything has to change."

"Please, Thaan."

The vendor turned away, reaching over with both her hands to bag mangoes for another buyer.

Hasmah fastened her headscarf tighter, finding comfort in its snug hold underneath her chin, in the way it shielded her. She traced different walks through the neighborhood to avoid places she had been. But people knew her, and after a first pass even the new alleys were aligned against her. They wanted her out. The entire neighborhood seemed to take up the call:

"Buddhists only."

"No rice here for you."

"We don't carry your people's dry spices anymore. Go back south for that."

When Hasmah walked the *sois* she had a train of children skulking after her, their sandals rasping on dry cement—*witch, witch, witch*—like sweeping brooms. Hasmah had expected the giggles and games, the heads peeping around corners, but a bold menace surged from these children like the rhymes they sang to herald Hasmah's coming: "Make way! Give way! How many mice will she catch today? One, two . . ."

Then the small, hard-eyed leader got the idea to throw fireworks at her, gunpowder-packed paper triangles that—to Hasmah's ears, trained in the frustrated, secessionist south—sounded like gunfire.

The children scattered in surprise at the strength of the fireworks, the shots reverberating along the cement corridors between the buildings. Hasmah staggered against a wall and cupped her left ear, her head filled with whistling.

The following morning there was a bright point of blood on her pillow. Hasmah took the pillow to the washing pool, where she scrubbed the stain against the concrete stairs, the rhythm and rasp soothing her until she sensed again their attention; and looking up she found herself surrounded by the children. They lined the concrete pit, pointing down into the water, where her pillow was shredded. Hasmah had scraped right through the pillow, through the skin of her hands, which she bared, releasing pink feathers like petals across the pool.

THE PHONE RANG. Its color, once sold to her as pearl, was the yellow of an old bone.

"Aren't you going to answer that?" Nam said.

"That's what they want."

A week ago, Hasmah had picked up the phone to a man's voice on the other side. "Go back south." They were coming for her, and when she heard the knock on her door minutes later, she was sure it was the police. But when she opened the door, she found a woman crumpled on her threshold. No one else was in the corridor. *The little girls of our little girls.* It was a test. Hasmah gently, gently pushed the door shut.

Nam picked up the phone.

"What are you doing!" Hasmah took the receiver from her and held it against her chest.

"There's no one there," Nam said gently.

Beside the phone lay the envelope of money. Hasmah knew the cost of such work. She looked at the money, but she already had a count in her head: *How many mice today? One, two . . .*

She pressed the receiver to her ear. There was silence, then, distantly, a chorus of voices: "One more."

IN THE CENTER of the back room was a work bed with a vinyl cover. In the corner, a deep sink, its metal surface burnished from heavy use.

From a locked drawer Hasmah took a packet of pills. These would induce dilation and contractions. "Who's coming to collect you? Not the husband?" Hasmah gestured to a gown folded on the bed. "You can change."

The girl turned her back to Hasmah before removing her clothes.

"No, someone else."

Hasmah prepared the tray, clinking her spoon as she stirred a glass of a drink that was pillowy and pink. She tucked a straw into it and laid out four white pills, pure as milk teeth.

Nam cupped the pills in her hand. "How does this work?"

"Put them under your tongue. They'll induce contractions."

"Like I'm having a baby?" Nam removed the straw in her drink. "And this?"

"Cold milk with Hale's Blue Boy sugar syrup." Hasmah pointed to the bottle of pink syrup on the fridge. "I used to crave it when I was pregnant. It brings me back to a good time in my life. Now I give it to all my patients to prep them for the procedure. Pink youth, pink syrup."

When Hasmah was pregnant she would cycle, with straw mat in hand, to the outskirts of her town and make her way into the limestone caves. The cool caverns kept the hot flashes at bay and stilled her restlessness. Hasmah had imagined her unborn daughter calming as well, her quieted mood passing like nourishment to the baby.

Nam touched her tongue to a frothy drop on the straw's end. "You make it different."

"I make it the southern way, yes, with a little salt. Take the pills."

Nam took the pills. She drank the whole glass of milk.

"I like it." She ran a finger across her upper lip and sucked it. "Sweet."

"Stand up. I want you walking around. It will help the natural process." Hasmah lifted the glass into the sink and washed the foam out. "You know I've tried different drinks over the years. Guava juice. Bael-fruit tea. Pressed sugarcane." Hasmah called up a history of patients sitting on the work bed, the glass clutched in two hands, legs gently spread and rocking, childishly content. "Nothing works as well as the pink syrup. A child's drink."

It always brought to her mind a schoolgirl. One waiting for Hasmah in a crowded canteen, her pigtails dangling and a pair of cheap leather shoes buckled on. What else? A gummy smile unfurling, the straw between her pinked teeth, perhaps even a laugh bubbling up through her.

"When I look at you girls I can see my daughter as a schoolgirl."

"You said you didn't have a daughter."

"She doesn't show herself, but she's there. They all are, you know, watching us. All those we've lost. They come back to us." Hasmah could tell what Nam thought of this, her fingers playing with the pleat of her gown, eyes shying away from the subject.

"You don't believe me. No, why should you."

"And you lock the windows . . . to keep the children out?"

Hasmah wanted to laugh at Nam's attempt at sympathy. She thought about how she would reach into the girl and squeeze that cloying syrup. Instead, she turned to the sink and spoke with her back to the girl.

"You don't understand. Children like to play. They test their muscles. They have a fascination with things that don't quite fit their hands. That's why I have locks."

Sometimes they turned up the heat on the water, played the light switches like piano keys. They wrangled the locks, flushed the toilet. One morning Hasmah opened the fridge and found the dial broken and the walls lined with ice. The milk was frozen and her vegetables had turned to stone.

"When it's quiet, you can hear them singing nursery rhymes."

Nam paced to the wall and turned back. "You know, you scare people with that sort of talk."

"Am I scaring you?"

"Not me, no. Others."

"This place has always been afraid of me. A Muslim, they say, and even that makes them run."

"No. That's not why."

"That *is* why," Hasmah said.

"No." Nam reexamined the padlock on the window. "They say it's madness. That you're crazy."

Witch, witch, witch.

"I'm not." Hasmah thought back to the children and their fireworks. "You don't understand what it's like. They follow me in the streets."

"They see a hooded woman talking to herself."

No. Only a mother followed by the shadow of her daughter. "They sing songs, play games. They throw things at me."

"Who?"

"The children!"

Nam stopped and clasped her hands around her stomach. "What children?"

Hasmah brushed at the front of her blouse and realized that her fingers were stained pink from the syrup coating the bottle. Pink streaks all the way up her arm.

"You have it on your face, too," Nam said quietly. "You know, the reason they say it is because that's what your patients tell them. There are stories."

"What stories?"

"They say one woman caught you talking to something."

"No, not talking," Hasmah whispered. "Playing."

"Will you come out if I play with you? I'm counting now. One, two,"—two fingers raised—"and three."

It was only child's play. Hasmah in her apartment, eyes facing the wall. "One, two," aloud, and behind Hasmah her daughter giggled, teetered on raised toes.

"I'm coming for you." Hasmah shut the cupboards and doors. She tried to coax her daughter out.

But her daughter hid from her. She scattered laughter like pollen. It caught in Hasmah's nose: pink. The pink of cheap syrup. The pink skirt hem on the clothesline curling under her daughter's fidgeting. "I told you not to do that. Come here."

Hasmah never caught her. She could only trail the hiding places. But that smell. Pink and sour, like blood coming up in the throat. She knew the smell. It made Hasmah's eyes water, her throat swell up with grief, the flesh there sore to the touch, soft as fish cheek. She tore at it.

This is how one girl had found Hasmah, huddled against the kitchen cabinet with her neck gouged, saying, "Oh, child," when the girl asked her what happened. "Oh, child."

"*What* child?" the girl said.

"You know."

"No."

"I'll show you." Hasmah checked the nooks. She put her ear against the wall. She knocked, expecting her daughter to come out of the woodwork, like an insect. Tiny pitter-patter. She could hear a rattle like a children's toy sounding from the plumbing. She tried counting, her forehead resting against an arm resting against the wall. "Want to play?" Numbering up and up in a loud voice.

So Hasmah's girls had started to talk, to say the cowled egg had cracked.

"You nonbelievers. You cannot see anything that you cannot describe with your hands."

"But you can?"

Hasmah lifted her hands to take in the empty room. "Do you believe me?"

Nam had stopped beside the work bed. "Maybe if I see my boy. This baby born of a Buddhist mother married to a Christian, taken from me by a Muslim. Where do you suppose he'll go?"

Nam's breath caught and she braced herself on the bed.

"You feel it, right?" Hasmah counted pills into Nam's hand. "Here, the expensive stuff. It can make you dizzy, but it will help with the pain. There's water on the cabinet."

They would both need it later, when the real work came. Hasmah took two for herself and ground them under her teeth. She licked her gums clean of the white grime. She liked that bitterness coursing through her.

"I can feel him," Nam said.

"What makes you sure it would have been a boy?" Hasmah asked.

"I just know."

"It's easier not to think of what could have been, to remember that this is not actually a baby. It's not a boy."

"Why do you have to say that?"

"I tell you girls what you need to hear."

"Don't call me that. I'm not one of your *girls*."

"You're all girls to me. All of you with all of your own sense of righteousness, your own set of excuses. Not one of my *girls*," Hasmah mimicked. "You are *all* my girls. If you knew how many of you there are . . . But I know what you do. You make a witch of me to hide your own shame. Why are you so ashamed?"

"You're wrong." Sweat was seeping into Nam's hair, upsetting its order. Black eyeliner bled down from her eyes. Her face was still gently powdered, but that would all come away.

"I'm not like them. You don't understand what I'm giving up."

"A baby."

"My husband. You think leaving my husband is easy. You know what a husband is? I suppose you don't."

"I had a husband," Hasmah said.

"It's a living." Nam stopped, and then tried again, deliberately, but her speech was unraveling. "A living. Not so good, maybe, but you don't know what the alternative was like. Sitting at the bar in fishnet. And all I can think about is whether the cut-rate metal stool I'm sitting on is going to leave a welt later. When he leans me over the bed—will he notice?"

"You need to even out your breathing."

"Yes, I need to lie down."

"On your hands and knees. Up on the table."

Hasmah watched the girl crawl onto the work bed. It helped the process, but Hasmah preferred it because it curtained off emotion, hid it behind the hair that draped over their faces.

Nam gasped, features clenching and unclenching. "I need to wait. He'll come. He'll be here," she blinked and rubbed her wet face into the bed. "He'll be here."

"Who? Not your husband. A boyfriend?"

"Something like that."

"No, you won't be able to hold it." Hasmah laid her hand on Nam, but the girl jerked away and dug her nails into the vinyl.

"I can. Okay. I'm breathing."

Hasmah could see that Nam was close. The hard bed was already sticky with her blood, heralding the moment with its stink. Hasmah brought her eyes to the sink in the corner, anticipating the ritual to come, the motions of filling up and scrubbing down the metal sink. Hot water, pink and frothy, would brim as the old pipes worked at swallowing. The steam would carry up the smell to Hasmah, who would force herself to breathe, taking in the flesh and metal, the scent of her own nightmares.

Always in her sleep Hasmah returned to the moment she lost her daughter. The smell of the bed of a police truck with raised grooves, and Hasmah's body against it.

"There! That knocking," Nam cried. "He's here."

The floor heaved against Hasmah when she moved. Its lean left her dizzy. She tasted a bitter bile rising, had to kneel.

"Open the door. He's here."

Hasmah brought herself upright against the doorframe to the front room, but she didn't go to the door. The knocking had intensified, taken on a savage bent that scared her, sounding too much like many fists adding their voice to the surface, not only of the door but the walls, too, so that the apartment swelled up like a throat yelling its protest.

The shouting snagged in Hasmah's memory. She knew the sound of protest, and how quickly it could turn to panic. Hasmah had been snatched up in that panic when the police dispersed the crowd. She'd been pushed to the ground in the stampede to get away. By the time they carried her into the police truck, she was already coughing up pink froth, curled in upon herself. In her mind: *Please. Allah, please.* But she had lost her baby.

"What are you waiting for?"

Hasmah turned to the girl who, with quaking limbs, attempted to climb off the bed.

"You shouldn't move," Hasmah told her. "It's coming."

"The door—"

"It's not him. It's the Buddhists."

Make way! Give way! How many mice will she catch today?

"Can't you hear them?" Their voices were against the door, making it chatter in its frame. Their eyes blotting the window, their calls in Hasmah's head: *malefactor, spirit-wrangler, abortionist.* It made her tremble. The building trembled. It brought out the creatures in Hasmah's ceiling.

"Hear what? There's only him. Please. It's him. I know it. I knew he'd come. He's here for me."

"Quiet now." Hasmah hushed Nam with her hand. "Quiet down. Listen." Not to the barking of people in the hallway, but something else—lifting up through the wood floors, humming in the walls, reverberating up the plumbing into the gramophone of the sink where it coalesced into something like a chorus of children singing.

"They're here," Hasmah whispered, not daring to interrupt the song that had taken the shape of her youth, of her girlhood and that coastal town with the call to prayer soaring above it all, hushing them: the incensed husbands on the mosque steps; the chanting children (*one, two, three*); Nam's calls for help; even the people outside the door, who paused to draw a collective breath and muster for the final onslaught. But when the door splintered, it was her daughter that Hasmah saw marching in over the debris, her hair swinging and her school shoes clapping. Hasmah's daughter grinned, and her teeth were pink.

Exit Father

PING (1985–)

Ping had only come back to see her father burned. But even after the ceremony, Ba remained embalmed in other ways. He was there in the chili bushes that were planted in old car tires. Ba, who rubbed menthol oil hourly into his chest, had left his cool touch on the TV remote, the hard pillow he prayed into, the figurines in the red shrine. Beginning with Guanyin, the shrine's pantheon also included Jesus, a Happy Meal collectible, and a Snoopy cast in brass.

Her family preserved him, too, in the seating arrangement at the dinner table that night, his chair of honor kept empty. Ping's youngest sister, Sarai, said they'd promised Ba to take his ashes back home.

"He *is* home," said Ping.

"Chaozhou, the ancestral home. He wanted it to be you, Poong-ping," Sarai said, making her appeal with Ping's childhood nickname.

After dinner, she went out onto the small bedroom balcony to wait for sunset. Ping's childhood was stretched in her memory into a single twilight, an amber dusk suspending old Bangkok. She remembered the canal behind the houses, with the long-tail boats roaring past, prompting roars from kids at the fence. And behind the fence, their newly constructed neighborhood. The developers had understood that creating order (the houses came in three uncompromising varieties) meant walling out the city's gleeful chaos. Efforts at an imagined first-world neatness lasted only through the initial wave of home sales, however, after which that golden evening light on the estate billboard had begun to grade into night.

BEFORE PING WAS born, her father, Narong, had seen in his neighborhood the decline of his own life. Narong subscribed to a homespun ideology peppered with the Confucianism that survived among the Teochew diaspora. Coming of age in the era of home appliances and their myriad enhancements, he believed in self-betterment, the notion that a person could be upgraded. And so when Ping was born in '85, her father viewed the inadequacies of his first child (she was *she*) as a mere deficiency of bits.

"Firstborn. But new generation, new opportunities," he told his wife, Manee. He took to beginning sentences with "Even a woman can . . ."

This optimism was a symptom of money. His family had fled with it from the purges of the Cultural Revolution, which drove the clan down along the Mekong. Narong, only a child, had taken to Thailand with a boyish adventurism—he'd been brought up to believe that any abundance was his. In reality, their fellow Teochew families had long established themselves. Every pawn shop and medicine store, it seemed, was run by some uncle from back home. The tailors who cut his father's suits spoke Hakka. And all the machine shops had Cantonese foremen. In the corner noodle houses, Narong ate elbow to elbow with the former lords of old-world Guangdong.

Narong's old-money family put their wealth in what they knew: land, gold, and shipping. By the time his parents died, however, the land and gold had been sold to fund the failing export business. What money was left was parceled out to twelve children, tapped by wily relatives, and soon gone. For Narong, the golden age was a light behind him. If Ping was born in the evening hour, then by the time Manee added two more girls ('87, '91) it was properly dark and Narong's optimism had failed.

By 1996, Narong was working at a hotel in the heart of Chinatown called The Supreme Dragon. He saw the hotel as a display of the tastelessness of the newly wealthy Chinese. It wasn't lost on him that the people he waited on, arriving for business conventions, belonged to the new generation of China's millionaires, the "classless" society founded on the very rubble of his own family's home and their vanished class. These card-carrying members of the Chinese Communist Party who, having checked with Narong that the shark fin soup included in their meal was in fact bona fide, asked for extra portions in to-go containers. So that they might eat the stuff gloopy and disintegrated in their rooms later? No concern for the painstakingly low heat the fin had been cooked on in order to serve it up, as custom dictated, warm and whole. No concern that a status symbol taken in the privacy of one's room no longer carried much meaning.

"Tasteless pigs," Narong complained to his coworkers. "They have sold our gods and traditions. What do they even know of opera? Or poetry? But they can still quote the dead chairman."

Narong curated the audiences for his rants, performing these lines on the most impressionable ones: children of immigrants, Thailand-born, Thai-cultured. He knew not to risk a real immigrant who might call out his own ignorance. Those people, after all, had former lives. A stunning array of former acupuncturists, former chess champions, former folk musicians. The old bellhop still composed ballads for the *koudi*, a small flute the man had fashioned from blue PVC piping.

Then came the 1997 financial crisis, when that tide of easy, foreign money withdrew as quickly as it had arrived, raking through the shells of local businesses. The *sois* around Yaowarat Road were suddenly lined with the newly unemployed, men peddling those blue flutes, for example, or plying their other former trades. That year marked a rise in suicides and in self-employment. The immigrants became seamstresses, fruit vendors, cobblers, noodle hawkers—they were weeds flourishing in storm-ravaged earth, freshly turned and watered. Only, Narong, when he lost his job at the hotel, hadn't any other talents. Nor, in his shame, could he bring himself to visit his brother's business. He waited weeks before going to the docks, by which time his brother's offices had already been stripped.

In the months that followed, Narong, unemployed, walked new neighborhoods, skirting the streets he knew, that knew him, bypassing banter from the father-son soy-milk vendor. He no longer flirted with the dumpling woman. He got out ahead of the sun. "The heat," he said.

The manager of The Supreme Dragon, a man of old China who had taken the loss of his hotel as a captain does his ship, had produced for each of his staff a stack of photocopies of his handwritten reference letters. These letters Narong kept in his weatherproof satchel, flat between the pages of Ping's favorite picture book, *The Generous Elephant*. Having signed the reference letters with the house phone number, Narong slipped them under the doors of the city's finest Chinese establishments in the safety of dawn's shuttered hours. In this way, he avoided direct contact with both the managers and his own shame.

When he did find work again, it was at a restaurant locals called "that Chinese place behind the parking lot."

THROUGH THESE YEARS, Ping and her sisters were raised speaking not only Thai and chatty Teochew, but also the Queen's English. Their grandfather had endowed a British international school with the land for its inception, ensuring the girls an education beyond their means, and Narong prized the Western pedigree of his daughters' schooling. His own clan had been brought down by Maoist anti-intellectualism. Nightly he stood his eldest before him to chatter away in English. When she was old enough to realize that he didn't understand a word of it, she spoke song lyrics, nursery rhymes, taking delight in belittling her father. Always she managed to keep the melody from her voice.

"Mary, Mary, quite contrary. How does your garden grow? With silver bells, and cockle shells, and pretty maids all in a row."

Math, however, Ba knew. She was quick, but whenever she stumbled, she could see him bunch the fabric of his pants.

"Six by seven," he repeated.

"Forty-eight," she tried again.

Gesturing for her to step forward, he grabbed her around the thigh, and then with his other hand, pinched her hard, high up beneath the skirt where the bruise wouldn't show.

"We are a family of achievement," he said before releasing the girl.

In the kitchen, Ma sat her on a stool and rubbed menthol oil into her daughter's purple skin.

"That hurts," Ping said.

"You have to please him," Manee said.

But already the shoots of Ping's rebelliousness surfaced. She topped her classes but denied Ba the report cards. It wasn't for him that she had aced those exams. One evening, she responded to her father's math quiz in English, daring the old man to admit his ignorance or respond in kind. She turned up her cheek, her eyes flashing victory.

He beat her. Properly, with the cane of bamboo he had stripped from the garden years back as an instrument of fear, now of harm. He whipped it on the backs of her knees and chased her into the bathroom. She slipped and screamed on the white tile.

"I MADE YOU!" he shouted.

"I don't know you!" she cried back.

"Shut up."

"I don't *know* you. I don't know you."

"I SAID SHUT UP!"

And when she didn't he turned the cold hose on her, plastering her school uniform dark against her body. The damp cotton gave no protection, but as Ping was swallowed by her fear, a detached stillness came over her, as of an animal certain of its fate. She saw the episode, as she would later remember it, from the eyes of the others. From her mother and her sisters, frozen in the hallway door, and her father himself, bearing down.

Her deadening made Narong furious. He struck her harder yet. The cane snapped. He dropped it and began to tear Ping's clothes, the wet uniform screeching as it was rent apart. What did he hope to achieve? He lost sight of it as he bared this body not seen since she was a toddler and he had bathed her, in this corner, in this bathroom, soaping skin the coveted shades of pearl, of ivory, those symbols of wealth and status in old China—forbidden to him now.

Narong mounded the soaked fabric and returned to the dinner table to pick the delicate bones from the fish on his plate.

The next day the welts were red worms creeping across Ping's flesh. Her English teacher, a Filipino man, asked her what had happened to her arm. Ping replied that her father had beat her.

"You should try not to disappoint him," the teacher said matter-of-factly. Which the girl knew as a grave misreading of the situation. It was she who was disappointed.

Now she saw her father from a new distance. His antics, once spectacular, were now clownish. Take Ba's dinnertime prophesizing, as he foretold their imminent return to being a family of means. His brother's import-export business, into which Ba had invested his share of family wealth, would surely pick up, and the clan would rise anew. For his children, Ba demonstrated with two finger-legs riding the elevator of his other palm. (For years afterwards, Ping would envision class as a winch system by which, with the correct understanding of its mechanics and access to the right levers, you could propel yourself to a higher floor.) The ultimate goal of this elevator was to return them to China (here, he pointed up at the ceiling), where they would at last rebuild the family home.

"How many bedrooms?" Bo, middle daughter, prompted.

"Twelve bedrooms," he said proudly. "Not even including the ones where the servants slept. We had two courtyards where I would play with my older brothers. The space of the upper floors—you wouldn't even believe it." Their father rose and loped around their dining table, staring at the same old walls, only now seeing a vast enclosure. "You could wander an entire afternoon and not encounter anyone else."

What followed was a blueprinting of the house, which changed according to the contours of Ba's imagination, but this was another effect of wealth, that a bedroom could be added or subtracted without consequence to the whole.

Ping cut holes in her father's design. "I thought the stairs were marble?"

Well, there were many staircases.

"What about the rock garden? What about the brook running through it and the plum blossom trees?" Ping had seen such domestic scenes stitched into the tacky drapery at the market. She had a handle on the truth: His memories were a table runner.

He rose and told her not to speak to him that way.

She stood to meet him. "What way?"

Her mother said, "Ping, come help me with the dishes."

In the back-kitchen, Ma passed Ping the bar of hard soap, a baton of dishonor.

Ping took a washing stool and surrounded herself with sudsy buckets. She relished the task, the crisp citrus air and warm water up to her elbows. It was real work, not the make-believe of her father. She scrubbed his face from the crusted bottom of the rice pot. Scrubbed until the grains crumbled and floated away.

"He's right," Ma said at last. "You can't talk to him like that."

"Why not? He's just some nobody with no money."

Her mother's slap threw Ping from her stool, causing her to knock over a bucket. The water, still hot, sloshed against her legs.

"Concerning our family," said her mother, "nobody is more disappointed than your father."

A malleable woman with a round face, Manee was also Teochew Chinese, but of peasant stock. Whereas Narong as a boy had been fed a history of riches, weaned on resentment of his usurped station, Manee was raised practical. When rice was scarce, she stretched it into porridge. She had an ear for the weather and a pedantic manner in the kitchen. She was grounded in her faith, which revolved around two authorities: Narong (lesser) and Guanyin (greater). The goddess's guidance Manee divined through every form of fortune-telling, Chinese and homegrown. And she had stayed the mulish course of her days through Ping's childhood, slowly expanding the pantheon of their home shrine. But the quality of Manee's faith changed in 1997. On the day Narong lost his job, Manee went to the Chinese temple. An ominous gust kicked a calendar page down the street and she clapped it in her hands to make a worried assessment of the zodiac box. At the temple, she played a *siam si* set twice. Each time returned the same fortune. On her third trip to the desk, the woman who kept the scrolled prophecies said, "This isn't the lottery! Take your fate and go."

So in the months that followed, while Narong walked the streets unemployed, Manee had, without his knowledge, started a washing business, mixing the neighbors' linens in with their own and pocketing enough to supplement the groceries.

She had learned to wring her worry out with the grey water, distract herself, a technique she perfected to the point of one day forgetting to listen for her husband.

On that day, Narong discovered his wife ironing rich red linens, the bedsheet trailing from the table like the train of a gown. A sheet the color of good fortune. Startled by Narong, Manee let the iron sit too long. She snatched it up when it hissed, but already it had marked the fabric.

The children returned from school. Ping kicked aside the screen door while explaining to her sisters, Bo and Sarai, how she had pummeled this kid into weepy submission after he mocked her lunch kit. She halted, her story piled up against her surprise at the beautiful red sheet spread on the white linoleum. There followed an instant in which explanations—not expressions, but the shapes of stories— flashed through Ping. Then she saw her father standing with his back to her. He didn't turn. She saw her mother crawling backward in the corner, the corner of the red fabric held between Ma's clenched teeth; Ma in the corner on her hands and knees. When she saw her children, Ma let the sheet drop from her mouth.

Ping tried again to understand the situation. She took in the over-stuffed furniture, the staticky TV, the rosewood dining table, as if by triangulating these objects and the positions of her parents she might navigate the mystery here.

"Continue," her father instructed.

Without looking at the girls again, Ma wadded the fabric between her teeth. Slowly, because her hands caught the sheet when she rushed, she transported on her knees the corner in her mouth to its opposite.

What will people say, Ping thought, channeling Ma, *of this sweat-damp dress bunching at the hip, crumpling the image of a woman whose appearance was always immaculate. That her house and her marriage must also be crooked,* Ping mouthed.

Ma made another trip, each fold shrinking the remaining red. Hair webbed her wet face. With four more folds she had the fabric to the size of the parcels she wrapped, ready to return to the neighbors, a final task that was Ping's. For Ping was as complicit in Ma's business as she was in her father's punishment. Ping stood as witness.

Her sisters flanked her, their sweaty fingers fluttering in her hands. What must they be thinking? Bo a tripping, falling, skidding kid, and Ma with pink knees kneading the tile. And Sarai, only six, sucking the hem of her own shirt in solidarity.

The sight of her mother kissing the final corner flat onto the fold would fuel Ping's anger into her early adolescence. It was there when she watched the humiliation of her teachers, whose professional apparatus Ping dismantled with her questions, laying bare the clumsy reasoning and hack-job explanations for the scrutiny of her classmates. Her teachers hated and feared her. Her English teacher, now a Malaysian, finally confronted her about her attacks.

"How can you talk to your elders this way? Is this how you talk to your parents?"

Ping, now twelve, responded, "I give my parents the same respect they give me. What respect do *you* give me, teacher?" This unnerved the man, and he steered the class away from Ping's participation, never calling on her, never asking her to the front. This became the strategy of all her teachers. Ping's antagonism was a means of deflection, and she caught her attackers with the ricochet of their own shots, which she went to lengths to show didn't hurt her. The shots were all glancing.

It was a trick of ego-preservation she'd learned from her father, who, since the red sheet incident, had forbidden Ma from working ("No respectable mother is also a laundrywoman, a seamstress, a vendor"). Whose every paycheck went into pretense, maintaining the appearance of middle-class status. He bought rounds for his coworkers. He gave money to help revive his brother's business. He made sure the girls' clothes were immaculate. But inside their neat shoes, the socks had frayed.

One time, Ba went so far as to afford the family a meal at his restaurant.

They sat in the air-conditioned back room, its walls papered over with travel-agency posters advertising trips to southern China. Ping turned her scrutiny from the white-capped mountains of Yunnan to the menu. The outing was a mistake. Her father, coming to the same conclusion, toyed with his uncertainty. He was a tossed coin, two faces alternating to catch the light. One was authoritative and its obverse, which Ping didn't recognize, congenial and simpering.

"Narong!" said their waiter. He opened his body to the whole table. "Narong's family! Welcome. You want ice or no ice with the water?"

"Ice!" said a gleeful Sarai.

"No ice," their father said.

"No ice," the waiter agreed, and grimaced sympathetically at Sarai. He handed a notepad and pen to Narong. "Cook says the crabs are sweet and meaty today."

When the man left, Ba thrust the pad and pen at Ping. "Write down what I say. Black-pepper crab, stir-fried *phak Kwangtung, phalo* duck tongues . . ."

Between words Ping glanced up at her father, seeing him clearly: a person still uncomfortable with his station, language, and nation. A man far from home. He could read, but he had never learned to write Thai properly.

The waiter came back and checked the order. He smiled. "Your daughter's handwriting is excellent, Narong."

It was an uneasy feast. Ma refused to look anywhere but at the dish before her. The girls responded to the friendly attention of the waiters and turned their eyes from their father's diminished person, loyal to him in this moment to spare him his shame, which was also theirs.

"Finish that," he told his daughters. "You think this food comes cheap?"

The food was abundant and the bill, when it came, too small. The waiters had covered much of the meal. Ba turned red. He bought a round of beers for the entire staff and then hurried his family out.

BY THE TIME Ping was fourteen, she and her sisters were sleeping in the living room, and the second bedroom was rented to a family of three. The family's father worked behind a counter in a Chinese medicine store, while the mother had established herself on a nearby corner, selling bagged food sets to the morning merit-makers who exchanged the food for better fortunes. Their only child was Joey, thirteen and horny.

Ping didn't know much about sex. Some of her giggling classmates had called up graphic photos on a school computer, but Ping had neither a computer nor the privacy in which to view porn. So although Joey was a year younger than she, and shorter, sporting a swanky overconfidence, Ping allowed his advances. It was an education. Better to know than be caught out, trailing a peal of laughter, the teenager's death knell.

They locked themselves in the bathroom with a greasy magazine of Joey's that revealed, page by page, every imaginable type of sex.

"Do you want to try that?" he said one day.

No. She wasn't stupid.

"But how will we know what it feels like?"

"We won't," she told him.

Joey looked at her like she was missing the point. "Don't you—"

"Get your hand out of your pants. I'm going. Only, wait until it's clear before you leave."

The boy worked his proximity, leveraging the allure of this magazine, and finally, when she was stranded in her parents' bed recovering from a body rash, his beseeching won her over.

He asked her to lift her shirt under the guise of seeing her rash, which his father had prescribed a cream for. Delirious with boredom, she complied. They both stared at her breasts. The rash had dried to scales, which were beginning to flake, and her skin crackled under his fingertips.

"Gross," he said.

"Yeah."

He spread the magazine. The woman on her knees, mouth open, and the man standing. This, also, was sex?

"Do you want to try it?"

"Sure." She sat up.

Joey unbuckled, unzipped, unveiled, while Ping studied the picture, the tongue, seeing the red sheet spilling from her mother's mouth. Then the pink nub of this boy was pointing at her, thrust at her, and she tipped back her mouth to laugh. *This* was the source of disparity between her parents? She was hysterical. She barked out her laughter. *This!*

Joey folded himself back into his pants and fled. The next day the rash had spread to the boy (his father didn't say where), and soon the family moved out, the brief covenant up.

———

"FIRSTBORN," HER FATHER threatened, "education is your ticket out." The international-school scholarship only took Ping through middle school. At fifteen, she'd been thrown into the footrace that was the high school entrance exam, finding herself hobbled by that luxurious Western curriculum, with its digressions and idiosyncrasies and variety. She thought of her new competitors as cram-school automatons, kids with the middle-class privilege of rocking in their seats while repeating-after-me before computer screens. Kids in after-school cubicles with their instant noodles bloating in a cup, trying to remain awake in the face of six hours of prerecorded lessons. Even if the students dozed, they did it with headphones on and Ping, for one, believed in sleep hypnosis.

Her father had afforded her a month of science tutoring. Outside of that, Ping had a night routine and some textbooks she had lifted from the teachers' lounge. And still, she was closing in on the scores she needed. She snacked on coffee-flavored caramels. She muttered English mantras, snatches of music or movies that she reinvented in her prim Commonwealth accent: "You set them up, I'll knock them down." Her night desk was a stool on the balcony, a mosquito sheet draped around her, a necessary configuration to keep the light from waking her sisters in the room they all shared.

Around midnight, Ba returned from the evening shift. She switched off her light and watched him take the path across the patch of garden—long since turned to mud and paved with rotting planks—that led up to their shabby townhouse. From this vantage point, she had watched her father arrive in every shade of mood and moonlight.

Tonight, she saw his childlike glee, his arms weighed down with two plastic bags, the remains of the day. He would insist they eat it hot.

"Poongping!" he called up, spotting her. "Get your sisters."

In the room, her sisters had burrowed into the sag at the center of the old mattress.

At these witching hours a truce emerged. It was likely traceable back to some feudal custom, a protection afforded dinner guests, but Ping was convinced it had to do with the hour: midnight. At the change of day, the way between past and present grew short, requiring less to knock her father backward into history, his childhood wafting to him from something as simple as a soy-based broth. A sudden bite of ginger might release an essence of a day when he was eight and the path to the future was yet paved with gold.

It was noodles. Ba spun the revolving middle of the table, acting the role of a game-show host. "What'll it be tonight? What'll it be?"

He gave his firstborn the first pick. Ping chose wontons, knowing that Bo favored the porkballs while Sarai had earlier whispered, in English, "I want the fishballs." The broth was lukewarm but rich.

"You won't find a better-prepared broth in the city," Ba boasted. "Not in this city. Not even in those stuffy hotels."

Only Ma excused herself from the night ritual, finding it extravagant to eat after dinner. In the years since the '97 crisis, her Buddhist zeal had advanced. She was by now at the stage of an ascetic, an artist of restraint in a family where the one thing they could agree on was excess, all of them wanting more from their lives.

Ping had noticed a desperate edge in her mother's faith. Ma spoke of a "pure happiness" the way Ping's alcoholic chemistry teacher dwelled on the double distillation process of hard liquor. Bliss was nearby, Ma knew, attainable even in this life if only one could recognize what were the false, immediate pleasures, and extract from those sugars of everyday existence the purer essence of true happiness.

On religious holidays, Manee foisted her beliefs on the children. The family joined the queues outside a Yaowarat temple, musty incense carried out into the street where the girls stood. Bo scraped her sole idly on the curb and Sarai played her little game with the vendors, inquiring into this or that trifle, as if she were a person who could actually afford such items, her chatty considerations always culminating in, "I'll just have to come back after the temple!"

Ping stood with hip thrust critically, memorizing the photocopied book in her hands. She was a week from the exams, but still her parents insisted on these charades. The queue was interminable.

"I can't stand this," Ping said.

"How will you pass your exams?" Ma said.

Ping spread her book and held it up. *Factor Theorem,* read the page.

Ma shook her head. "Your gods are not our gods."

THE EVE OF her exam also happened to be her birthday. It was a Sunday, and her father was working the midday shift. He would return for a family dinner, a feast in the making: curried crab, fish and taro steamboat, oyster omelet. Ma excused this extravagance with frequent depreciations of her own artistry.

"I've tried to cook you your favorites tonight. I've tried but I couldn't work in a *phalo* with this spread. Too much egg. You'll have to do without. And the crab isn't as fresh as the vendor promised. And—"

Ping, who'd only come into the kitchen to steal a branch of lychee, touched Ma's shoulder. "I'll be upstairs."

This was the exit she had worked toward. If she could test into one of the best schools, then she would board, leaving home at last. And yet, even now, she was feeling the pang of loss. Perhaps it was the evening's unusual harmony, a confluence of light and her mother's good mood and her father, returning now, carrying a whole duck strung up on a hook, a puppet he had to maneuver carefully to get through the gate. He saw her up on the balcony.

"Poongping," he cried with satisfaction, "a duck! I am coming up." He passed below her. Soon she heard him on the stairs, and then he was standing right beside her, gripping her by the back of her neck. His fingertips were cool with menthol oil, and he worked them into the bones of her spine, as if feeling for something she'd hidden from him.

"Childhood hasn't always been easy for you, I know. But soon you're leaving us. We are proud of what we've made in you. Even a woman." Ba's fingers paused, as if contemplating his own words. The hand clamped around her neck and shook her. "You will remember me," he commanded her, "when you are gone."

She was silent beside him. It was nightfall and the neighborhood was changing, the amber light fading off the reservoir where the conquering algae made gains from the shores, closing like stage curtains over the remaining life. Soon it faded from the water bottles fencing Ma's plants by the curb in domino rows. It faded from the pink bougainvillea that had gone rogue, and from the top of the wall coated with beer-bottle shards. Finally, the street in front of the house was dark. In the distance, she could make out the Skytrain whispering past, not stopping but announcing itself, the grim horizon streaked by its light, a last filament of gold.

TWO MONTHS BEFORE his death, Ba had called her.

"Poongping," he said. "Your father." As if she could have forgotten that voice. Ten years hadn't been enough to cleave her from the fear and resentment. Like old times, he drilled her with martial efficiency on the status of: her graduate degree, her relationship, and his grandchildren—were there any? No? Well, it was for the best because—

"Who gave you my number?"

Sarai, of course.

"What do you want, Ba?" It was the first time they had spoken since she'd left Thailand for graduate school in the U.S.

The occasion was his diagnosis.

"Are you trying to make me feel guilty?"

"I've picked the temple. And the arrangements. The cost . . ." he began, and broke off. He gave a number.

"What do you want?"

"I want five days on display at least. Seven would be better. I've chosen the temple where my own father was displayed. Those funeral rites were attended by thousands. The wreaths from the dignitaries were enough to fill a second chamber. Do you remember the place? They use real gold in the murals, I've been told."

He didn't have the money, she realized.

"Poongping," he said. "Firstborn. Please, the room must be big enough to accommodate everyone. There is your uncle's side and the managers of the Dragon and the cousins from Lat Phrao. Seven days of rites. Then a waiting period before the cremation."

And she let him speak, hearing the man from her childhood who paced circles around the dining table, telling his girls what his life would be.

Parade

LARA, NAM & RICK (1991)

The street outside the temple was already ornamented with red flags, the many flapping tongues heralding the Year of the Monkey. Lara stopped to swing the tail of a firecracker braid, itching to ignite the dawn: Wake up! But Mom was dragging on her arm, and the girl got her legs tangled in newspaper pages kicked down the street by passing traffic. Mom stooped to hoist free the left leg, now the right leg, and said, "You do this to me intentionally, Lara."

Lara had made them late this morning with what Mom called her Year-of-the-Ox behavior.

But it wasn't morning so much as daybreak. Actually, it was the predawn for which there is no word, nothing to voice a child's indignity at having to be up before the figurative rooster. They weren't *monks*.

"Mom, I don't want to go to your stupid cult." Lara had turned her face from Mom's questions: How does it look, this skirt, these pleats, the sandals? Mom adjusted her glasses in the mirror. Sufficiently pious?

What did it matter? Mom would just be furniture in the corner, convenient and foldable. Lara bit into her pillow, already decided on arriving late, her hair kinked, her mood disheveling the atmosphere the parents blanketed over their crazy spirit-medium sessions.

They didn't enter the temple itself but its back room, a bare manufacturing bay responsible for the pendants, dashboard idols, and bead bracelets with which to accessorize one's zeal. Half-chiseled statues flanked the walls, each week their features more defined. Some even grew limbs.

The other kids were circled up. Mod, a neckless boil, smirked at Lara as she took her place beside him. On her left side was Kwan, whom they sometimes called Robocop. She was autistic. Lara bullied her to gauge her reactions on a human scale. All the kids faced outward except Tony, who preferred to sit alone in the center, with the parents making the biggest loop around them all, as if to say, "Here are our bodies embracing yours." It was the sort of line they quoted from the booklet.

Nobody knew if Tony was actually this kid's name. His parents didn't participate. They were from the other end of Bang Na, beyond the ring roads where it wasn't even Bangkok anymore but a province Lara and the others referred to as the countryside. As in: "How's life out in the rice paddies?" When actually it was the same cracked concrete and shophouses they all knew.

They never said that to Tony himself, of course. Never made fun of his *farang* name either. Tony was the only kid that looked like he actually needed the help. His mother tried with the baseball cap; she dressed him in collars and long sleeves. But you couldn't costume over a boy that pasty, that bald. It was said that his skin came away at the touch, not in flakes but ashy, like talcum powder, which is probably what his mother used to cover up the patches where her goodnight kisses had burned an imprint into his forehead.

Tony was twelve, though his height said eight, and his doctors said that he might not reach adolescence. The reason he was here— the reason they all were—was to summon help.

The group had its obvious cases: Fon with her milky eye, one-armed Amrit, and Jojo, who choked up her meals. Jojo'd been saddled with a throat that swallowed backward, her neck seizing and her chin jutting out; whenever she ate, all the watching kids took gulps themselves, willing the meal down. Jojo ate soup mostly, but on occasion attempted a meal with substance, a real test of the sessions' efficacy. The food always came splattering back into the bowl her mother held waiting.

The rest of them stowed their uglies on the inside, or so the story went. Yod got seizures. A couple boys were just poor. One girl's dad beat her. He took a coloring-book approach to hide his abuse, bruising her within the margins of her clothing. Poor Kwan laughed at all the wrong things. Once Lara had accompanied her to the toilets, where Lara had listened to cascades of flushes followed by Kwan's laugh. A halting, clapping laugh, it clattered against the bathroom tile and sent an unnerved Lara back to the circle. Let the robot find her own way.

Mod's dad was also from the U.S., and for most sessions he sat beside Lara panning the parents' efforts in English: "This is like *The Exorcist* meets Care Bears. Bunch of amateur spirit mediums aren't going to sort *me* out."

He claimed to be dyslexic, said his brain stuttered when he read. His writing was even worse, the letters arranged all wrong, some of them not even letters. It looked to Lara (who wrote in cursive) like a box of cereal had spilled across his page.

"You're probably just stupid," Lara told Mod once. The boy had swung around and stabbed his ballpoint pen into her arm.

They had gaped at the pen shuddering below her shoulder, shocked that it was ink spurting from the wound, viscous as blood. For the children it was a confirmation of what their parents had always claimed: Their insides were all wrong.

And what was Lara's defect? Everything, her mother said, went wrong around the girl. The others heard an allusion to the circumstances of Lara's birth, that she was an unwanted child, raised alone by her mother. But no, Dad was at home, if hovering at a foreigner's distance to what he called that Thai mumbo jumbo.

"Where've you been?" Dad would ask in English.

To which Lara would answer, "Temple."

"Again?"

"Yeah. Again again."

At which point Mom ducked into the kitchen and a resigned Lara arranged her feet together and conjured up the untruth du jour. "I set go eels in the temple pond."

When the occasion did arise to free beasts, Lara always volunteered to handle the eels. They were disgusting, plopping out of the bag all balled up. She dispersed them with a stick, reasoning that if she could show mercy to this mess of entrails, surely the gods could spare Lara a once-over.

"Set free," Dad corrected, "set the eels free," which made Lara feel like maybe Mom was right about her being a failure.

Lara had gotten an earful of it over some truly dull sessions. While other kids slumped on their cushions like orphaned puppets, Mod would slink his wormy mouth to Lara's ear and tell her:

"You were an unwanted baby. You were supposed to go out with the garbage. Your name should be Ratfood."

"Ai! You shit!" And then it was Lara messing up again. Lara proving them right.

To believe the parents was to believe the booklet, and the booklet said the history was bad. These kids were in need of a karma transfusion.

MOD WAS PRACTICING his side shuffle, bumping Lara with his hip, saying, "Buddy up, buddy up. It's red-carpet time. Bets on who they're summoning today?" He held out his hands. They were like soggy mittens. At least with Mod she could gossip. He winked and rolled his eyeballs back into fluttering lids, displaying his yellow-whites.

"Sicko."

"I'm here for the cure," he intoned.

Kwan had slumped down on her pillow. Tony was on his back with arms behind his head, as casual as if he were floating in a pool and not waiting for one of the adults to summon a long-dead monk into his body. The parents were cross-legged, offerings splayed before them on trays. They revved up with loud throat clearing, which was the cue for Jojo to make another round with the spittoon. Lara spared her mother a look. Mom was aligning the betel leaves on her tray, trying to get them to fan out prettily. It was Mom's way of working through her nerves, like the time she had taken up origami using real money.

She had returned from that art class with a red bouquet folded from hundred-baht bills.

Mom held the flowers up. "You like?"

Lara said, "It looks like a golf trophy."

"Nam," Dad said, "how much did you spend on that?"

"Class is five hundred baht."

"No." Dad pointed. "*That.* How much?"

"I don't know, *kha*. Maybe four thousand?"

"Better earn it back." He shrugged and returned to his paper.

So Mom spent the evening unraveling the roses, running a hot iron across each of the crinkled bills. Lara draped herself over the back of the sofa, saying it reminded her of the newly minted bills she was given in a red envelope each Chinese New Year.

Mom held out a hundred to Lara.

"Hey! It's hot!" Lara pinched its corner. "I can keep this?"

Mom promised Lara that if she came to every booklet session, this year's *ang pao* would be full of ironed hundreds.

"Okay, well, I want, like, a stocking's worth of hundreds," Lara said, conforming as always to her father's traditions.

THE LAST SUMMONING session had yielded no guest, the parents turning over the booklet like they expected an answer sheet. But to sidestep the guest was to forgo square one, showing up with all the trappings of worship—incense, candles, lamp oil—and no fire.

This session the group was rigid, the conversation gagged by their wadded anxiety. But five shifty, sniffly minutes was all it took before a woman began to yip. When she opened her eyes and looked upon the group, Lara could tell that something in this guest was different.

"And . . . they're off," Mod whispered.

Lara dropped Mod's hands and submitted herself to procedure. The adults came out of meditation. A procession formed in front of the woman, parents offering their plates of betel nuts and betel leaves and of the pantry miscellany, those juice boxes and wafer bars past expiry. The guest chewed through the ritual, her saliva running red from the betel leaves.

Eventually she held a palm up to quell the children, but Tony already had his eyes closed and who knew how much even registered with Kwan. Lara gave her best Queen Mother wave, but seeing Mom roil in the corner, she amended the gesture, brought her hands together in a respectful *wai*.

"What's your name, child?" The woman spoke now with a man's voice, its sound sputtering as if transmitted from afar, the mouth just a radio catching a signal.

The circle of children fell away on either flank.

"Lara."

"Closer." The guest gestured at her own face. "This one's eyes are bad."

The woman's hair had come undone, haloing around her head like some cartoon madness. Section III of the booklet cataloged standard guest behavior—irregular motion, for instance, voice variation, gender confusion. Lara could see the mental bingo game playing across the faces of the adults. Section III also allowed for undocumented behavior. This woman sucked her front teeth, apparently gleeful to have them all.

"Who are your parents?"

"That's my mom." Lara pointed. "And my dad, well, he's not here."

"Do you have an offering for me, child?"

Lara presented a cast-iron teapot on a tray. The tea was Tie Guan Yin, Iron Goddess of Mercy. It had over-steeped and came out richly perfumed.

"Tell me what's wrong with you, child."

Off to the right, Mom's eyes asked Lara not to sink this opportunity.

"I'm told I was born the wrong way."

"And are you a good child? Have you tried to correct your karma yourself?"

Again Lara read her mother for cues. "I guess I sometimes get into trouble."

A chuckle like tires on gravel. "Well, your guest today is merciful. I forgive you. Come and I will bless you."

Only, the woman's laugh had displayed her teeth, as red as if she'd just worked them over a bloody shank. Her eyes were wide, the skin there strained like pulled linen.

Lara shuffled backward, away from the customary blessing. "Do Tony first," she said. "He needs it more than me."

She grabbed Tony's collar, dragging him from where he stared into the ceiling of his imagination. She offered the boy up the way she did dinner bones on her stoop to the loitering mongrels, a variety of ridgeback street-bred for its viciousness.

The woman seemed not to notice the substitution. Her hands found Tony. She called up a chant that was beyond what the kids had been taught to sing into their pillows. Its sound, distinct from Pali or Sanskrit, was jagged and breathless, the rhythm primal, and the adults, drawing close, felt compelled to respond.

"Join your energy with mine," she instructed.

What happened then was unprecedented. They each touched Tony.

One thing the kids held certain: Only the actual guests may touch the children. And even then, the guests, like monks, never touched women. But today Tony was being *touched* and it was coming from parents who hadn't handled their own children in years except to steer them onto a school bus or beat them for that last test score. The rule against contact had preserved the theory of Tony's crumbling skin, impossible to disprove until now. And *had* it now been disproved? Lara craned her neck but Tony had disappeared beneath the adults' snarled limbs.

The children peeled off from the session and snuck outside, suddenly shy after the naked intimacy of the gesture, like being witness to a mother breastfeeding. Lara could feel her fellows condemning her for selling up the purest of them, for exchanging a better soul for her own. But in their silence, there was the relief of not being picked, too. Even Mod, a veteran of another booklet group (same booklet, different circle, nominal success rate), had been cowed into a conspicuous silence.

It was normal for a child to be singled out for a deity's favor. In fact, each of the kids prayed for the patronage of a specific god, drawn from a lineup of Hindu through Taoist pantheons. Lara had chosen Guanyin, thinking that if any of the higher-order guests had the authority to pardon Lara her birth crimes, it would be the Goddess of Mercy, mother to the guilty.

LARA DIDN'T ALWAYS understand the guilt she had been born into; she knew only its restrictions on her happiness, how it reared from the past in moments when the family was trying its best, like two years ago, when Dad had pledged his participation to the Chinese New Year festivities, going so far as to wreathe the driveway in firecrackers.

Lara and Mom had watched from the street as Dad cradled a match to the mother fuse. It sparked and out-scooted Dad, head low as if dodging ricochets, a man's face made young by a boy's delight. Buoyed by a triumph with the firecrackers, their misgivings drowned out, the family had gone on to see the parade down Yaowarat, the city's original landing ground for Chinese immigrants.

Each neighborhood had its own mythology, but no legend was so widely enshrined as that of Somboon Supajirakul, a man known to children for having led that year's procession outfitted as the fabled monkey king. Lara remembered him straddling the armrests of a rickshaw pedaled by a kid in a matching monkey getup, the monkey king brandishing his staff as if preceding a conquering army. Following him in the vanguard were legions of dragons batting their formidable eyelashes at the little girls, as fire-breathers threw up red plumes.

Children wrangled for vantage, clambered up parents to see their patron deity, mascot of misfits and rascals. Impish by nature, the monkey king was never tamed except when the bigwig deities involved themselves, those times in folklore when he had properly overstepped the boundaries: Down fell the hand of Mother Guanyin to snuff his fun, pinning him under the weight of her righteous severity.

Lara had been riding Dad's shoulders, bucking with excitement. Only now they had lost Mom. "You see your mother?" he asked irritably.

And so their totem pole of two revolved to find her among the parade-goers.

"There!" Lara pointed.

Taxi drivers had used their cars to cordon off a section of road for dancing, tuning their radios to a single station cycling *luk thung* hits, clinking beats that struck an old-timey chord for Lara but that her father associated with the poorer region for which such music was an anthem.

Mom said she had taken Dad up-country once for a weeklong tour of her hometown, where the heat drew out the aroma of the *karawek* flowers that vined bus stops, and where even the relative cool of a corrugated roof overhead could feel like seeking shade under an oven coil. Dad orbited the neighborhood on a borrowed moped, making a breeze for himself. The trip had been cut short after he couldn't cope with the food, pungent and hot—what Mom craved made Dad's stomach run.

"She's dancing." Lara clutched her father's head, trying to reconcile the mother she knew with this woman laughing among taxi drivers.

Lara had seen this version of Mom before. Once, desperate to source her condition, Lara had rummaged through her mother's possessions. Was there some document denied to her—birth certificate, medical record, transcribed prophecy—that might have spelled out her origin?

What she exhumed was teenage Mom in her up-country days. In the photograph Mom stood on the back of a motorbike, her hands clutching the head of a smiling, steering boy, his right arm looped around to brace her. The warmth in the boy's hold, the comfort Mom had with her fingers twining his hair—these details went unappreciated. What the picture captured for Lara was a Mom who had kicked off her sandals miles back on that dirt track. This was not meek old Mom dressing up for the occasion, Mom doubling up on donation goods. Not Mom whose best contributions barely dappled the dinner-table conversation among Dad's friends. This was the Mom she saw that day of the festival, stepping to the music of her youth, opening her arms to Lara and Dad as she spotted them from afar: "Let's dance!"

"Forward!" Lara spurred Dad.

He didn't move.

"Lara, come!" Mom called out, soft-shoeing half the distance between them.

But Dad wouldn't let Lara climb down. "I don't want you dancing with those people." Turning, he called to Mom, "We're going home. Stay if you want."

Mom looked down at herself, trying to understand what had gone wrong.

As she followed them home, she transformed once more into a woman uncomfortable in her body. A small-stepping Mom, her heart rate economical, blood vessels tightened with unspoken anxiety.

Lara envisioned that young, barefoot teenage girl restrained like the monkey king under the hand of Guanyin in those old tales, whining through the centuries of captivity: What have I done but lived more, lived harder? Lara wanted to bow to him. Where was the man possessed by the God of Fun?

Well, he was an alcoholic, if you were to follow the tale of Somboon Supajirakul to its fade-out. Not that Somboon himself mattered, really; the myth of the monkey king had consumed the man. Children chiseled at the foundation story, refined their legend. Now was the year of the monkey king's return. The parade of the Year of the Monkey was to be his reincarnation—only not in flesh but jade. It's said Princess S. herself commissioned the statue, carved from a single cloud-white stone as if fashioned from the stuff of the heavens.

THE CHILDREN HAD engaged in the latest round of mythmaking, seeking consensus as to the height, pose, and vessel of this year's favorite when Tony was returned to them.

"Hey, man," Mod said. They were on the stairs outside, tiered according to an established hierarchy, with Mod and Lara at the top. "What do you think, will the statue be child-sized, man-sized, or giant-sized?"

"I don't know." Tony rubbed his eyes as if recently woken up. He seemed relieved not to have to describe what had happened. "Hope it's big, though."

"So you're coming to the parade later this month?" Mod asked. "We're all going to be there. It'd be fun if you were there, too. But it's okay if you can't come. I mean, we know your parents are, like, old-Chinese strict."

Tony livened at the invitation. "I'm going to ask them if I can come for the parade."

"That's cool, man. We'd like to see you there." Mod glanced around at the other kids. "So, like, do you have to ask your parents when you need to go piss, too?"

The closest boys sniggered.

"Shut up, Mod," Lara said in English, making room for Tony. She considered this moving over an apology. She had a system for managing her misdeeds. This system involved Lara punishing herself. For instance, she would skip tonight's dinner to make up for having disappointed Mom during the session. In this way she sought to keep her karmic scale in some approximation of balance. It was her own rudimentary code of ethics. The higher-up in Lara's imagination was a Buddhist-Taoist mishmash she called her Iron Goddess of Mercy, a vengeful, needy deity that had to be mollified regularly. And Lara tried.

She tried with Dad, played dutiful, trailing his interests in jazz, even baseball. She sang standards for him. On good nights Dad turned down the volume and reduced the radio to a background accompaniment, making space for Lara's own voice, the part of her they were both proud of.

Then there were times when Dad responded to Lara's efforts with a glazed expression, his affection clearly distant. And, look, the song was already over, as the radio station fuzzed into its next program. It might be an hour before they played something else that Lara could match her voice to ("You're my Billie Holiday reborn," Dad liked to say) and in that hour Dad returned to the world of his papers, his work, didn't notice Lara slip into the bathroom where she sat against the door, legs splayed, blaming her inner imbalance for this day's failures. Her karma was bad. Her fiddling with the nail clippers escalated into trying them on her forearms. Was it adequate punishment? She nipped the skin. Again. The clippers bit clean through. The pain was clear and sharp, like a purging fire. She made a formation of cuts that later scabbed, scarred, became a row of crescents luminous against the dusk of her arm. *I am my own Iron Goddess of Mercy*, she thought.

Mom came out of the temple rubbing her glasses on her skirt. The children stared up at her.

"Are you all right?" she asked Lara.

"You've got betel juice all over your mouth," Lara told her.

"I don't even like that stuff." With the back of her hand Mom smudged the red stain across her face. "Better?"

"Mm. Can we go?"

TONY DIDN'T COME to the following session, and a week later they found out that the boy had died.

Lara imagined Tony's parents at his bedside when whatever force had held the boy together departed, the parents helpless as his form began to dissipate. She saw Tony's father sobbing, shaking the body down to an ash that shrouded the parents with the same grief later displayed on their faces like masks the color of talc.

The woman who had led the prayer for Tony stopped attending entirely. Jojo's mother withdrew the girl, and the diminished session they endured was fruitless.

Outside afterwards, the kids tried to reapportion the weight of their parents' disappointment.

"You want to know what I think our trouble is?" Mod asked. Had Amrit been present, he'd have raised the obvious, his stump, preventing Mod from embarking down a familiar warpath. But Amrit had left, too.

"Our parents hate us." Mod surveyed his audience. "Other kids don't have to deal with this, right? Like, I'm serious. What would we be without them? Normal, probably."

Mod was met with the usual nonresponse: kids toe-sketching in the dirt, sucking candy, disrupting ant highways.

Lara was engaged with her own question. What would our parents be without us? It had boiled up the night before, as Lara tossed and turned in bed, rewriting her day's disappointments for posterity. Only, what had surfaced from the presleep murk wasn't the wan boy Tony but Mom—Mom dancing. It was easy to trace Mom's dancing steps back to the hidden photograph of her on the motorbike, where she and Lara looked so much alike. That same curtain hair, middle-parted to frame their shy faces, dead straight and black as if they'd never seen those women's magazine ads pushing shades of foreign, lighter brown. Even hairdressers remarked on the blackness of Lara's hair: "You have nothing of your father's coloring." And seeing herself in her Mom's past, Lara imagined her own future as the same as her mother's. As if that photograph had captured Lara herself, destined to follow the same dirt trail to the present. Lara, awake last night, began instead charting a divergent course, originating from that picture but running parallel, divided from the real present as if by a great valley.

The Mom of the far side was, as Lara conceived her, a teacher, fulfilling Mom's often-expressed desire to teach English. But Lara's actual Mom, in voicing that aspiration, would botch the English: her tenses, her pronouns, her pronunciation, her every English sentence a juggling act.

And what else had this Other Mom found on that timeline unaccompanied by Lara and Dad and their easy English banter that left actual Mom straggling? Lara became convinced that the parents had misread the booklet. *Mom,* she wanted to say, *Mom, you've got it all wrong. You've tuned your body to the wrong station, you know?* The channel Mom needed was not one of some red-mouthed monk airing knowledge accumulated from his many lives, but rather a signal in counterpoint to Mom's own, carrying with it the message from a single life: Mom's other.

LARA WENT BACK inside the temple, spiked her incense into the sand tubs and bowed before Mother Guanyin, certain now that they had it all backward. They were praying to the wrong pantheon. They had gotten hold of the fledgling deities, heaven's counterpart to their own circle of duds. What was needed was not soft, feckless Guanyin but her grim equivalent, a steely goddess whose mercy was punishing, bracing but cold and bitter as old tea. An Iron Goddess of Mercy.

Mod and the others followed her inside, Mod still ranting.

"How come all of the prayers we're taught are pleas for forgiveness? We didn't do it. Our parents are the ones who screwed up and we're being punished for it. That's why Tony died. You know? His parents messed up." Mod retreated then into the sullen mumble ("karma dumpsters") that was becoming his signature. He was taking on puberty. Acne had besieged his face, another case, he had claimed, of his parents' wrongdoing manifesting in him.

But he found his mark among the kids. They went about their temple obligations with impudence, treading on the entrance threshold, pointing their rude feet at the dais. Had the parents seen their children stepping all over tradition like this, they would have condemned the behavior. But the adults were busy expelling their own malcontent. A row of them stood at the shrine, using sheets of paper to fan the length of their bodies in encompassing head-to-heel sweeps.

"Go," they whispered, as they worked to usher out their own unhappiness.

"GROUP'S DEAD," MOD said.

It was the first day of Chinese New Year. It would be their last meeting before a two-week break.

"I've seen this before. They take a holiday, and then nobody comes back. You'll see."

Parents kept their hellos curt, trimmed their prayers. They anticipated a clean slate, borrowing against their futures for an unencumbered state of mind. The children hankered to get outside, where people were already queuing for the Year of the Monkey parade.

Lara picked her scabs, slipped the crusty skin into her mouth so she could taste metal. She knew Mom watched her, in the red-rimmed way of a mother mourning the loss of a child, discovering in the place of her daughter a changeling, a teenager (nearly), whose flaws were displayed not on her face, but tallied painfully across her arms.

Last night Dad had finally noticed.

"What the hell happened to *you?*"

Lara offered a vague explanation about karma, about righting wrongs.

"You did this to yourself?" Dad said, holding Lara's arm out to Mom. "This is your fucking cult stuff."

Mom took the arm. Counted. Her fingers read the raised scars, treated them as strikes against her parenting. Lara could feel the accusation in Mom's touch: You do this to me intentionally.

Lara fled the fight that ensued. She went to her usual place, upstairs straddling the windowsill, collecting what rose from the heat of their argument. Mom sobbing and shrill. Dad's words wine-limbered.

"*Your* problem," he kept saying. "*Your* history. *Your* daughter."

Until Lara couldn't listen to more.

She dug through the medicine cabinet and found an inhaler, an item from her bronchitic youth, days when Mom discovered her on all fours in the middle of the night, her cough a hound's bark, her throat bulging. There was no air. Mom would fill the bathtub with hot water, a film of Vicks scumming the surface, the rising steam thick with menthol.

"Shh, Lara." Mom cooing, smoothing back Lara's hair.

And Lara would fall into a happy half-consciousness, as she did now with the old inhaler in her mouth, puffing until the cartridge turned cold. Her vision strobed, all the sounds around her communicated as if through the back of a fan, everything muffled, stuttering.

Then Lara was on the carpet and the air-conditioning was speaking to her. No, that was Mom downstairs. What was she saying? Lara cobbled together the fight; it came to her in fragments, ugly, the language broken.

MOM FROWNED THROUGH the meditation, straining, Lara could see, to summon a being with answers, someone who might save the group. For the first and only time, Mom wanted to channel. The group prayed for answers, but the session ended without activity.

"That's a wrap!" Mod said brightly, interrupting what Lara realized was her own hope.

"Come on," he said. "Parade's coming."

The kids went out to the street, jockeying for a view. They could hear the procession beyond the bend in the road. The spectators set off firecrackers as it passed them, giving the impression that the parade was igniting the shophouses as it galumphed through, cornering finally onto the thoroughfare, where the music was briefly overwhelmed by the crowd's response. The entourage of dragons, acrobats, and musicians was lost to the main spectacle, a wooden barge skirted in blue ribbons to look like it was rolling by on a high tide.

"What the fuck?" Mod said in English.

The children had seen it, too. On a plinth in the center of the barge was a child-sized statue of the monkey king. Not even the height of an especially robust kid—a wimpy little thing, more like a standing baby hewn of regular sea-green jade.

Lara heard the collective disappointment of the amassed children in the sudden muzzling of their rows, her fellows probably thinking, as Lara was, that a cruel joke was being played on them. This was their mascot? But there it was: diminished, crude, too small to wield their outsized myths.

The nearby adults seemed not to have noticed, and when the parade reached them any shortcoming was overcome by the frantic bursts of released firecrackers.

It was all a sham.

Lara slipped back into the temple alone. She took the inhaler from her pocket and puffed, filling her mouth with its cold kiss. She puffed again. More. She breathed deeply and the cloud from the inhaler mixed with the firecracker smoke funneling through the production bay. As the smoke withdrew its hold over the room, the statues were disrobed of their mythical fog.

Then Lara noticed another figure—to her right, a luminous shape that made a nimbus of the smoke framing it.

Lara recognized the form from one of her early memories. She was five, and to escape the nighttime smother of that year's hot season she would bring her pillow downstairs to the cool tile of the kitchen. One night she found Mom slumped there, crying, her shaggy nightgown made resplendent by the moonlight, so that Lara had afterwards wondered whether it was actually a mirage that had carried her back to bed.

Here in the temple, Mom sat completely still, three burning sticks of incense clutched in her hands. Her incandescence had that smudged quality found on an old TV, its antennae unable to hold the picture quite still.

Lara brought her hands together in a polite *wai*. "It's not you, is it, Mom?" Lara would have recognized Mom's soft posture, the signature way her body folded.

This Mom managed only a mumble.

"Can you hear me?" Lara asked.

The eyes—her mother's—swam back and forth in the bowls of her heavy lenses. Finally, the darting attention seemed to harden into a sort of recognition.

Lara brought her head lower, practically bowing into Mom's lap, the next question a whisper.

"It's you, isn't it? The Iron Goddess? I can see you in there." Lara imagined skin of a brushed bronze and eyes that were mirrored tiles, like those adorning temples across the city.

"Child—"

"Don't," Lara said angrily. "Don't 'child' me. You *know* me. *I* asked you to come here. See, I have questions you need to answer." Before her she saw her mom lying in a crescent shape on the white linoleum of the kitchen.

"That memory . . . Is it even real?"

Lara wasn't sure whose voice spoke, Mom's or the goddess's. Less than a breath: "Yes."

"*I* caused that, didn't I? My birth ruined our family."

"Yes."

What could she do with that answer? Lara sagged. She thought of pieces of Tony floating apart. Of marriage like a bamboo raft pulled asunder, not violently, but by gradual drifting. The anger that had been her center released now.

Lara took Mom's hand and placed it on her crown. "But you can make this right," Lara said.

There were sudden smacking sounds from the entrance. The kids entered beating one another with wooden clappers, pretending to hand out blessings. "Good fortune! Good health! Good wealth!"

Mom's eyes flickered. The guest's attention drifted.

"*No!* Please don't leave. I need your help to make it better."

The kids: "Happy Year of the Monkey!"

"Wait—I'm sorry. Can you still hear me? I'm sorry." Lara jerked out her left arm, displaying an arm filigreed with small scars, pink and white lacing her skin to the elbow.

"Isn't this what you wanted to see?" She slapped the arm with her other hand, snapping the guest's attention back. The guest watched the red blotch resolve to Lara's natural color. "Isn't this what you want—to punish us? See?"

But the goddess was about to depart, the gaze reaching out like guiding hands in a dark room, braced on the furniture, ready to heave into the air. And Lara could see in that departure the receding of the other future they might have followed: Lara left with Mom to stumble their dirt path, Dad already absent, while above them all the Iron Goddess of Mercy receded into the blue, unable to pardon them their many mistakes. And from a ridgeline across a valley young Other Mom, forever distant, calling to them, "Forgive my happiness."

"Please. You have to help." Lara grabbed the incense sticks, their ashy lengths like fingers wickedly curled.

"Please." Taking a breath, she touched the incense to her skin, felt a sweet jolt of pain. One of the stubs fell away. "Please." Again she burned herself.

Mom's hand clasped Lara's. It snapped the remaining incense stalks. For a final instant the two eyes settled on Lara.

"Child," said the soft voice. "Your mother wouldn't hurt you."

Stomping Ground

BENZ, TINTIN & PRADIT (1993)

When the monsoon begins to fall, plinking the tin roof of our shack, drumming the buckets upturned in the dirt, the three of us are outside putting up the last length of our rain wall. Garbage mixed with sand, it encircles our hideout like a mother's arms. We mean to see our shack weather its first monsoon. In our slum, if you're not careful, the rain will wash you away in the night, lulled and sleepy-eyed into another life as something better suited to Bangkok's wet season, a klong-swimming creature like a frog or a snake. Or something like us: strayboys. We learned early how to survive.

"Here it comes," Tintin says, clapping the sand off his hands. He leans his head back into the rain.

I move my stool under the shack's awning and light up a cigarette. Big is testing his new rain boots but the fat at his ankles forces him to roll the tight rubber down his legs like stockings. Big and Tintin are the only strayboys able to actually *grow* on what little we eat of boiled rice and vegetables now that the mothers aren't cooking meat, having renounced the pretty animals that make pretty dying sounds when you snap their necks for dinner.

"The rain won't breach *these* boots," Big says.

Tintin leans on the screen door to stop the wind from whipping it. "Too bad. It might wash that shit smell off your feet."

"These toes are cleaner than your teeth." Big holds his foot up to Tintin. "Smell. No?" He returns to digging around in the garbage wall beside me.

My cigarette's caked in mud, so I stub it out on the gummy face of Big's left boot.

"That's money you're hole-punching," Big says.

"You didn't buy them," I tell him.

"Didn't say it was *my* money."

Big found the boots yesterday, bobbing in our klong. Now that rain has juiced its waters back to chest-depth, the klong is murky enough to mask the riverbed rubbish. It's also heavy enough to truck treasure from upstream, where it feeds into a moneyed neighborhood of sunny homes with sunny-colored rowboats bleeding their sky blue into the grey water. Sometimes those people paddle down to this end. Our shack stands beside the bush and bramble wall that hides the rest of the slum. It's right out of a TV soap, all wooden slabs hitched to metal sheets—simple enough to catch their rich imaginations. Their prying eyes make me want to bite them, a snake tearing into some pretty Polly bird come up from Australia for a holiday.

Big uproots an umbrella and spreads its torn hood. He walks into the rain watching his feet. Mud wells around him and the water soaks his wide head.

"There's a leak in the left one," Big points out.

Tintin pulls out his cock for a piss. "Stand here and find out for sure." He laughs as he shoots into the mouth of a buried oil drum.

The bushes rustle. On instinct, I reach for a broom handle, but what barges through isn't a beast. It's two boys on monster bicycles in glossy red and blue. Each bike has enough gears, springs, and metal for some kind of war machine. Next to their equipment, my broom feels like a toothpick. Their tires gouge the mud as they slow.

One boy is white with yellow hair crisp and curled as *khai chiao*. The other's *luk khrueng*–looking but too broad in the chest and arms to count as half Thai, not even in the way of Big, who's barreled around the middle.

"Hi," the white one says in English. The only response from any of us is the pitter-patter of the accelerating rainfall.

Here's me on toe-points teetering about what to do with the broom. There's Tintin clutching his cock like it's a piece of fruit. Big's umbrella wilts above his head. It's not their brawn or bikes that has our trio dumbstruck from afar, thinking, *Really?* It's the pairing of those tires and this turf, the sheen of their new clothes next to our broken abode. It's them against us. It's enough to give any strayboy pause.

The boys look curiously at Tintin, who finally puts his peanut away.

"Let's go, Tom," the white one says, and with whirring wheels sets off in the direction of Monopolyville, the bright colors of their bicycles soon dissolving into the wash of rain.

In a slum the size of ours, you would expect a healthy helping of sexy, *suai* daughters. *Slum suai,* you know—the so-ripe-she's-bruised kind that end up in the sex bars. So you can understand our outrage when we're gifted only one. Chanel. Just one to handle all the hungry looks. Wherever Chanel walks, all us strayboys plant ourselves in rows like street-side weeds, heads swinging with the passing leg traffic. She's sixteen, the age, we've noticed, when girls attain enlightenment—impossible combinations of firm and soft, slim and rounded—only to begin the descent to dirt, recalled from that pink paradise to an afterlife as just another mother among the collective.

"The heavens open up," says Tintin, throwing his arms out in the direction of Chanel. "And . . ."

She's smoking a cigarette under the awning of Apah's shop. We shuffle in her direction, the three of us cooped under Big's broken umbrella.

"Hey," Big says. We bunch in beside Chanel, water plip-plopping off our noses, and arrange our hair: plastered flat (Big), spiked in tufts like a rice field (Tintin), slick side parting (that's me). A second's jostling and we line up, Chanel beside Big. We peer sideways, trying to trace the contours of her curves through her soaked cotton shirt.

"What is this, a peep show?" Chanel asks.

We lean back into line.

I find something to say. "We talked to two *farang* boys just now."

She's surprised. "I didn't know you could speak English."

"Mys name ids Benz," I say in English.

"Whaas you name?" Tintin adds, trying to do Teacher Somkiat proud with his exquisite pronunciation.

This exhausts our English. Tintin and Big look at me.

"Anyway, we didn't talk to them for long," I say. "They seemed pretty scared of us."

"They biked over by our shack," Big says, nodding.

"The infamous Big-Tintin-Benz shack," Chanel mocks. "So where did you set that thing up, huh?"

Guarded glances between the three of us.

"Sworn to secrecy," Big says.

Chanel snorts. Then she looks down, rubbing her arms. "Nice boots."

We look at Big's boots. He rocks back onto his heels and puffs his cheeks modestly.

"I picked them myself," Big says.

"They leak," I say.

"So?" Chanel fixes her eyes on me. "What's wrong with nice clothing, Benz?"

Tintin tries to tuck me behind him with two fingers on my arm.

"*I* think they're *suai*," he says. "About as *suai* as—"

"Yeah, but what do *you* think, Benz?" Chanel won't let up on me.

"Sure, they're nice."

"There's talk you three are earning money," she says.

Tintin takes his place at the end of the line. Big holds his breath and arches out of the path of Chanel's question.

"Maybe you'll pick out something for me one of these days?" Chanel glances down at her wet shirt.

"Clothes, you mean?" I ask. "Like a skirt?"

"Sure, I'd *like* a skirt. Big, is that an umbrella that you're not using anymore?"

Seeing the umbrella still in his hand, Big gives it to her and she walks into the rain, leaving us stranded outside Apah's shop.

"You boys go somewhere else!" Apah yells from inside. "You're scaring away the customers."

"Old man, there are no customers in this monsoon!" Tintin says, but we take off our shoes and shirts, ball them in our hands, and run away.

"YOU DIDN'T HAVE the sense to find an umbrella?" Mother Anisa asks, seeing us in the doorway. "I just mopped the floor, so you wipe yourselves off before you come in."

We take turns slapping the mud from one another's legs.

"What's for dinner?" Big asks.

"Mother Pranee is cooking rice soup with *khai chiao* and cabbage," Mother Anisa says.

"Same old shit," Tintin mutters.

We slip our wet shirts into the basket outside the kitchen and go upstairs to the bedroom. There are twenty beds stacked like ladders, a roof humming under the rain. The wind makes hushing sounds as it skulks in through the wood-board walls. The other boys are already there. Their heads snap up from their circle in the corner. It's the mothers that make them jittery. The boys are clustered around playing cards, a pile of cigarettes in the middle. Gambling, like sex, drinking, and drugs, is banned in the house. It can get you booted out the door, which is not what any strayboy wants. Half of us here paid a pretty price for entry: past lives built on beatings, drugs, jailed parents. The other half are sons of one or another of the collective's mothers. With that half—the Fatherless, they've dubbed themselves—it's hard to say who belongs to whom, the mothers, of

former Chanel-caliber beauty, being tight-lipped about their histories. All we know is they once tried to rise above the slum, but have
since come back down.

"Got anything to gamble?" Op asks. Op's the unspoken leader,
and not because at seventeen he's older than all of us, but because he's
the unspoken son of Mother Gai, our household's head hen.

Tintin takes two bent cigarettes from his pocket and looks at me,
but I shake my head. The boys return to the round, reaching over
heads and hands to lay their cards.

"You were at your hideout, huh?" says one of the Fatherless boys,
barely ten. He's out of the round. He bets cigarettes but doesn't smoke
them, keeps a small stash in a tin beside his mattress.

"Maybe," I say. We sit down beyond the circle. Our wet shorts
spread damp shadows on the floor.

"Whatever," the boy says. "Your hideout's boring anyway. What
do you even do there?"

"Some *farangs* let us ride their bicycles," Tintin tells him.

"Whose bicycles?" he asks.

"Two *farang* boys from that neighborhood up the klong," Tintin
says.

"How come they let you?"

"What do you care? Their bikes are taller than you."

"Even *I* took a turn," Big says. "And I hate exercise."

"Like I believe you. What color were they?"

"One red. One blue," Tintin says.

The round ends and the others turn to us.

"What kind of bikes?"

"I say we go joyride through *their* neighborhood."

"How much you think we could sell one for?"

"What, a bike or a boy? Depends. How white are we talking?"
says another boy. "I know a buyer who pays a pretty rate for pearly
white skin."

Op cuts through the clamor: "The *farangs* are trouble, okay? Don't be bringing their trouble here, or you strayboys"—Op says like he's not actually one of us—"will be out on the street before your next meal."

Op is all about fortune-telling, dealing out doom like we're toeing the rules to a game he invented. A lose-lose game. But that's okay. We know what it is to lose everything and keep playing. Still, there is some power in Op's prophesizing. Because, eventually, we all prove him right. If not by a rule-breaking mishap, then simply by puttering along at the pace of life, gaining on the finish line of fifteen years old. That's the age, the mothers concluded back when they put up an ante on their futures and pooled their efforts into this house, that boys become men and are man enough to make their own money. Op, of course, holds the biggest trump card of all: He won't ever leave the collective, his fifteenth passed him by. In this house, Op's as permanent as boiled rice, as the mold clutching at the corner tiles in the showers. He's also all we have in the way of a father. Me, I'll be fifteen in a month.

THE MOTHERS LIVE downstairs, where the walls are concrete, cooler in the hot season and quieter in the rainy. We eat on two long tables off the kitchen. Tonight, Tintin, Big, and I are the center of chitchat, stirring up the suppertime *sup-sip* like it hasn't been since that time some kid fell into a klong and crawled out with a rich man's wristwatch caught on his shoelaces—or so he said. Tonight, the others, having heard about the money we've made in the last couple months, want to help us spend it.

"You should loan the money out," says one of the strayboys. "My own pa did that before someone decided they'd rather give him to the police than pay what they owed."

"Where'd you get it from, anyway?"

"Some diamond-eared woman got off the wrong bus, probably, and then they mugged her." Once the story gets going, they all pile in, talking over one another.

"Thugs."

"Nah, those fancy women don't ride buses," Tintin says. "They don't even leave the house except at night."

"You know that?"

"I do." Tintin runs his fingers along his arm, as if admiring his own color. "It's in the skin. You think the sun has ever seen that skin? It's butter. Soft butter like Bpa Tong puts on my rotis."

"Those fancy women can butter my roti anytime." Another boy sniggers.

"Who asked you?" Big says.

"I'll bet they stole one of those bikes. Sold 'em to Apah."

"I'd steal a bike if it got me the hell out of here."

"I know! Take the money and buy a street-food stall. 'Krapao! Khao Pad!' for the rest of your fucking life. Ha!"

"At least you'd never be hungry again."

"No, it should be a noodle stall. Your kids would have long arms and legs and live forever. That's what noodles do to people. My grandma told me before she died. She died because she didn't eat enough noodles when she was a kid. She only ate rice, so she was fat and short."

"But *we* only eat rice," Big muses.

"Just shut up."

Nobody scours the pot for the last scoops of boiled rice, as we usually do. Mother Gai comes in to tell us that tonight the mothers will wash the dishes. We have a treat, she says, a visitor.

"The older boys might remember Pi Pradit, who left us years ago," Mother Gai says fondly. "He's a police captain now, in our own district."

Pi Pradit steps through from the kitchen now, bowing under the low beam and then straightening like a returning hero, which is how the mothers see him. His grey-green uniform is tight around his stomach. He's tall for someone who grew up hungry. We make our *wais* and bows because the mothers want to see that, too.

Op goes to the front, but the other boys back away, not out of respect but fear, especially among those of us who haven't harbored here long. I arrived late, at twelve, and I'll tell you there isn't an honest job for a strayboy out there. We know the world this man polices, just like we know that the police are the worst of it. I don't care that Pi Pradit may have spent a few upstanding years in this house; once you're bent, no ironing will shape you up. It takes a broken boy to spot a broken boy, and twelve years under my father's boot will break the best of boys.

This happened the year before I moved into the house. I found myself in a fight, frozen above the boy and raising a metal pipe. For what? Cigarettes for Father. I took them from the boy. You would be surprised what a cigarette could do for my chances of sleeping safely through the night. Stick one in Father's mouth and he deflated for the time it took him to torch those two inches of tobacco. I tried to keep him smoking forever, which is why I had a pipe in hand, a boy beneath me. I tell myself I was beat, bloodied, berserk. I tell myself that it was my father's face. I surprised us both when I struck him. I left him bloody. I don't know what happened to him. I didn't even know the boy. Another story disappearing into the klong with the rest of the city's debris.

Pi Pradit tells us what **he does** and how he shares the money he makes with the mothers who once fended for him. The mothers expect a return on us. Why a house for boys? Because only pretty girls **can** earn money, and with all the *farang* men swooping in from the first world, there aren't many pretty girls left. And why strayboys? Because we make our own way.

Pi Pradit beckons me over afterwards and asks how old I am.

"Fourteen."

"Almost out. When you're out—when any of you are out," he says, bringing in Big and Tintin with a wave, "and you need a job? Come find me."

"I don't want to be a policeman," I tell him.

He laughs. "I don't mean a job as a policeman. Understand?"

"Yes," Big and Tintin say in unison. "Understood."

Those two are proper strayboys like me, not Fatherless kids who grew up cushy. They're afraid of Pi Pradit.

"Benz?"

"I understand."

But when I age out of the collective, I'm not taking up under Pi Pradit's wing, no matter the pickings, the winnings, the boxes of cigarettes on offer. I'll choose where to lay my own bets. Fifteen years is enough time to know what type of work I don't want to go back to, not for some top spot on the food chain, expending every ounce of energy to be the big fish like Pi Pradit.

He draws us into a smaller huddle with his hands and I can smell the garlic and chili in his teeth. "I hear you've already started a little business of your own." He smiles at our surprise. "I like that. Men with initiative. We could use your type when the time comes."

"It's not a business," I say. "And it's not illegal either."

"Yes, of course. And look, I understand. I won't breathe a word of it." He kneads my neck with his fingers. "Just remember you've got your older brothers, like me, watching over you. And I always like to know what my little brothers are up to—that they're not straying from the path."

Visits likes this bring out the bravado. As we climb the stairs, it's the Fatherless boys who talk biggest.

"I'll own a whole building. My name across the side in bright fucking white."

"Whoever makes a million first has to buy us a new house and we'll all live there."

"I'm not living with you."

"I'm living alone."

Op the prophet keeps quiet through all of this.

One of the other fourteen-year-olds turns to me on the stairs. "Pi Pradit likes you, Benz. You can ask him for work after you age out."

"I'm not asking him for a damn thing."

"What, you too proud? Too busy playing with your *farang* friends? Where are your bikes, anyway? Show us the bikes."

"Like we even want the bikes," Tintin says. He pulls his shirt off for bed. "We're making our own future."

"If you're talking about that shack on the waterside," the boy says, "you're dreaming. It won't last the monsoon."

"It will," Big says. "Right, Benz?"

"It will," I say quietly.

"Plus, it's not a shack," Big says. "It's a *business*."

"Three little businessmen. What do you know?" The boy climbs into bed. "More like three shits in a rain-fat klong. If you're smart, you'll stick with someone who can swim against the water, like Pi Pradit."

A younger boy from the next bunk turns to me. "I'll buy my own bikes someday. What do you want, Pi Benz? What'll you buy?"

I lie back thinking of Chanel.

WE HAVE FIVE crates full of glass soda bottles and ten garbage bags of crushed plastic bottles: a week's worth of wealth from combing the klong. Using a wheelbarrow made from a plank and bicycle tires, we take the bottles to Apah's shop.

"How much?" I ask Apah.

He taps each bottle he counts, meandering back and forth up the rows.

"I told you," I say. "I counted them already."

"Weigh the plastic for me," Apah grumbles.

Big has already picked out a Popsicle, but he's waiting for Apah to finish before he unwraps it.

"Good," the old man says, and hands me the money. It's less than half of what he'll get for recycling them, but enough for now.

"Where do you find them?" Apah asks.

"It's all out there in the klong."

"None of the other boys bring back this much," he says.

"What does it matter?"

"Some people ask questions, you know? Maybe some people don't like it when boys make their own money."

"Tell them they can come ask me."

In the week since Pi Pradit's well wishes, we've been warned twice now about our new trade. Two days ago Mother Anisa took me away from washing duty to tell me that I was a clever child—yes, smart from the start—but whatever my trio was up to, it was drawing bad attention, she had heard. I told her it was all perfectly legal.

We had started scouring the klong a couple of months back, after finding the empty plot behind the high bushes. At first we were just looking for supplies to build the shack. Boards, beams, bits of metal—whatever washed up. But we kept looking even after the shack had begun taking shape. There was wealth, we saw, below the sediment blanketing the klong.

Then, when Tintin dredged up a badminton net from the deep middle—the klong having been hobbled by a week's worth of mudslides—it was my idea to string the net across the water. And it worked, too. We brought in enough bottles to visit Apah's twice in one morning. Now we do this every day. Tintin swims to the far side and we walk the net up the river, raking the bottom.

"What do you do with the money?" Apah asks.

"We're buying ourselves a future, you know? Someday we'll be able to buy whatever we want, even a bicycle."

Apah returns to his stool behind the counter. "You're dreaming, boy. Where would you find a bicycle?"

"How much would you pay if I brought one in?"

"I don't deal in stolen goods, kid."

"I'm not a thief. You never know what the klong might give up." I glance at Tintin and Big sucking their Popsicles outside. "Hey, can I see the clothes you have for sale?"

Apah points up at the t-shirts hanging on hooks from the ceiling.

"No, uh, the women's stuff."

He shows me a wooden container brimming with plumes and

ribbons. Not much for clothing. I root around with my hand and come out with a short black skirt with a strip of silver stars stretching around the hem. It probably belonged to a little girl. Apah sells me the skirt for more than anyone ever paid for it in the first place.

CHANEL HALTS OUTSIDE the shack. "I thought this place was a secret."

I open the door and follow her in. "We built it. We make the rules."

"Where are your boys, anyway?" She strokes the wind chime we made with cut-up soda cans.

"Tintin went back to the house to change. A monitor lizard shat all over him when he tried to move it from a tree. Big went with him." I light a cigarette.

"Could you sleep on this?" Chanel asks, bouncing on the wooden boards beneath us. "Bet you could dance on it." She demonstrates, twisting, bowing at the waist. She steps up to me, places her fingertips across my lips, plucks the cigarette out and drops it. She leans into me.

"Careful! Don't burn us down, all right?" I move around her to crush the cigarette. "We worked hard on this."

"That's what I like about you," Chanel says, walking her fingers up my arm. "You're making money, but it's clean work. At least, you *seem* clean. But what do I know?" She looks down and brings her feet together. "I mean, look at the length of this skirt you bought me. You would think I was trying to seduce somebody."

I had taken the skirt to Chanel at her house. She had me wait in the front room while she wriggled into it in the back. The door between the rooms dragged on the swollen floorboards, and she left it open, enough for me to see the fabric slide up the narrow bell of her hips. She turned and caught my eye before coming back through.

"We'll put in window shutters next," I say, tapping the empty frames. "And, with time, lighting."

Chanel sighs. "So, Mister Business. Why start all this? Why not just put yourselves in Pi Pradit's pocket? No lizard shit in there."

"We'll make our own home. Ours from the ground up."

"Big boy in a small man's world," she says, backing me into a wall this time, her lips on the line of my chin. "So." Her fingers find my skin beneath the t-shirt, her thumb in the socket of my navel as she pushes down.

She handles the buckle of my pants with one hand, the other around my neck, pulling my mouth into her. Her clothes come off in what seems a single swoop.

"Except for this," she says, flicking up the front trim of the skirt. "I like this."

She straddles me, whispering, "You can touch me."

But I don't even know where. "I've never—"

"Oh." Chanel stops. "You're just a boy after all, aren't you, Benz?" She reaches down. "There." But she lingers above me, close enough that I can feel the wet brush of her. Her expression is playful, as if she's waiting for me to move. She holds me down when I try to thrust upward. Her grip belongs to a slum girl, one hand steady enough to keep the chicken's head on the block.

"I know what I can do for you,"—she lowers herself an inch— "but what can *you* do for me?" Her hips roll forward, slowly, and then back. "What will you give for more of me?"

"Anything."

"Give me a price, Benz," she breathes, pushing down onto me. "How much am I worth?"

THREE WEEKS INTO the season and our klong has shed its banks. At night the water climbs against our rain wall, reclaiming the garbage, piece by piece. We spend the mornings fortifying the shack and waiting for the water to recede. In another province, this monsoon has already taken two homes and a baby boy. Now, instead of growing up to be like us, he'll get to be something else. Something better maybe.

When I asked the morning monks about rebirth as I offered up food once, they told me that it doesn't work that way, said I should learn to see beyond my own immediate concerns. But then, what do the monks know? They don't even earn their own food. They might have an answer if they went to bed hungry as often as we do.

At noon it's still raining. The klong is heavy, its middle tow quick.

"Can you swim it?" Big asks Tintin.

Ankle-deep in the water, Tintin's naked except for the white underwear plastered against him, the end of the badminton net tied around his stomach.

"Do I *want* to swim it?" Tintin says.

"Maybe if you start farther upstream," I say.

"Maybe I won't drown then, you mean?"

"We have to take risks," I say, "if we want to get anywhere."

Tintin turns to me. "Yes, but *who's* taking the fucking risks?"

"You want to let all that loot wash by us?" I point at the waterline. "A week's worth of floods, huh? Think how much glass and plastic is down there."

"We can tie you," Big suggests. "We'll tie our end of the net to something solid. We can pull you to shore if the current's too strong." Big looks around. The only trees that haven't been cut up for walls and floorboards are saplings, bowing under the rain. The monsoon's eroded any certainty of the ground, and our shack itself is about as solid as our dwindling garbage wall.

"Big," I say. "We'll tie it around Big. Right? He's the sturdiest thing around."

"Big?" Tintin says, but I'm already circling the rope around the globe of Big's belly. I tie a knot and tighten it like a belt.

"Hey! Go easy."

"You sure, Big?" Tintin repeats, less than sure himself. "We can wait a day. The klong may be slower tomorrow."

That's a day's earning away from what I'll buy Chanel next: a beautiful piece for her hair.

"Just do it, all right? Before the water rises."

The klong has crawled up within arm's reach of the rain wall by the time we're ready. Big stands dumb with the rope around his waist, Tintin behind him, braced for a running start. I'm downstream from them, standing near the shack.

Tintin shivers. "Cold."

"Go on," I say. "The swim will warm you."

"Wait." Big pulls off his boots. He's sealed the hole on the left side by melting the rubber together. He forces the boots over Tintin's feet, gripping Tintin's legs at the ankle.

Tintin flexes his toes in the boots. "Thanks." He tugs at the badminton net to give himself some slack, then takes off running, the boots leaving pockets in the mud.

Tintin's body strikes the water and immediately shoots downstream in the fierce current. The rope snaps taut, jerking Big onto his face.

I yell at Tintin to come back, but his arms furiously work at the water, trying to move forward. The current twists him so that the net spools around his body like he's a spider's prey, caught and bound.

"Stop!" I run to Big who is down on his knees trying to anchor the rope as it drags his great heft into the shallows. "Let it go! He's getting caught in it."

Big blinks the mud from his eyes and releases the rope in his hands, but it's still tied around his waist and he falls sideways, winded, groaning as the knot burrows into his flesh.

"Hold it. Hold the rope while I untie it." I dig my fingers into the bulge of Big's stomach. Only, the knot is a clenched fist and I can't pry it apart.

I hear people coming through the bramble behind me, attracted by our shouts.

I look up. It's Pi Pradit and another policeman. My fingers are still on Big's stomach. His swell stills as he holds his breath.

"He's drowning," the other man observes.

Tintin writhes in the water, the netting crossed around his face, and I imagine him laid out wide-eyed on ice like a market fish, his pungent smell turning into something unknown, lacking the familiar reek of life.

"Help him!" I urge.

Pi Pradit signals and the other man reels Tintin in with several long pulls, all the way back into the shallows, garbage ensnared alongside him in the net. His body becomes another piece of the riverbank now, adorned with punctured cans, plastic bags clinging to his skin. He chokes up water.

Pi Pradit squats beside Tintin and draws his knife. "Looks like this net belongs to a badminton court. You boys been playing with stolen goods?"

Tintin sees the blade and curls into the mud, covering his ears with his hands. He coughs into his knees. Pi Pradit holds the net out for the current to tow away.

"We didn't steal it," I say, trying to grab the net, but the other policeman pushes me back.

"Risky business you had here," Pi Pradit says. "Whose idea was this?"

"I told you, we didn't steal it. We weren't doing anything illegal."

"Have you studied the law? No? Well, you might not know, then, that all businesses have to pay a tax."

"It's not a business," Big mumbles.

"What?"

"It's not a business," I say.

"Yeah, well, old Apah says you've made some money. Sounds like a business to me. It's been a month now. Or more? Look, your safety is not a right, it's a privilege, and we only offer our protection from harm to those who pay their taxes."

"I'm a strayboy. I make my own way."

Pi Pradit laughs. "No you don't."

I look past him. "Tintin, get up."

Tintin climbs up onto his knees only for Pi Pradit to press him back into the watery mud.

"We don't have any money," Big tells him. "We spent it all already."

"Did you?"

Tintin groans as Pi Pradit pushes him deeper into the wet mud, which rolls up around him, now, yielding to his body.

"Stop it," I say. "We don't have the money, okay?"

"Earn it back," Pi Pradit says simply. He kneels on the back of Tintin's head to make the point. Tintin kicks, his scream caught in the wet earth. "Which of you wants to be responsible for Tintin drowning?"

He releases Tintin and steps back. Tintin vomits onto the ground. He paws the dirt out of his eyes. Big kneels to help him.

"But listen, because we all come from the same collective, I'll see what I can do for you. For the mothers."

I look at Pi Pradit. "You threw away our net. Now it will take us weeks before we can collect enough to pay you."

"There are other ways." And although he doesn't say it, I know that Apah has mentioned the bicycles.

"You want me to steal," I say.

"Who's asking you to steal? I'm asking you to pay what you owe, Benz."

"We won't do it," Big says from beside Tintin.

"Shut up, Big," I say, and Pi Pradit nods at me. He waits for my answer.

THERE IS NO answer. He could drown Tintin and take me in. I would grow old among other boys who didn't play by police rules. It's not even about the promise of Pi Pradit's business protection. If the police wanted money, they would have taken it already, as it was being earned. This isn't a tax; it's conscription.

I'll go. The fences in that neighborhood are easy climbing, kid stuff. I know because we clambered on broken ones as boys. It will be behind the cars, the red bike. An automatic bulb will blink on. No chains, no angry dogs, the only sound my scratching soles. I'll find the switch for the mechanized gate. It will make a click-clapping noise as it unlocks, the doors swinging wide for me to wheel the bike right out.

The police might take me immediately. More likely, though, they'll want me in the slum as a power play, a spectacle that will earn them a reward from the wealthy ones who don't understand that these police are ours, not theirs. I'll be let off for the minor theft because favors beget favors. Because, for that small service, for the time not spent in a boys' prison, I'll owe Pi Pradit. Another debt of time. Not a lot, but enough; enough that I'll belong to them when they need me next. They'll find a need. There's always work for another soldier on their stomping ground.

I'll wait for them at the shack. The monsoon will be falling heavy on the hard roof. Under the ceaseless rain, I'll watch as the klong brushes aside our garbage dam and laps right up against the walls, forcing the boards apart, undoing all our work. The water will come up around my knees, and I will remember our first days foraging. Three strayboys bobbing at the glint of glass, an ebbing klong connecting us, the water giving up its elements. Here plastic. Here glass. A bamboo basket floating behind us filled with what we gathered.

I'll think of Chanel turning before her mirror in a too-small skirt, the stars catching a fluorescent bulb. Big and Tintin sweating in their bunks, hoping for my footfalls on the stairs. Tintin still coughing klong water into his pillow. Downstairs: our mothers, counting hours. And finally the police, drinking and gambling before making their slow way to me.

Only, before I hear the boots coming through the bushes, I'll take that bike and heave it into the rain swell, the thick monsoon klong, hoping that some luckier boys downstream might someday haul out my prize and keep it for themselves.

Goodbye, Big E Bar

PINKY & PRADIT (1996)

My father, El-Vitat Pohndee—that is, Thailand's original Elvis Presley—is dead. He's left me his costumes, which I'm restoring, as if to embalm him in the essential regalia. I've chalked a map for my embroidery, plan to work the fabric by hand. Still, these clothes, like old pelts, will never regain their former luster.

He's also left me the bar, the Big E, but it is going under. Gone are those tidy tourist families with their wind-up cameras come for Thai Elvis, Mommy whispering behind her hand, "Do you think it's a transvestite?"

I sent flyers to the old guard. "Closing Night!" I hired a band, kids from the jazz college who roll their heads as they play. "Cheap booze," I said. "End of an era." In America, see, Elvis may be long gone, but here at the Big E Bar, we're only now laying the King to rest.

My FATHER MADE his name performing in the love hotels that became synonymous with Americans on R&R. Back then it was rock and roll versus communism. All they played on the Armed Forces Network was Elvis. Vietnam was burning. It was the GIs who gave Vitat his nickname, El-Vitat, after Elvis. Almost the real thing, the soldiers said, lulled, lost in the women and the seats that were plush and red like tongues.

In 1969 Father sold the Gibson SJ-200 he'd refurbished by hand and flew all the way to Vegas on that money. He returned with a candid photograph: Elvis captured through a break in the crowd. The other Thai impersonators learned from LPs, and later videos, but the closest they knew to an authentic performance was El-Vitat, who managed to impersonate more than just a voice. He knew what it felt like to be in the presence of the King.

I'm his last child, the twelfth of twelve children. "Too bad it's another girl," my grandmother said. All of us were raised by my mother in El-Vitat's family house, away from the vulgar spotlight of Father's career. My siblings had long fled Grandmother's regime. After I was born, my mother left also, to live with my eldest sister. Grandmother said my mother was irresponsible, some whore. Grandmother said she loved her son, and also that she would never forgive him for sullying the family name with his clown getup.

I was twelve the year Grandmother died. "It's Vitat," she had confirmed when the doctor told her she had a growth. "He kills me." By then Father had wrangled a real following. A side attraction in the big guidebooks, he found a backer in a corrupt police major and opened the Big E to secure a permanent stage for his performances.

He moved me to his apartment above the bar, the rooms small enough that one didn't expect much in the way of privacy. The walls were constructed of heavy brick and plaster, but Father's bedroom was my only route to the toilet. At first I regarded the journey with a child's terror of the dark, but it was light I dreaded, that snap of a switch followed by the overheard fluorescence *ping-ping-ping*ing to awful intensity. "Oh, it's just you. Get out."

I finally halved a milk carton and within a week had mastered this makeshift bedpan. By then, however, I was curious, and waited for my subtle friend, the quarter moon, to steal in and look at my father without his looking back.

He was older in his sleep, the moonlight carving out his face. I thought at first that he mumbled, but having battened down my heart, I recognized the sound: the grinding of teeth, the murmurings of a man rehearsing.

From my first week, Father had me helping behind the bar. I was directed by the fattest woman I'd ever seen. She snuck sips of rum and had to sit on two stools. Still, she was kind to me. As she worked, her hand hovered at her chest, always plucking the shirt from her body. It was better like this, she said. The men let her be.

When Father fired the woman—Rita was her name—I ran away. Soon I was lost in Bangkok, watching the rain from the awning of a supply store. When asked by the police for my address, I could answer only: El-Vitat's bar. It was evidence of his reputation, Father boasted, that the police knew right where to bring me.

After Rita, the most constant presence in my childhood were Father's friends, Rick and Pradit.

Rick was American and an amateur Elvis himself. He had a rich voice but a quietly magnanimous way of looking down on the crowd, as if he had bestowed rock and roll upon us. A vehicle for stupid Westernisms, he seemed to enjoy dispatching these references in our conversations.

"Pinky, how're you doing tonight? Need a friend? A Hyde for your Jekyll? Gin," Rick clinked his glass against my water bottle, "for your tonic?"

Pradit, on the other hand, was a police major and effectively the bar's owner. He had other establishments, like Venus, his most popular club, where Father took me on his nights off. Pradit wore two large amulets: one with a portrait of Elvis, the other a carving of King Bhumibol. He also kept an entourage of three women. Always three, and in cocktail dresses that were forever being tugged down. They came and went with him, and whenever he caught a man looking, Pradit would say, "I've seen them all naked. So can you."

Pradit called me "Good Girl," saying it in English, tearing "girl" into two syllables: *gah-url.* "Get a drink for my helpers. Good Gah-url."

I once plucked up the courage to ask why he called the women his helpers.

"You're right! They should call *me* the helper." Pradit patted my head when I didn't understand the joke. Didn't I know? He ran a charity. Wasn't he always looking for a poor girl whose life he could save? He had a better record for lives saved than the Red Cross, probably. He did a good thing.

That was true on occasion. More often, though, he just ended up replacing them as they aged. They came and went in cohorts, while Pradit maintained his reputation for a workforce that was young— they truly were *girls.* In his club, age, as opposed to time, was the marker of change. Inside Venus, I, too, had aged.

I was initially bound to the front room of Venus, sitting with the women idling between customers. The new ones always told me I had Vitat's looks. They'd lean back as if to take all of me in and then tell me it was the eyes. I had my father's dark, unblinking eyes, which appeared never to see the crowd but something beyond it. Father dressed me for these nights out in clothes tailored by his friends, men who worked stiff northern silk to cling on my narrow frame like a Western gown. When the women asked, I told them I was twelve rather than the small fourteen-year-old I actually was. I did this to spare them having to address my father's absence ("I'll be upstairs, fucking," he had told me himself). And to keep up the ruse, I occupied my helpers with a twelve-year-old's questions: *Do you have to curl your hair all the time? What about when you're sleeping? So, you're a bartender? Do you speak English? How well?*

Eventually, age caught up to all the women in Venus, just as it had caught me. I was soon sixteen and no longer pretending. A man in a suit bought me a drink. And another the next night. We were stuck at one drink per night for a month. Finally, he kissed me. The next time, he booked a private room and dropped his pants but kept the suit jacket on, which confused me. We had plenty of time. My father always left me alone for hours. I undressed fully, as if to demonstrate how.

The man said he preferred anal sex. It hurt and then it didn't, and on the toilet afterwards I reflected on this fact. "On the shitter?" he asked through the door. Yes, I was. "Don't come in." This sputtering: a dirty trick. Sex was not a fair exchange. He came. I emptied my ass.

Of all our customers, the locals were the most frustratingly inconsistent. They showed up for live music but drank elsewhere, though I believe they loved my father.

It was expats, though, who really enjoyed the Big E's nostalgic charm, our falsely remembered America. Laughing at the store-bought "antiques" dotting the room, they insisted there was an authentic Thai-ness to the kitsch, to the bar's wood paneling that had been kicked in from years of enthusiastic feet-swinging. The wall behind the drinks was a checkerboard of old record sleeves printed on cheap paper.

Father charmed the tourists, wanting to show them how classy a Thai could be.

"You have to find the right Thais," I had heard him say once, to an intimidated white couple. "Where are you from?"

They said they were from Wales.

"Great Britain!" Father exclaimed familiarly. They said yes, they were from Newport, and did he know it? "Newport, yes," he mused. And then, "It is because we send only bad Thais abroad. They don't know how to behave. Country people. Poor people. Immigrants." He sighed. "And they go and they don't throw garbage in garbage bin and you English, you think, 'These Thais such barbarian!'"

They were Welsh, thank you.

On such nights, I took over the job of humoring Rick. I poured him an extra finger of whiskey and let him unpack his American lore. He explained for me the importance of the great duos: Simon and Garfunkel, peanut butter and jelly.

"The king and the King," he said one night, pointing to the poster by the stage. It was a blown-up photograph of our King Bhumibol meeting Elvis. Rick said that speaking obliquely was his first lesson on arriving in this country, where he discovered laws governing talk.

"I wasn't used to that. In the U.S., it's always First Amendment this, First Amendment that. You get me?"

"Obliquely?" I asked.

"Sure. As in, Elvis, in place of 'King of Thailand.'"

I didn't understand. Why would he need to talk about our king at all?

He smiled at that.

Other nights he complained again about his daughter, who was suddenly a teenager.

"Not much younger than you," he'd tell me. He said raising a teen was like a game. "Tell me about soccer practice. Tell me about your best friend." And despite the attempts he said he knew nothing about his daughter. Lara. Teenage Lara always executing some violence against herself. "I'm cutting, Dad." Chiseling her sexless body, once childishly chubby, but budding. Who the hell were these kids emulating?

All this he said without properly looking at me. He told me it was the intensity in my eyes, what he called my faraway look, that disconcerted him. Really, he didn't understand that my attention was reaching past what was before me, searching out my father on the stage.

When Rick felt my attention moving beyond him, he'd eventually get up onstage to sing himself. His wife was often in the front row, mouthing along to the lyrics.

Unlike Pradit, Rick could also be generous. He volunteered to accompany me after I had been bullied into my only public performance, my eighteenth birthday gift. My father said performance was a rite of passage. How did I expect to carry forward his story? If anything, I was already a decade overdue.

"Don't worry," Rick told me. "Me and you, a duet. Like Rocky and Bullwinkle."

But only one of us was a hive of writhing, humming nerves. I bumped Rick on the way to the performer's bench that birthday night, sloshing beer over both our outfits.

Rick stared down his front. "Guess it can only get better from here."

"So sorry," I said, attempting to pat the froth on his chest with my fingers.

"Your dad looks pissed. Sure that wasn't on purpose?"

Father directed us around the bar and into the costume room, which ran below the stairs. His collection was arranged chronologically, 1953–1977, and hung from two rails. At the end was a full-length mirror, giving the impression of an endless wardrobe. I thought of the hours my father spent here, rehearsing his introductions, altering his persona and the fit of his clothes. He loved that mirror. Vanity kept him true to his art.

"What's that smell?" Rick sniffed. "Embalming fluid?"

The mops and cleaning supplies were stored here. Father used to say the smell would also keep the insects out of his clothes.

"You could set the air on fire in here," Rick said.

I picked out a suit I had recently retouched—white with streaks of sequins along the lapels. I handed it to him.

Rick turned a slow circle looking, perhaps, for a dressing room. I made it clear this was it. Wanting to seem professional, cool, I turned and stripped to my underwear.

I pulled a rhinestone vest over my bra and approached the mirror. I could see Rick undressing. He was fat in the top-heavy way of tall men: a bulbous belly on a boy's calves. Rick was watching me, too.

He came behind me, against me, and looking in the mirror, he touched the tattoo on the inside of my thigh. It was of a card, the nine of diamonds.

"Why this tattoo?" His hand, too, a question. "Why here?"

I stopped the crawl of his fingers, shrugged off the nuzzling at the nape of my neck, then turned around and kissed him, childishly—smack. "For luck!" I said.

Too late, I should've said. My father had inked my memory, such that I couldn't feel a man's stroking fingers on my thighs without thinking first of Father holding a swimsuit stretched for me: "Left leg, right leg. That's right."

I touched Rick's top button. "Father leaves this open."

I WAS RAISED motherless, see, but with women proximate. My father's women, who, after spending the night, would take upon themselves the task of making my breakfast, of checking over the components of my school uniform: belt clip, pin, ribbon. They braided my hair. Initially, I had loved their affection. It was a currency I could hoard, thinking these women must have assigned me value: See how important she is to her father?

Eventually, though, I came to understand that they simply didn't know what to do with him in the morning. You fuck El-Vitat only to wake up beside old Uncle Pohndee. What could a woman do? And so she busied her hands with something familiar—girlhood—while waiting for the legend's return.

In my teenage years, I modeled myself off these women he brought back. I stole their clothes and makeup. My first thong was black, cheap. I took what they had.

Then the nine of diamonds, his favorite woman. One morning, with Father gone, I watched her lying twisted in a blanket. I sat beside her, smoking, and peeled the covers from her thigh to see in full the tattoo, its red ink purpled by age. When I looked up she was watching me. She asked for the cigarette and sat up to receive it. The blanket fell away. Her left breast showed the stain of a bruise the same color as the tattoo.

Even his infatuations had their life spans. But he wasn't a man to confront his audience. He hid on the roof, flicked ashes at the pigeons, reclined on the low wall, and lorded over the morning street. By the time the day grew warm I would step in, explaining to them his solitary dawn routine: walking the backstreets. He could be gone for hours. Most of them understood the significance of a man's absence, his silence. Only the few who had actually grown to know him forced themselves back into our lives.

His favorite, true to her indomitable character, outdid them all. Pillaging the bathroom, she emerged with her body painted the purple of Father's hair dye, the bags of which she had exploded against the tiles. She called for El-Vitat. He didn't come. She threw herself on his bed, and then hurtled down the stairs, marking the bannisters and the old posters. I was impressed. Finally, as she bore down on the costume room itself, Father intervened. He dragged her to the street, but not before she had marred a number of shirts on the 1977 end with her indelible prints.

I never asked about his relationships and their cycles. I understood the rotation; by maintaining young company, my father stalled age, an impression necessary to cast El-Vitat as he hoped to be remembered—in his dazzling prime.

There were other ways we worked to maintain his youth. Obviously, the hair dye, which I applied, and so frequently that his scalp held a grey shadow. His health was more difficult to manipulate. He considered it a personal betrayal that Elvis had bloated himself with barbiturates, a deterioration that eroded what he left behind. Intending his own incarnation as a corrective to the original, my father pursued a maniacal exercise regimen, which took place both in the bar and in the apartment. "People have eyes, you understand?"

His fans, he meant. And he wasn't about to let them see Vitat laboring in a scrappy t-shirt darkened by triangles of sweat. Instead he worked our staircase, up and down for hours, wearing first into the varnish, then into the meat of the wood. For all his self-preservation, he died young.

I found him one day at the bottom of the stairs, unconscious, his leg broken. The bone had split clean, the doctor said, after applying a cast. She brought me outside the shared ward.

"The problem is his heart," she said. There wasn't enough muscle, apparently, to carry his weight. "Has he been fasting?"

I didn't understand her question.

"The likely cause of his falling down the stairs is a stroke. It can happen if the heart loses too much of its muscle mass, which is the case here. Is this his normal weight?"

I said I didn't know.

When I returned to his bedside, I saw that the doctor was right. There were hollows below his jaw and his arms were little more than veins braiding bone. He looked like a child in the oversized bed.

Yes, that's him, I thought.

His customary jacket was draped over a chair. Dry sweat salted the collar and the once-smooth sheen of its back had cracked into scales. I fingered the cuff, feeling culpable. I had this idea that Father's essence was somehow bound into the fabric of his clothes, and in the past few years, the mending of such jackets, his costumes, had been reluctantly turned over to me. Detail work strained his eyes, and he did his best to oversee my replacement of zippers, repair of holes, oiling of leather, and glazing of his one mink jacket.

"Pinky, what are you doing?" he would ask at intervals.

I remember one time, I was sitting cross-legged with my arm through a jacket sleeve to give the fabric body while I restitched an area of sequins that had grown bare. I held it up to show him.

"They are antiques," he said. "They are irreplaceable."

Never had I prompted such watchfulness from my father, drawing out his total, if begrudging, attention.

Hovering in the hospital ward, I began to think about how my work with the clothing had increasingly consisted of shrinking him. I took in waists, tightened shirts, narrowed collars. Keeping pace in these with his loss, I hid his condition. We didn't own a scale, but yes, he had a practice of weighing himself in his reflection, in his estimation.

Did he know his condition, and had he considered, as he tum-bled, his precious legacy? In his magazine interviews, Father managed some proactive eulogizing, oversharing as if to shoot for the scale of a biography. But the editors always cut it down to the essentials.

I folded the jacket over my arm and sat.

He was sedated, and I watched without the threat of that childhood light being snapped on. In sleep, he became the man of my youth. A man who once caught me, not with the light, but with his hands, on a night he was too drunk to recognize his own daughter. His hands found me but lost their way tracing an unfamiliar navel; he sought my breasts. His hands hurt me. "Oh, it's just you," he said finally.

The ward emptied out in the night, and I watched him, watched until those familiar features grew strange, his face drawing down on one side, like earth slipping from a mountain.

I watched him make choking, clucking noises. His left eye was open—it drifted. He shuddered and attempted to raise himself.

A buzzer called in the nurse.

I REMEMBER MY one performance onstage. I ran my thumb around the hem of my vest, feeling the jagged stones. How did he do this, night after night? I closed my eyes and inhaled—the scent of cleaning fluids, layered and soaked into the collar—a smell I associated with him; it was clarifying. The dress-up, I realized, was only the trigger for memory. Through the jacket, you remembered the man, could shrug right into Elvis, work your arms through *his* sleeves, sing with *his* voice.

That night, I had stepped onto the stage as El-Vitat himself would have in his prime. I looked down on the devoted crowd, imagined looking down on myself and beyond, into the infinity of lights. Always he fixed his eyes on something above, such that my life was spent covering the distance between where I stood and where his eyes were trained. How to position myself for his attention? My girlhood was right here. *Look here!* Or he would miss it. Too soon, I was a woman, and then the woman at her father's side in a hospital ward, swearing that if he died she wouldn't—no, she would never—carry forward his story.

Easy

LARA, NAM & RICK (1997)

In '97 we bought back our old townhouse on the outskirts of Bangkok. We came down from the brief condominium view Mom had framed in her mind as the high-water mark of our family's achievements. The townhouse had a plot of earth in the back that Dad used to call a garden, and Mom had once been satisfied potting green and fragrant plants there. When we returned after the economy collapsed, Mom had the washer dragged out back so that the house itself felt bigger.

The occupying family had divided up our home, and I went cautiously through the new territory.

"The Thai-Chinese are all like this," Dad said expertly. "They make walls, you know? Like to live in little boxes." Mom, part Chinese herself, allowed him this.

What we returned to was a Thai-Chinese aptitude for making something of nothing: three rooms of a former family room, and a wealth of square shelving that we would leave empty. Even the luxurious expanse of wood ceiling had been claimed and paneled over. They'd torn out the kitchen and reconstructed it in the old maid's room. My bedroom was halved.

Dad landed a soft punch on one of the partitions. "Just cheap drywall, huh? Nice."

As if to prove his point, he set about taking down the walls with hammer blows that Mom and I counted from our rooms. He used an eggshell paint to hide the scars. Between morning rains and after-noon humidity, the paint took whole days to dry, but he checked it on the hour, brought his nose close to that surface sheened in river sweat, pitted and porous as skin. In those weeks, Dad gave himself entirely to the reconstruction of our home.

MY INTERNATIONAL SCHOOL was a luxury we maintained. I was fourteen and in love with a boy who had ears like cymbals. It was all I could do not to clap my hands on either side of his face and kiss him. His name was Tom Bell, but the other girls called him Tommy Bell. Tom called me Laura, like a wholly white girl, when actually it's Lara, like Sahara, the desert. I never corrected him.

"Hullo, Laura," he'd say, and I'd nod mutely because we all knew what I thought of his attention, that Irish brogue of his. We all knew too much about one another: who had touched whom in the music rooms last week, what the note slipped into Shruti Singh's locker said (*curry cunt*), and why Charlie Ong walked around with both hands in his front pockets. We knew that Bow Wattanakorn's father shot himself in his Mercedes before the debt collectors could take it away. On her last day at school, we signed Bow's white polo: *See you soon. Sad to see you go.* And, from one idiot boy, *Get well soon!*

DAD WORKED ON the living room wall while I watched television. My soap opera was muted, the actors' emotions seeming to outgrow their faces. Dad had complained about all the Thai chatter, a poor accompaniment to the rhythm he had going in his renovations.

As an American, my dad was seen as culpable in the regional col-lapse. The U.S. is where the easy money that made the bubble had come from, and it was where the money had fled to. Dad could only fall so far; there was always "back home."

Still, he was unsuited for unemployment. And measuring his worth in working hours, he had to do something.

"We were meant to live by our hands," he said.

"Right, like hand-to-mouth."

He laughed. "A person should know their way around a toolbox is all. Come the apocalypse, it's the blue-collar workers who'll inherit the earth."

Dad had worked in finance.

"This is Thailand," I said. "Ninety percent working class. We'll be fine."

"They teach you too much at school." He swung the hammer like a golf club at a stray piece of plaster. "You know, no one warns you that your kids are a helluva lot less fun when they grow up."

Two months with only this hammer to handle had added to his bulk. But these were an old man's muscles, his shoulders like worn tires.

"There's grey dust in your hair," I said.

Mom came in to check the disorder. As if to oppose Dad's new-found broadness, she had adopted the mannerisms of a bird of prey, hunched, stalking Dad's efforts, her censure biting into him like a hooked beak.

"Dad says it's the end of the world," I told her.

"Yes," she said, surely recalling a newspaper cover image from last week, the baht's value falling into the graph's underworld.

"Don't be stupid," Dad said to me. Then, to Mom, "How's my Kit Kat?"

Mom hadn't responded to that in months. She looked over his work, and then at me.

"What a mess," she said in Thai.

"It's a mess all right," I echoed, in English, for Dad.

Satisfied with this transaction, Mom left the room.

Dad laid down the hammer and surveyed his wall. "Why do I feel like you girls are teaming up against me?"

SCHOOL WAS STARTING to feel like musical chairs. Within a couple of months our hundred-strong class had shed seventeen students. The expat kids left with plenty of fanfare, hosting goodbye parties where the parents got smashed and said things like, "You know, I never *did* like Singha beer."

As for the Thai kids, they made quieter exits, disappearing between schooldays. For them it was as much a matter of familial shame as money. Sam Meath and his boys took up singing "Another One Bites the Dust" during morning registration until Sam's dad, a confectionary executive, was himself transferred. When Sam left, someone drew a penis on the back of his shirt. Too many goodbyes. We didn't know what else to do with all that canvas.

AT HOME I asked Dad for a sip of his beer.

"Yesterdaaay, all my troubles seemed so faaar away," he crooned, and handed me the bottle. I took it in gulps to get the bitterness down.

"Easy, you."

The living room was now furnished with a folding chair that Dad used for his breaks. He was one of those serene drunks. Beside the seat empty bottles were lined like well-stocked bowling pins, just waiting for Mom to barrel through with the quiet precision of her fury. My mom was not the type to wail. A childhood under the bamboo sting of Grandma's broomstick had taught Mom to hush up. Instead she stacked the replicating bills neatly beside Dad's bottles.

Mom caught me in the hallway. "Now he's teaching *you* to drink?" she said in Thai.

"Don't worry." I felt hot.

She gripped me tighter. "It's your studies that make me worried, though. What next, drugs and sex with those *farang* boys?"

EASY   123

"Yeah, right," I said in English. "I'm not like *you*."

The language stung and she snatched her arm back.

It was a few years before this that I'd discovered that power. I must have been ten when I noticed my advantage in her missed plurals and the way she botched idioms: "I'm feeling down weather" and "Speak to the devil!" And so I switched to English whenever we fought, pulling the linchpin on her authority, watching it unhinge and spin to pieces.

"Keep *up*, Mom," I said.

It was Thai against English. Dad, imagining we did all of this to spare him the intricacies of our quarrels, removed himself. He let us hash out our war in a battle that replayed itself all through my childhood years, until the ground had scarred beyond recultivation and Mom and I retreated from each other permanently.

DAD SUITED UP every morning, but I knew he wasn't actually going to interviews. He always came back blushing the red of brick dust, the grit of his guilt caught under the nails he picked at. He was going out to visit housing projects under construction; I knew because I used to go with him on weekends. Dad had worked with land development companies. They made large industrial parks, factories, and condominium plots. But his passion was in the smaller projects of residential architecture. It was his habit, coming back from my volleyball matches, to drive us through a neighborhood under construction, a housing community modeled after American suburbs for newly middle-class Thais. He ignored gates, was undeterred by homes without stairs. And the workers were too timid to challenge a white man.

Mom must have known, too. But her method was quiet, like the way she used her small body to box out Dad at the sink, taking the sponge from his hand if he tried to help with the dishes. She made this appear natural, just as she had made it ordinary to turn away his affection, bearing only her cheek to his lips.

"Let me, dear," Dad would try. "I can do some dishes."

"I wash," she said. "You work." Her anger had come down since we moved back to the townhouse.

" 'Temporary' move?" Mom had yelled at the time. " 'Easy' move? Only you *farang* are so *easy* to come and leave."

After that, Mom wouldn't even afford him the warmth of her rage. It put my dad off-balance. He relied on her affection. Within these multiplied walls of dressed-up cardboard, the sound skipping right through, I knew what was not being said in private. One night I listened outside their door. I expected a squabble, maybe a push-and-shove followed by sex. But all I could hear was Mom's soft snores, which had grown faint, as if she were withdrawing even that sniff of life from Dad's presence.

THE STUDENTS IN my school's set-one English were all Commonwealth kids—Singaporeans, Indians, Malaysians—their parents savvy about what Received Pronunciation could do for their children's opportunities. It embarrassed our British teachers that the native speakers weren't up to snuff. By native speakers, they really meant the white kids.

"Due to decreased student enrollment, we're combining our class with set-two English," our teacher told us. That was how I came to sit next to Tom Bell.

Inevitably: "Hullo, Laura."

"Hi, Tom," I managed, before pretending to have forgotten my copy of *Great Expectations*. He spread his book between us and kept a hand pressed on it like a wrestler pinning down his opponent, roughing up the spine in a way I both loved and hated. Freckles ran up Tom's fingers. I pictured the freckles on his back, or those trailing up his thighs like a line of crumbs leading me to X-marks-the-spot.

Chicken skin, Mom would have called it.

Back then I was still peeking at the white girls as they came out of their clothes in the changing room. I wondered at their allure. In the last year their underwear had grown tighter, smaller, sheer. The effect? Their blemishes were all the more apparent. And yet Tom Bell only dated white girls.

"You're one of those book lovers, aren't you?" Tom said, when I ironed out a dog-ear fold with my thumb.

"What?"

"It's okay. My mum's like that, too."

I SKIPPED THE next English class to follow Dad downtown, my motorbike taxi weaving in the wake of his car as it navigated its way to a construction site.

Posters along the perimeter promised Bangkok "another level of luxury." Diamond Heights, they called the condominium. Two buildings. Swimming pools for every unit.

They had erected the honeycomb cores of the twin condos—thirty stories in concrete—but there were as yet no windows or outer walls. I slinked easily after Dad through an opening in the gate.

I had started to wonder about his disappearances. He had lived in Thailand so long that it seemed reasonable for him to yield to its behaviors, that practice of keeping another household. "Minor wife" was the Thai title for such women, as if it were a privilege. But the only other home Dad was going to, apparently, was vacant.

He saw me coming through the fence and smiled, maybe to hide his surprise.

"Going up?" He held back the gate of a construction elevator.

"Please," I said.

"Okay, then—all the way up now."

He took us to a penthouse where we sat with our legs dangled out over the edge. The view was of the twin building, like staring at a blueprint, the sky our drafting paper. Graffiti was the only embellishment to the grey concrete, and in what had been intended to be private balcony pools inky swamps had formed. Halfway down I could see where a can of spray paint had been smashed against a wall, exploding a comet of red.

"Your mother and I are thinking about what to do next. If it continues to be this bad, I might go back to the U.S. for a while, you know? Work there until things smooth over on this side."

I swung my feet. "Why can't we all go?"

"Your mother doesn't want to move."

"Then she can stay here on her own," I said.

"Try to understand. What was the point of marrying me but to improve her life? She didn't marry up to play a maid."

There was movement below. Two men with gleaming coils over their shoulders were moving through the building opposite us.

"What are they doing?" I asked.

"Stealing the copper to sell, I expect."

The bigger man carried a stepladder. They were quick, opening panels in the walls, one man stripping the rubber off the cables, the other coiling.

We watched them work up three stories before Dad said, "Let's go. Probably not safe to be up here."

I COULD TELL Mom had made an effort with dinner. The pasta, angel hair, was coiled elaborately, dressing up its simple tomato sauce. The meal was a reminder of tables laid with excess in this house, the dinners of my early childhood. They had made me feel rich once, as I'd stand up on my chair, surveying the wealth of options. Mom's own meal had always been huddled around her plate, two curries and raw vegetables that vined out of their bowls, a collection of food I often compared to a swamp. As for Dad's side, it looked like a color sample for Hay Stack: the few sage leaves washed out in a butter sauce with pasta.

"I really like this. I do," Dad said, and made sure Mom looked at him.

"Tomato," Mom nodded.

"Pomodoro, pomodori," Dad singsonged, happy, I knew, that we were all eating from the middle bowl, having adopted a homegrown superstition he adapted to mark out his own omens: one household, one dinner.

"Where you come from?" Mom asked, to which Dad lied blithely.

"Oh, I met an old contact at an office development company. They've paused their projects but seem actually to be weathering this pretty well."

Mom asked if this was Khun Pin's company, and I translated for Dad.

"Oh, no. An old acquaintance," Dad said, responding to my translation but looking at Mom. "I was just curious."

Mom cleared away dinner and Dad unfolded his newspaper. On the cover was an image of Thai policemen ransacking the offices of a foreign company.

"It's hard being a foreigner in a recession," he said, setting the newspaper aside. "The Thais blame *us* for their mess."

He reached below the table for a box. It was wrapped in signature pink and white twine.

"For my girls." He smiled like a boy. A boy coming in from the mud bearing pocket-gifts of live creatures mixed with chewing gum for his mother, oblivious of the beating to come.

Mom said to me, "What is this supposed to mean?"

I didn't answer.

"Ask him," she said.

"Ask him yourself."

We knew the box, the string, the cloying scent. It was the bakery at the base of our old condominium. A charming Parisian place that reminded the residents of how far above the rest of the city they could consider themselves. Mom had loved it.

Mom turned to Dad. "No job but you waste money. Soon no house?" She pointed at me, jabbing with each phrase. "No school. No future. No good. What I want cake for?"

What *had* he been thinking?

He raised two empty hands. "Guess I just thought we all might like to share something nice for a change. Been pretty bleak lately. How about we cut it up and then decide?"

"Decide what?" I asked.

Mom said, "You eat. I clean up. Only in the slum they don't have maids."

"Why don't *you* get a job, Mom?" I asked in English. "You want to live big so bad, *you* go and make it happen, huh? Do it yourself."

"Don't talk to me that way."

I nodded toward Dad. "Speak in English so that we can all understand. Go on, tell him."

"Actually, Lara," Dad said. "We *have* been talking. And we think it might be best for me to move back to America. Back home."

There was work, he could send money, and we could afford my last years of school.

"She's doing this to you," I said in English, "isn't she? Making you go."

But even then he defended her. "No, she isn't."

"We need you here more than we need money," I said. "Other jobs will come."

"Sweetheart, please don't worry—soon as things pick up again, I'll come back."

I said to Mom, "You're sending him away."

"Your father has to understand. He has to be responsible. Tell him that," she said, her eyes never leaving Dad. "Tell him."

I LET THE house divide us. It was easy enough, given all the walls still left over. I staked out territory and avoided common spaces. The family room stood empty. Mom left me food on the kitchen counter. Dad existed in a periphery, the sounds of his living always a layer removed, a room away. His only presence was in the traces he left:

shaving cream in the sink, his sock buried in the sofa, the bread crusts he never ate in the trash. These were the things I would try to piece together after he left, needing some semblance of his order, the way my life had come to orbit his, even if only to avoid him.

On the day of Dad's flight, I left the house before he was awake. Unsure of where to go so early in the morning, I found myself at Diamond Heights, looking over a city that had become a graveyard of office towers and housing projects. I'd keep returning to the empty building over the next months, skipping classes to sit in its hollows while I read about the debt suicides. The newspapers ran stories of debt being sold to loan sharks. Of businessmen shooting themselves. Of businessmen shooting their families and then themselves. Some of those fathers were jumpers. In other homes across the city fathers were being dragged to jail. Others were running away to their second lives, those minor wives and backup families. It was a father conspiracy. They all had a plan B. You could trace their exploits, if you wanted to, in the home-shaped shells they left in their wake, all the invoices totaling their obligations.

WHEN MY NEXT school break approached, Dad booked me a flight to go see him. We couldn't afford two tickets, so Mom would stay at home.

On the last day of English class, I told Tom Bell I was leaving for the U.S. I needed something to work right then, and I could start with his attention.

"What? What're you on about? Like a holiday?"

"I'm leaving. Flying tomorrow. America. To go live with my dad."

"You're *leaving* leaving?"

"That's right." I fished out a marker. "Will you write something on my shirt?"

"Well, sure. Didn't realize you were off as well. How does 'I'll miss sharing stuff in English' sound? And 'Goodbye and good luck'?"

I nodded and angled my chin up so he could lean in to sign my front. "Oh, and it's actually *Lara,* Tom. You'll remember me? *Lara.*"

"WHAT DO YOU think?"

Dad walked me through the two-bedroom house he was renting, a house built to hold heat through winter. He had a dishwashing machine.

"Looks pretty permanent," I said.

"Funny you should say that."

"Why? What's funny?"

He had lost weight since resuming desk work. I pictured Dad bigger, less than a year younger but at the height of his health, it seemed, marching through the house with his chest too broad for his shirt, earning his keep with bare hands.

"You're not coming back, are you?"

"You'll be out here soon anyway, right—for college?"

I waited for him to invite me to stay in the States so I could tell him what I thought of him: just another foreigner passing through, a white man with minor wives, a colonialist. What had the papers said of them—foreigners—in recent months?

Dad didn't ask me to stay.

"College, right?" he said again. "You'll be out here soon?"

"And Mom?"

He ran his palm along a pristine dining table. "Well, she wants to be in Bangkok, doesn't she?"

MOM CALLED THAT night and I answered the phone. I told her I was coming home and Dad wasn't.

She asked to speak to him.

"He doesn't want to talk to you," I lied, in Thai so that she understood.

"I want to speak with my husband."

I switched to English, "I told you, he doesn't want to talk to you."

"Please."

The line was bad. Or she was crying, I don't know. Something couldn't contain her voice.

She tried English: "Please."

Feasts

PING, PINKY & PRADIT (1999)

Pinky let me come to dinner so I could learn from her. "A girl needs to know how to negotiate with a man."

But what was negotiation to this guy? A buffet. He wanted it all. He leaned over his plate of crab shells and pointed a roe-red finger at her.

"Am I being too blunt?" His gaze slid from Pinky to me and back.

It was my first time eating crab, and because I didn't know where to prize and where to suck, I'd filled my hand with regurgitated pieces of shell.

"Adults can take the truth. And you," he told Pinky, "sure look like an adult to me."

Under the table, Pinky squeezed my hand until the crab shards cut into my palm.

Nobody ever explained to me how Pinky and I were related. Back then I didn't think to interrogate our relationship. I was still a child, accepting "cousin" as I accepted the "family" we visited on Chinese New Year, those house stops on a pilgrimage of refusing and then accepting food. The dining table was the common ground, and in the kinship of shared rice, Pinky was a sister.

I was fourteen when I moved into her apartment in central Bangkok. My new high school was in the city, a two-hour bus ride from my family's outskirt neighborhood. We were too late signing up for the dorms, so my father arranged for me to stay with Pinky. Ba wasn't about to let go of this opportunity. In a regular feat of overkill, I'd tested into the best high school in the country. And so I spent my last months of middle school basking in local glory, passing bus stops flanked by posters boasting my score, my face, and the name of the tutoring company (the posters' sponsor) where I'd taken a mere month of lessons. In the photo I wore the dazzling white uniform they'd given me on the morning of the shoot, my hair trimmed to a regulation pudding-bowl bob, my pocket stuck with unchewed pens. I'd given the camera a thumbs-up, like I was egging on kids younger than I, who, with the help of this cram school, could pin similar honors on their little lives.

Of course, such tutoring had nothing to do with my success. Only in chemistry had I learned anything new. To hold the cram-school veterans in thrall, my science tutor employed sexual analogies desperately. More than the analogies, though, I was shocked by *her*: a *thalueng* woman. It would have been nothing in a man. Vulgarity was their jurisdiction. I knew this like I knew Boyle's law. Abandoning the *why* of it—why this relationship between x and y—I marveled at the *how*. Were such women allowed to exist in that distant place of adulthood? The tutor proved only a prelude to Pinky, however, who would show me the true boundaries of my prudishness, and how to overstep them.

Pinky was twenty-two and, according to my mother, studying science at university. This turned out to be cosmetology at a training school. Her apartment was small, a bathroom connecting our rooms. When she wasn't using this bathroom, she left the door on her side open, so I did the same. I would lie on my bed and watch her passing beyond the doorframe, the sound of her radio soap operas carrying straight through to me. I grew to differentiate the characters on the radio, even if they were all performed by the same troupe of six actors. In my head, these actors sat around a shared table. Their seats were surely labeled *Adult Man, Adult Woman, Child Boy*, and so on, but they donned and discarded their characters like so many masks.

Pinky, too, had different faces. There was her bedtime face, a layering of clays, serums, jellies, and balms. And then the daytime face, which was not, as I'd imagined, also layered on. Rather, Pinky's makeup seemed to reveal her flattering contours, the lines of eyebrow and jaw, the color in her lips.

I twisted out her lipstick and looked longingly on the red.

"This is expensive, isn't it?"

Her glance told me this was the wrong question.

"Does it *look* expensive?"

The skill was in the intimation. Was she rich? No, but glamorous. Especially beautiful? No, but the way she wore clothes surely was. And always, Pinky was poised. The kind of poise a woman might need, for example, to suck the tender flesh out of a crab claw as a man described, over a plate of carcasses, what he'd like to do to her body.

I WOULD ONLY see Pradit that first time over seafood. He wore a black polo with *SIG Sauer* stitched on the breast, the fabric tucked tightly over his belly like every man who had been through the police academy. His fingers were stubby carrot ends but they picked apart shellfish with precision. There was a mean edge to his neatness. He reminded me of every one of my PE teachers whose fitness suggested a militant home life, sleeveless shirts, a knife collection.

When he was done telling Pinky what he wanted, he presented her with a bag. It looked expensive in that brand-namey way. The letters made a golden swirl across the side. Pinky placed the bag in my lap without looking at it. They were playing a game I didn't get, but I knew that to look would be to lose.

He spoke directly to me then. "And what are you supposed to be?"

I put my elbows on the table. Made myself look at him.

"I'm Poongping."

He repeated my nickname, drawing out the vowels to make me sound like a child.

"Ping," said Pinky, "is my apprentice."

His eyes didn't leave me. "With some work, maybe."

In the back of the taxi she unwrapped the bag, handing off the tissue, layer by layer, which I proceeded to fold into neat triangles. She unveiled the box (red, maybe actual leather?) and then the bracelet within (very gold). It was the color duo of every Chinese gold store from the ones in my backwater neighborhood to that Chinatown landmark, Hua Seng Heng. Which is to say, I wasn't impressed. Nor was Pinky.

"Mannish," she announced. She turned the bracelet to check the name etched on the inside. "But the screwdriver it comes with is real gold, I think."

I took the bracelet. It had notches along its surface shaped like screw heads. I saw none of the typical markers of women's jewelry. No florals, no flowing lines. It was bold, solid. Gold the way men wore gold.

THAT NIGHT I stood before the bathroom mirror. The week I'd moved in, I'd had my hair cut short. The rainy season had begun and rather than surrender to nights of hair never drying, a perpetual wet patch on my pillow, I'd had it clipped as close to the head as school rules allowed.

His words came back. *With some work, maybe.*

Pinky leaned on the bathroom doorjamb. She knew what effect his words had on me: "Fuck him anyway. Come on, what can we do with this?"

I said I didn't mind my hair. It was a look.

"You look like the stuff that clogs my drain."

At her dresser mirror she gummed her hands with hair wax, worked it between her fingers until it was warm and sticky as sap. She pulled her fingers through my hair. The look: punk via the schoolyard. Her face turned blank and still as she worked. The difference between us had never been so obvious as now with Pinky behind me. I had my family's signature moon face, which was shaped, my father claimed, by generations of prosperity, a jowly wealth bestowed to me. Picture that against Pinky's slim face, her small mouth, everything delicate except her large, overlapping teeth—the reason she smiled only with her mouth shut. She caught me watching her and smiled now, but I didn't smile back. I don't know why. Resisting the instinct to play along, I guess.

I was alone for dinner the next evening. Back home, my father ran meals as a series of if-then conditions: If I wanted custard buns, then I had to eat the cold pig ears. If I wanted the ginger steamed perch, then I had to finish the bitter melon stir-fry. Alone at the supermarket now, I bought instant noodles, eggs, Yakult, and a dozen strawberry ice cream bars. I could see the cashier had the urge to comment.

"Prize money," I told him, and fanned the bills.

Eating with a comic book propped against my water glass, I started with the ice cream, bar after bar, relishing the bite of strawberry shell, the pillowy sweet cream within. I imagined myself into Pinky's adult autonomy, the pleasure of doing whatever you wanted. Only I never made it to the noodles. The sugar sent me to bed, where I licked the pink residue from my lips, my face turned toward the silence on the other side of the bathroom. I'd grown used to the radio and its voices, which somehow made the apartment bigger; always, it seemed, there were other people with us, in other rooms.

MIDNIGHT. FROM THE kitchen, the thud of blows landing. I stepped out of my bedroom. The only light came from something turning in the microwave, throwing its yellow sideways onto Pinky, who, in her sleek cocktail dress, was driving a cleaver into a piece of meat the length of a man's forearm.

"Oh, shit—sorry." Her voice was high and strange, reaching for casual. "You want some food?" Was she drunk? I'd never spoken to a drunk person. The air was sticky-sweet, and from the pot on the stove I could hear bubbling.

I moved closer. The slab on the cutting board was a side of crispy pork belly.

"*Khao na mu krop.*" Pinky looked proudly over her purchase before burying the cleaver into the rind again. "I know the best vendor."

The microwave pinged and the room went dark. Instead of reaching for a switch, Pinky opened the fridge door, left it wide and worked by the wedge of its cool light, dividing the steaming rice into two bowls, and then topping them with the sauce off the stove. She moved the cutting board with the pork to the table.

Every evening, she pushed this table against the wall for space, but instead of moving it back now, she took a seat and drew out the other one for me.

"How's your swinging arm?" She held the cleaver out blade first.

I turned the pork over, soft side up, and chopped it into clean cubes.

"Fasting and then feasting," she said to herself pleasantly.

She ate greedily, her face low to the plate. Could it be *that* good? I took a bite. Crunchy skin, juicy fat, the meat layer itself a little dry. The sauce dripped thick and brown, but it was too sweet, even over rice. I sat sideways and watched Pinky by the partial light of the fridge. *Ma would never,* I thought, as Pinky crunched and swallowed noisily. The gold band, too big for her wrist, slid against her hand and she worked it back up her forearm to the pinched flesh where it stayed only briefly. Irritated, she finally took it off. She didn't even need the screwdriver; it slipped right over her knuckles. I picked it up, turned the gold in my hands, and watched her until, impossibly, she reached the last piece of pork. She pointed at it.

"It's yours," I said.

She picked it up with her fingers. "And what've you been doing? Did you start school yesterday?"

"Yesterday was Saturday."

"Saturday. Yes."

I asked what she was doing.

Her eyes rolled lazily. *"Indulging."*

"He didn't feed you?"

"He asked me where I wanted to eat. So I told him. But when I saw him eating the pork, I—couldn't."

I asked what Pradit did for a living. She said he owned clubs, massage parlors, bars. He'd put up the money for the bar Pinky's father had run, which is where she'd met Pradit. She said he was a man who ate off his own menu. "You know what I mean?"

Sure, I thought. I knew enough not to ask if it bothered her. No, the right question was, "What was the sex like?"

It was a bluff, of course. Although I'd once seen a porn magazine, the contortions involved in the images were so absurdly far from possible that, in my head, sex was still conducted by the stick figures with molecule heads introduced to me by my science tutor.

Her knowing glance. She sat back. Grease-tipped fingers drummed the tabletop, wanting more. She was letting the question slip away. Always, she would temper sex for me, dialing down the radio as the descriptions escalated toward the bedroom. During the rape scenes on TV, which appeared with penultimate-episode regularity, Pinky always switched the box right off.

"Well?"

And so she told me, focusing on everything but the penis. She talked about Pradit's constellation of moles, as if the man's chest were some great night sky we might count ourselves lucky to gaze upon. She described his clothes, how they reeked of money.

"Which smells like what?" I was sullen. I thought she was hiding the good stuff.

"I don't know, like something kept in a box."

"Out of reach," I supplied.

Her eyes caught mine. "But not for long."

The closest she came to the sex itself was the wiry hair she said got stuck in her teeth; for Pradit, of course, was bald.

I told her I was going to bed. As I rose, she took my wrist, fingers closing around the bracelet there. I had slipped it on while she spoke.

"You like it?"

I didn't respond.

"Keep it," she said.

"He'll say something."

"He won't even notice."

IN CENTRAL BANGKOK the rainwater stayed longer than in my old neighborhood, the water sloshing lazily from one penned street to the next, none of it ever running down. That, to me, was the city: a lingering, brown wash. When the storm finally broke I went out for lunch and carried noodles back for Pinky, who was just rising. Was she hungry? No, she'd never eat again. All she wanted to do was watch soap operas from the trove of tapes under her bed. We settled on one about a flight attendant who falls in love with a pilot, Pinky relishing the extravagances of the life of an "air." She had applied for a job with Thai Airways, she told me.

"In the interview they asked me why I wanted the job, and I told them it was because I wanted to sleep with a captain."

"You didn't!"

"I didn't." She smirked. "No, what I *did* tell them was what I wanted. I wanted that mile-high living, those glory shots from Paris, from Amsterdam. I wanted to touch snow. But what they wanted was 'service.' What they wanted was English that's better than mine."

"But you have the looks."

"They said that, too. Don't worry. I'll make it someday and send you a postcard from New York." From her wardrobe, Pinky picked out black heels and a red scarf—her idea of a flight attendant's uniform—to complement the white bathrobe she was still in.

"You look silly."

She gave me the dead eyes of an actual flight attendant who was not amused, and then proceeded to clack into the kitchen before returning with a Yakult that she served the way the attendants served wine in the show, leaning over suggestively, cooing the words. "A yogurt-based beverage for you, madam?" But after I took my drink, she leaned over me, making the same offer to the "sir" beside me. Her eyes, I saw, were on him.

The spirit left her then. "I'm tall enough, I guess. But my arms are disproportionately short. Can you tell?"

"You look just like the women on the show." Onscreen, the characters were kissing in the first-class cabin.

"I'll get there!" She pointed at the TV. "You need a five-year plan, right? I've got mine. Pradit is a step. All these men are steps." She raised her foot in demonstration, planted it in midair as if on the backs of the tower of men who would take her where she needed to be.

PINKY RUINED HIGH school for me. Even after moving out eventually, I was never able to see beyond my classmates' pettiness, their small secrets and passing sadnesses. Their contained lives, compared to Pinky's one of extravagance, seemed like so many cramped, windowless rooms. Not so different from my own, really. High school became four years of competing for the government scholarship to go to a university abroad: a five-year plan, Pinky had said. I, too, was trying to leave the country.

Even though I was finally living away from my father, I didn't exactly have freedom. Money, that was freedom. Saturdays I went to the mall, where every storefront showed me what I couldn't have. Whole hallways of forbidden wants that circled back on themselves, the escalators looping infinitely. Like other kids doing weekend school activities, I wore my uniform—my way of leveling the field—while always keeping that golden bracelet prominent, intimating, as Pinky might have said, *more*.

Pinky was always gone on Saturday. Of course, I went through her room. Maybe she expected it. I put on her bathrobe. But what looked like ivory on her was only yellow fuzz against my skin. I tested my way around the workshop of her makeup table. In a chest under the bed she had a collection of odd clothing. Leather jackets studded with rhinestones, sequined suits, belts laced with seed beads, rings of gaudy semiprecious stones. The clothes looked large for Pinky. Of her family she'd only mentioned her dead father, whom she called a magician. She'd said he was a master at possessing the dead. Only after he died, Pinky felt that, actually, it had been *she* that he possessed.

On Sundays Pinky dressed me in her old clothes and we revisited the places she had been with Pradit. She ate everything she hadn't the night before. It was her own magic, the bottomless hat of her appetite.

First the food was familiar. Shrimp and popping mushrooms in the herbed richness of *tom yam*. Fatty Hainanese chicken rice. Stir-fried pickled mustard greens with eggs, side of stewed pork knuckle. But soon we moved on to pink fish (salmon, she told me) served almost raw, tossed in lime and chili, curing white at the edges, slipping around my mouth like a second tongue. We ate sea urchin right out of its prickly shell, a fort of black spines, each of which, Pinky said, studying my reaction, was poisonous. I held the flesh in my mouth, tasting first brine and then, underneath, a sweetness.

These meals were also her stage for unveiling Pradit's gifts. She had the right showmanship to pull this off in a restaurant, drawing attention from the waiters, irritation from other diners. It embarrassed me that she took up so much space when the city was about the opposite. Always, she deprecated his gifts. There were perfumes in bottles cut to glimmer like jewels ("stuffy"), opalescent pearls ("fish scum"), and flower bouquets ("vulgar" or "short-lived"). Then, having unveiled them, having gauged their effect on the public, she made the gifts disappear. On another Saturday, I discovered that she kept the gifts in her wardrobe, each one sealed in a clear bag, folded into their original tissues and boxes.

That my gold bracelet was the exception to his gifts, the only one that was actually used, made it more precious to me. I remember I had this fantasy at the time that my bracelet was a piece of long-lost treasure, the type of daydream teenagers have in which the whole world has been quietly watching you, waiting for you. This bracelet, you see, was at the center of my arrival in public life. I imagined walking into the pawn shop on Pinky's *soi* and having the man appraise the bracelet. *"Poongping,"* he'd say gravely, *"do you even know what you have here?"*

We ate Japanese cheesecake dusted with gold powder. Hot buns filled with salted-egg cream.

"Lady Dior." Pinky set her new handbag on the table. "I suspect it's a hand-me-down. See this wear along the seam? He said it was a bag fit for a princess. Yeah, Diana, I told him—and look what happened to *her*."

We ate giant Ayutthaya prawns spilling tomalley, dunked in chili-lime sauce. Oysters shucked tableside.

"They're fishermen, Pradit's family. He worked his way up the trawler's ranks, I guess, and then sold the ship as soon as he owned it outright. Then he put all that fish money into the soapy massage business. But you can still smell it on him, right, the coastal reek?"

Of course, Pinky had also said Pradit was once a police captain. She'd said he was the son of generals, too.

"Okay." I could see I was not responding the way she wanted.

"Even his cum," she added, leaning in, "tastes like washed-up seaweed."

This was so shocking that I laughed with embarrassment. She sat back and laughed, too—deliciously, like she'd gotten what she wanted.

After a week of exams during my second school term, she took me out at midnight for salted-fish porridge and inky preserved eggs. The restaurant's almost-dawn closing time made it a likely stop for second-act feasts after hitting the clubs or enduring a wedding reception or a funeral chanting session. There was a celebratory pitch even to the post-funeral types, the return to the everyday heralded by that most common greeting exchanged as the mourners left the temples: *Have you eaten?*

A silk scarf with a bird-of-paradise print. She used it to wipe her mouth.

I could tell, through his gifts, that Pradit misunderstood her. In a game of doll-like ornamentation, Pinky didn't go in for pearls and silks. Her accessories of choice were drawn from that box of odd clothing under the bed: worn leather and rhinestones, black denim. Or that's what I thought *I* understood about her. And what did I know? I've always wondered about those Sunday feasts. I had thought it was about her weight—her appetite, forced into a small shape all week, at last allowed to unfurl.

Now, though, looking back on it, those meals appear more like reenactments, the way I'd seen police remake a crime, trying to understand all the elements from the theater of their own re-creation. Pinky, I think, was retelling a story. She wanted it her way.

Except what was I in all this? Maybe she brought me for my wide-eyed newness, my predictable marveling at the tasteless wallpaper, the faux-brass lamps. Maybe she liked being able to explain this world to me. If the conversation lagged, she always slipped into her game of flight attendant. "Tea, miss?" She topped off my glass. "Chicken or fish?" she said, holding two identical dishes and asking me to imagine, to see as she saw. With that incantation, she called me back into her world.

"Did you know that airlines have machines, simulators, that actually teach people to walk through turbulence?"

Only once, at the end of the school year before I went home for the holidays, did we go out for Western food. It was a Friday night this time, rather than a Sunday. My father was picking me up the next day. Pinky had been promising me chocolate mousse. Our taxi pulled up to an Italian restaurant with a brick façade, glass facing onto garden, the interior glowing like a hearth.

As soon as we were inside, I could see we didn't belong there. Pinky had dressed up for the occasion in this absurd creamy white, full-length, balcony-bra dress; she looked like she'd stepped straight off a pageant stage. Everything about the restaurant said moneyed indifference. The velvet on the chairbacks was bald. Tapered candles drooped over tarnished brass candlesticks. The floorboards showed paths of wear leading to the kitchen doors. The other diners were older, all of them men, their collared shirts bagging, pink faces slack from wine, themselves so many set pieces in the restaurant's picture of glamorous decline.

We were asked for our reservation.

"Oh, I don't have one."

"I'm sorry, but we're full tonight."

"We can wait," Pinky said.

"Yes, but we're full *all night*." There was no mistaking the woman's implication. Pinky, though, had her real heels on, and she spoke from that height.

"Listen, it's a special occasion. My sister has just completed the school year. She'll be leaving tomorrow. We're here for a nice parting meal, good wine, and chocolate mousse. I've talked up the mousse."

"All the same—"

"We'll just have a drink until something frees up." Pinky sat herself at the bar. "Ping, right here." She tapped the seat beside her.

As if to distract me, she started on the Pradit stories again. She used his name, but the men she described were not Pradit. Just as, I imaged, there were other incarnations of me out there. Or of Pinky, a woman not sitting at this bar, not getting drunk on white wine, telling a girl about a man who was a traveling salesman for Pilot pens. A man who was a government bureaucrat sidelined after uncovering bribes to a superior. A man who got his start opening brothels around the old American air force base in Ubon.

We didn't eat. The bartender served Pinky wine and the tables emptied, the diners passing us on the way out. I couldn't look at them.

The final time the hostess came back to ask us to leave, Pinky pressed a thousand baht into the woman's hand. "I'll keep this between us," Pinky whispered.

The woman unfurled the note and laid it on the bar beside our drinks bill. "I'm sorry, but the check is for three thousand."

THE NEXT DAY, walking home from the bus stop, I went into the pawn store. The pawnbroker turned my bracelet under his jeweler's loupe.

"Did you steal this?"

"It was given to me."

He studied me over his glasses before pressing a button to release the security door. He beckoned me back behind his desk. "Whatever your story is, I hope you didn't buy it. It's a fake."

He put the bracelet on a scale, tapped his fingers along a shelf of catalogs before pulling one out.

"Ah, here." He flipped to a page with photographs of a bracelet. "See? A fake."

"How do you know?" I leaned over the catalog. It was my bracelet exactly.

"It's a good one." He handed me a magnifying glass. "But the placement of these numbers is off. It should look like this, in this picture. Also, the weight's wrong."

"Is it made of gold?"

"No. Gold-plated, maybe. Say, a woman's been coming in here every week with fakes like this. Good fakes, I mean. You didn't buy this from her, did you? Because I've been trying to warn the locals about her. Even the packaging she has them in looks real."

"No," I said quietly. "It was a gift."

He could see I was disappointed.

"Hey, girl, if it doesn't matter, then keep it. The detail work is good. Those screw heads look close to the real thing. Who's going to know the difference?"

It was Saturday so Pinky had already left the apartment. I put the gold bracelet back in its red box. I went into her room to hide the box among the others, but when I opened the wardrobe, the gifts in their sealed plastic were gone.

I couldn't leave it there for her to discover. Instead, I dragged the chest out from under her bed and nestled the box among that treasure of rhinestones, sequins, and costume pearls.

I thought of Pinky every day after I moved out, but I never went back to see her. Like the actors of her radio soap operas, I'd discarded my mask, and it was impossible to go back to being who I had been, sitting at that bar, keeping eye contact so as to avoid looking at the departing diners, and seeing in Pinky's eyes that awful appetite.

YEARS LATER, DURING my second year of university in the U.S., I was in a grocery store when an old man working the vegetable aisle greeted me.

"You're back, then," he said. I'd never been to this store before.

"Did you end up seeing all the places on your list?"

I found I couldn't disappoint his earnest expectation. "I did."

"Paris and where else?"

"Amsterdam." It was the name that came first to me. "And—"

"Rome?" he said, as if recalling this name.

"Yes."

And I let the man lead my story with his questions. I can't say why, but as he spoke to me of my travels, I became certain that he was speaking to Pinky. That she had been here before me. That she had made it to those cities she promised me postcards from. Paris, London, New York City. In naming them, she had possessed my memory of these places, so that when I did finally reach each of the cities myself, I saw them as she must have. I imagined myself as Pinky in a restaurant, appraising the men over a tray of oysters, fork turned between fingers, the tines picking only the finest from the ice.

Captain Q Is Dead

BENZ & TINTIN (2000)

Aweek after Benz and Tintin had come off the construction job, off without full pay, Tintin's mangled hand was still pink as a pig's knuckle. He had cleaved it with an industrial staple. Now it was souring, adding to the bathroom's dank, yellow perfume.

"I need to wash it again," Benz said. "Okay?"

He had Tintin pinned against the sink, his chest flat on the big man's back. Rum wafted from the bottle Benz held poised to flush the wound.

Tintin resisted his lesser weight.

"Hold up." Tintin took the bottle and swilled the alcohol in his mouth. He raised the rum as if to toast the ruddy faces in the mirror and said, in a beefy voice fit for a commercial, "*Captain Q. It's better than rubbing alcohol.*"

They laughed, their eyes meeting in the mirror—Tintin's squeezed and red, like two welts.

"Shit, Benz. What are you even doing with a friend like me?"

Benz looked into the sink bowl where blood-marbled water coiled down into the drain. He motioned for the bottle.

Their room, the top story of a narrow old boardinghouse, was pressed up against a corrugated roof that seemed to glow under the midday sun. The floor was a jigsaw of thin mattresses, bedding of the men they boarded with.

"Two things to always buy in bulk," Tintin said, dropping the final, empty bottle into a case labeled *SAMPLE.* "Toilet paper and rum."

Benz was sweating on someone else's blanket now, watching the roof burn.

They were out of money, these two scaffold monkeys. They'd turn twenty-two this year and had known each other since they were twelve. Wherever Tintin climbed, Benz had to follow. But too often it was down a hole, a job mucking street sewers beside convicts.

"What am I doing with a friend like you?" Benz would observe whenever Tintin fucked them out of good work, say, by arriving drunk at the site and shooting staples through his hand.

Today was Benz's turn to be drunk, awfully, in a way he hadn't been in months. He usually let the big man drink the lion's share, but now he outpaced Tintin, upsetting laws laid down years ago, during their adolescence, a time when boys realized that even among the poor there could be disparities.

A difference in smarts, for one thing: Benz outperforming his poverty, boggling teachers, topping his classes. And height for another: This was Tintin's territory, a difference Benz couldn't comprehend at first, the trouble his friend had with arranging his big legs beneath schoolboy desks or that the skewer vendor treated Tintin as an honorary adult, referring to him as "Pi"—older brother.

Benz learned the meaning of their difference when, following a job running back-kitchen booze, the boys were rewarded with a plastic bag rubber-banded at the top above a full quart of precious moonshine. Benz, thoroughly drunk on half of what his friend downed, relied on his clearheaded friend to conquer a staircase, realizing then how easily Tintin bore his weight, to say nothing of the alcohol.

Tintin's ability to outdrink the other boys had crowned him with a new sort of cool. The other arena of adolescent respect was, of course, soccer, a sport long married to alcohol in the advertisements that were lore for strayboys with nowhere to spend their afternoons but in a scrum around the television in Apah's corner store.

For Benz those afternoons had been a time of magic. Ask a younger Benz about The Flying Dutchmen. Ask him how many saves Oliver Kahn, The Titan, had made (more than Superman's career total, for the record). And there never was a zero to hero like Maradona. World Cup '86, the "Hand of God" goal—Benz could tell you how he did it: superpowers. Over the players' hearts, in the customary place of a hero's crest, would be stitched the logo of a leading beer brand. *Carlsberg! Heineken!* To the boys these represented distant kingdoms, key centers in some vast sporting empire. Boys with their own rags-to-riches futures rolling from their mouths, unfurling before them like red carpets. They swore themselves into the cult of Singha beer. They bowed back to the Manchester United legends, lifted fists to toast the screen. "No, *you*, Roy Keane!" The boys laughed, sloshing imaginary pints. "Thank *you*!"

Adulthood had since fallen, sobering and black, over Benz. He lifted himself to the sink and washed. On the tiles, split open, lay Tintin's pus-caked bandages, a carapace picked clean of meat.

They found their way to a warehouse address.

"Looks like the scene of a crime," said Tintin, standing with arms akimbo as he appraised a building boarded up and neglected by all but the local graffitists. The moon was up, and they found an open door.

Inside, the petty crime boss Nai Somyod ran a garage, having inherited the business from his recently imprisoned brother. He knew little about crime, Somyod, and even less about cars.

Benz walked a circle around an old Camry, surveying its value. The front had been crushed, Somyod told them, when the driver rear-ended a municipal bus, which, like a tank, was constructed of steel sheets.

"Entertainment system's gone," Benz said. "Gasoline's been siphoned, but the fuel tank's intact. There's good aluminum in the wheels, copper in the wiring. Rear end's whole. Could take the lights, bumper, back wheels."

Tintin stood by a table laden with tools, flicking the blade of a dusty power saw.

Reaching inside the car to check whether the passenger-side airbag had deployed, Benz noticed a splatter of brown crusted into the ceiling fuzz. "Airbags are spent," he reported.

"Let me see you take it apart," Somyod said.

"You want us to work for free?" Benz said.

"Just want to know you have the skills."

"Oh, Nai Somyod," Tintin said, yawning luxuriously. "Child's play."

Word of this job had come to Benz along the childhood grapevine, a network of orphans who, as boys, had learned the value of junk. Boys who at twelve could swarm an abandoned car, pick precious metal from carrion already scrapped over by scavengers less hungry. Their troupe would romp through neighborhoods and come down on anything untethered. They even dared one another to steal into the rich areas, not for the cars—expensive vehicles with an intimidating gleam—but for the trophy of a hood emblem, the standing star, Benz's namesake. He had kept a row of emblems fixed to his orphanage bunk in ascending order: C Class, E Class, S Class.

Benz handled the nimble work now, stripping and spooling the wiring, thumbing the little brass screws from the tire rims, while Tintin, his injured hand hidden in a sleeve, jacked up one side of the Camry and started the oil draining into two blue tubs. Then he went to work on the wheels.

Somyod paced around them, shoulders curled, arms aping out by his sides. He didn't speak. They worked by the illumination of a half dozen car headlights that had been pulled from their sockets and set up in a circle, the trailing innards looped back to a noisy generator that fumed the air. Now Benz understood where the gasoline had gone. So the building was without power, off the grid; nobody expected to find them here. Under the staring lights Benz couldn't see the ceiling, but he knew there were no windows. What looked like a tough, dark moss was spreading toward the island of scraped and oil-stained concrete in the center of the space.

"What sort of building is this?" Benz asked.

Somyod had been hovering over Tintin's attempt to saw through a rubber tire and strip it from its wheel. Twice now Tintin's hand had slipped, and Benz noticed that his grip was bloody.

Somyod looked up and gestured into the darkness. "It was a movie theater."

Benz could make out a poster now, hand-painted, like a weathered mural sinking into the texture of the wall: half a tank roaring over a hill, the gun muzzle exploding in a white flame that appeared to have consumed the rest of the poster. What remained of the English title read *Battle of* ———.

It was not long before the vehicle had been flayed of its fiberglass body and its components heaped into piles of copper, plastic, aluminum, glass, rubber. All that remained was a steel skeleton—a car in its elemental state.

"We tore that *apart*," Tintin said.

The universe wants to return to its natural state, Benz remembered being told by the chemist and moonshiner who had once caught young Benz and Tintin sneaking into his distillery. "Chaos."

"Is that a threat?" Benz had asked, surrounded at the time by the chemist's boy workers, Tintin's and Benz's equivalents, only smaller than Tintin, and stupid, unlike Benz, which is why the chemist had spared them punishment. He gave them the alcohol they wanted and put them to work. Two years later the man was killed in the fire that razed his distillery, what everyone knew to be a police purge, those same officers the chemist had bribed when all parties were still profiting from the situation.

"Never had such a sweet job," Tintin said when they went to see the building's carcass the following day.

"There are other ways to get alcohol free."

"Oh, not the money." From the rubble Tintin unearthed an

empty bottle, its interior seared black. "We'll never find drink that pure again."

"WHERE DO YOU get the cars?" Benz asked Somyod.

Plucking at the piled treasure, Somyod recited a tale involving Japan, abandoned cars, shipping containers, his brother.

"Japanese people won't even live in used *homes*." That's what Somyod said: "used." "They throw them out, bulldoze them, build them new. If only we could ship those back, too. Ha ha!"

This after Benz had filed off the Camry's VIN number, which identified the car as local, Thai-made. Whatever, better to be lied to when it came time to get out. So they didn't ask Somyod when the work came in—older makes that Benz knew were easy-stealing, still bearing the marks of a break-in, a split gearshift lock on the passenger seat, ignition wires swinging loose.

"Amateurs," Tintin muttered, rolling up a window to find it a shattered stump.

The cars arrived predawn, in time with the rooster calls from Bangkok's outskirts, the rumble of ten-wheelers downshifting, halting after thundering overnight from up-country. The activity drowned out their minor operation: the unloading of cars with license plates clipped off, with the hubcaps already poached sometimes, to which Somyod said, "What the fuck is this?" to the small, rough-hewn men who did the unloading. "You stealing from me?" But nobody was afraid of him; and recognizing that the cogs of this operation were the competent men his brother had assembled, Somyod began to absent himself from the production line.

In four weeks Benz and Tintin dismantled dozens of cars. They worked by their own rhythms, taking turns to go buy food, to sleep on the bedding they had dragged in. They worked to the radio, American rock-and-roll oldies, Benz silent but Tintin chiming in on every "hound dog!" What they knew of the outside came stuttering through the speaker. They hardly even spoke to the truck drivers, who didn't converse so much as maintain a constant Isaan patter, teeth chatter-ing, up on *ya ba* or M-150, the lifeblood of Thailand's workforce.

Benz and Tintin finished their meal (lunch, was it?) and lay back on blankets, the Beach Boys crooning over the radio, and drank themselves happy on rum. What had been rent money now supplied a case of Captain Q bought from a friendly customs officer.

"Holy water." Tintin splashed rum over his hand and flicked it in Benz's face, imitating a streetwalking monk. "Bless you with good fortune. With money and women."

"Stop." Benz grabbed the hand and sensed a jolt from Tintin. "Oh. I thought it had healed."

"Doesn't really hurt. Just habit."

Benz's finger drew a line along Tintin's skin, scrunched as if chewed, but whole.

"I can't, you know, make a complete fist, but otherwise it's like new." Tintin turned his hand and flexed as if trying on a glove for size. "What did I tell you? Holy water."

DECONSTRUCTION OCCUPIED BENZ in a way their old work as bricklayers or welders never had. Childhood sessions in a temple had done a number on him, belief in the Buddhist cycle running deep, and he couldn't help feeling he was returning the cars to the earth.

Tintin, though, was restless. He disappeared into the black end of the hall where rats had made a plush nest of the heaped theater seats and nibbled warrens through the cushion foam. Back there was a room with flaking walls and a termite-laced desk, its wood sheeting curling up like a figure rising from the grave. Up a short flight of stairs was a projection room with, Tintin claimed, a working projec-tor and reels of good film.

"I reassembled it and greased the parts." Tintin's black-tipped fin-gers rubbed stripes into his pant legs.

Benz anticipated the question. "Want to connect it to the genera-tor?"

"Can I?"

Gasoline was precious, but Benz wanted to settle his friend down a bit if he could.

A day later, with extension cables roping up the stairs into the projector room, Tintin got the bulb sputtering. A sun flared on the wall, lifting Benz from his efforts prying apart an airbag hub.

"Hello!" came Tintin's voice from the back. The silhouette of his hand appeared in the circle of light and wiggled its fingers at Benz. "Watch that spot!"

The light obscured and then seemed to condense as an image came into focus. A flashing countdown, curtains, a comic book, credits.

"*Superman*," Benz whispered, recognizing the emblem that now appeared.

"No sound!" Tintin called.

Benz stood up. The picture transitioned into a scene on another planet.

Tintin trotted up behind him and squeezed his shoulders, shook him. "Still—our own theater!"

"That's fine. No sound is fine," Benz said softly, the images a rising wind that billowed the screen of his own memory.

As a boy he had seen a few *Ultraman* episodes thrown against a white sail staked out in a field beside a temple, its fabric perforated with flapping vent triangles. This was the setup of the primitive roving cinemas that projected off the back of pickup trucks. The operators would make a parade of the evening traffic in their outskirt neighborhood, calling the children to the curb with news of "Ultraman's battle against Gomora! Hin Tong temple at sundown!"

The horns of the temple's shadow closed slowly around them as they hunkered down and waited for dusk, the movie image finally cleaving from the last light of day to reveal a cityscape and then Ultraman's signature glowing eyes. The children raised a cheer before quieting down to sit rapt, hardly noticing the offscreen man with a microphone live-dubbing the dialogue from scrappy notes. The man's voice chased the image, a delay as natural to the viewers as thunder responding to lightning.

At the halftime break car headlights snapped on, illuminating tables spilling all manner of candy. There was something for everyone, the microphone man announced. Bamboo spears and plastic pistols for kiddie turf wars. Household items to satisfy the parents. There was the broomstick man with his trundling bicycle-cart sporting a tail of chicken-feather dusters.

And Benz and his boys, proud, poor, skirting the light, awaiting the return of the free show and the story of a man winning a war against monstrous forces. Against all odds.

That night Benz lost Tintin during the break. When Tintin returned he had a plastic bottle—bartered, he said, from old man Chart in exchange for repairing the wire around his hen patch—a job Tintin would never finish.

"What is it?"

"Chart's liquor."

Tintin stood above the other twelve-year-olds, a shadow, but the car headlights caught the crystalline moonshine he tapped casually against his leg.

For all of them it was a first attempt at drinking. Benz held the alcohol in his mouth, afraid to swallow it.

Tintin watched him. "Go on. It burns through you. Like it's purging something." He swept his hand over the spotlighted bustle below them: the children thronging, the parents herding, and the vendors calling, telling them that there was something for everyone.

"Like you could burn all this away."

THEY PUSHED TOGETHER their mattresses and ate their meals from the Styrofoam they were delivered in. They kept the rum within reach.

"It's clearly very toxic," Tintin said, speaking for the silently mouthing captain in their current film, a space adventure. The voice he assumed was wooden and fully annunciated, like a radio host's.

Benz asked what the hell that voice was supposed to be.

"That's the voice of Captain Q," he said, unusually solemn.

Silence drew out the spaces in the movie, and there were the long spots of ruined film where they lost the picture completely. To Benz this was like watching rain against a dark windshield, the oncoming headlights parsed, appearing as mere flashes in the water curtain.

"You suppose the captain's dead?" Tintin asked.

"Not yet."

The picture flashed back on suddenly, an alien exploding through a man's chest.

"Fuck!" Tintin yelled. They curled their legs instinctively.

Then everything turned splotchy again and they fell apart laughing.

The film reel ran out before they reached the end. They agreed that somebody had to survive.

Benz raised the garage door.

"This is the fucking life," Tintin said in a voice still possessed by Captain Q.

They had bought several half liters of beer, and Tintin was alternating between that and the hard stuff. "Drinks and movies and sex." He looked around. "Well, no sex. But you know the ladies love rum. Mix it up with some sweet Hale's Blue Boy and a little soda water, a little bubbly. They love it."

"Okay."

"We'll go drinking and I'll show you how *much* they love it. How they want to put it in their mouths."

The thought floated above them while they remained on their mattresses.

"Remember how Paeng used to claim she had white blood?" Tintin reminisced. "That her father was an American GI, or something like that. She would rub water into talcum powder and try to hide her face. It dried so firm she hardly moved her lips when she spoke. I always wanted to take a chisel to it. Just"—he lifted his fist and drove home a hammer—"you know?"

Benz said nothing.

The bats chittered up in the old airshafts, their black forms swooping in through the garage door, dotting the dusk, seeming to bring in the night.

THE NEXT MORNING Tintin remained where he was ("Captain's out," he mumbled), so Benz handled the delivery himself. The driver was shifty, sucked his brown bottle of M-150 like a pacifier.

"Where's the boss?"

Benz hadn't seen the man this week.

"We haven't been paid," the driver said.

When they rolled the cars into the open warehouse, waking Tintin with the blaze of morning, Benz noticed that the drivers had half stripped the cars themselves—crude but effective work. He looked from the missing parts to the driver, who lowered the bottle in invitation.

"I'll tell Somyod you're looking for him," Benz said. But by the next delivery Somyod still hadn't come for the parts. Benz lined the inside walls with car components, but there was no hiding the spent cars now crowding the lot outside.

THE HOT SEASON arrived overnight. They had to keep the door shut against the heat while they worked, but they knew noontime by the swell in the day, the heat filling every bit of the cavernous space. By afternoon, the floor was hot enough to bake their soles, their backs, so they switched to working nights, using the daytime to sleep.

And then there were no more cars. The deliveries stopped. No one came for the parts.

"We could sell them ourselves," Tintin suggested. But neither of them knew where to find the buyers. And there was the problem of the police.

Benz rather enjoyed the feeling of having been forgotten by the world, as if they had stepped out of a gridlocked road.

A week passed in which they used too much money while expending the stockpiled gasoline to keep their films running. Benz hardly watched, just lying back on the mattress so as to observe the movement of light overhead. It was dusty enough inside that he could watch the projector rays braid above him. He listened to the voice of Captain Q take on each movie's leading role. But only the lead, so that each film was a monologue, a man in conversation with friends who had departed, whose only response was silence.

They ate less, didn't leave for food as often. The heat had made them sluggish, even after Tintin found an old fan, creaking at the neck and missing one of its metal blades, which threw the gait of its revolutions.

"*Wum, badum, wum,*" Tintin would mimic absently.

Sleeping side by side on a mattress to share this single wind, they woke often, tossed against each other, sweat patching where their bodies touched, the floor grit that coated them turned slick as graphite.

"Sorry," Tintin murmured.

"It's not even evening yet," Benz said.

Tintin rose and went into the bathroom. Benz, restless and awake, followed. It was a bare room with a latrine-style drain dug around the wall. The tiles—blue—were uneven and spat up trickles of water when stepped on. A toilet squatted absurdly in the center. This had probably been a mop room reoutfitted after the theater became a factory. Light chipped through the slatted cinder block wall.

Tintin was in his underwear, dousing himself from the drum bucket. The water, running warm from the hose, reeked of sulfur. Benz halted in the doorway, eyes adjusting.

In their world of narrow men Tintin had always appeared as out of place as the Michelin Man. Built like steel rebar, he was a man of rods and girth. The opposite of Benz, whose armature might as well have been a noodle. Tintin's chest was wide and his legs rounded with muscles that tensed now to every shock of water he threw over himself.

Tintin tossed Benz the pail.

"Make yourself at home." He turned on the hose and slid it into the drum bucket to fill.

Benz looked down his slender body as he washed. The sun had marked him dark as drain water, save for the halo of skin at the lip of his underwear.

"White," Benz remarked.

"Your *farang* parts!" Tintin laughed loudly and pinched Benz's hip. "White as toothpaste. White as Made in America."

Benz reached back and grabbed Tintin between the legs. "You want to see your face light up?"

He gave a squeeze, expecting a comic, stuffed-animal yelp, but Tintin hesitated. The underwear fabric was ridged and wet, soft and rumpled as flesh.

Tintin clutched Benz's hand with his own.

The hose slipped from the bucket lip. It thrashed on the floor and Benz released Tintin to subdue it.

THE FILM WAS called *Rocky*. They exchanged the bottle during the opening credits, drank quickly, didn't take their attention from the men fighting, locked, heaving against each other.

And then Tintin pulled the rum from Benz's mouth. He leaned into Benz to set it down, breathing noisily. He rubbed his thumb against Benz's hip bone. He stretched the elastic of the waistband, dragged the shorts to Benz's knees.

The bottle clinked onto its side.

Benz wanted to speak. There was no dialogue onscreen.

Tintin said nothing. He had his tongue in Benz's navel. He wrapped his hand around Benz's cock and filled his mouth and Benz tried to tell what was tongue and what fingers. His breaths didn't come. Tintin's other hand climbed up Benz's chest, grasped his neck. The fingers found his mouth and entered him, salty on his tongue, forcing his head back.

Benz was too drunk to perform, the alcohol and heat blunting his anxiety. As if he'd have known how to perform here anyway. Instead he stared, head back, at the poster of the tank with its clandestine opponents. "*Battle of*," he read.

His teeth caught the ridge of scar tissue on Tintin's hand. And then he did after all—thrust upward, pulsing, spent, suddenly embarrassed by the hold he still had on Tintin's hair.

Tintin rasped his mouth against Benz's thigh, leaving a warm smear, a residue Benz would later hesitate to wash, noticing the way his leg hairs had aligned to the gesture.

In the movie, a couple was ice skating.

Tintin washed his mouth with beer, swallowed, and slipped his underwear off. His penis—how many times since childhood had they bathed together—was thick and it stank.

"Take it," Tintin instructed. "Put your hand around it."

Benz hesitated. He recognized the voice Tintin affected: deeper, hollow.

"It's okay." Tintin guided Benz's hand. "It's not us. I'm somebody else. You know me."

THEY WOKE TO the clatter of the garage door. It was still night and Tintin was naked. Three flashlights swung through the room.

"Oh. You're still here?" It was the Isaan driver and his men. "We thought you'd be gone by now."

Benz stood, feigning alertness, though his eyes were still fogged from the press of the mattress. What was the driver doing here? Benz searched for a reasonable statement: "We've still got these parts to sell."

The man's light turned to the wall of parts. "That's right. Which is why we're here to pick them up."

There was no threat in the statement. It was the casual way these men had with violence—no malice, just a tired inevitability.

Tintin joined Benz. He was still naked. "We're waiting for Somyod."

"Man's run. Or, who knows—maybe dead. Anyway, that's up to the police now. We came to burn the place down."

"Why?"

"It's what the police want, right? So nobody has to answer any questions." The light beam swung briefly down Tintin's naked front. "And they'll be coming soon, too. Nobody's paid them, see. Nobody's paid the junkyard and nobody's going to pay you scrappers, either, so . . . Time to go." The driver gestured at his men.

The components were piled high, so the men pulled from the bottom, allowing the parts to tumble and scatter across the cement floor. They backed their pickup right into the theater, casting Benz and Tintin in the red of the taillights.

Benz went to the tool table. He listened to the men loading, and finally laid his hand on a steel-head hammer with a cruel ripping claw.

Tintin, beside him, took Benz's wrist in his fingers. The wound had reopened.

Benz released the hammer, hovered his fingers over the raw tear. "That was me."

"Yeah."

The driver watched them. He held up a can of gasoline. "We were going to burn it down," he said, "but you're here." Behind him another man had lit a cigarette.

Benz held Tintin's hand.

"I'll leave it to you, then," the driver said, clanking the can down. "Give you time to get your stuff out."

At the doorway he stopped and pointed up. "You'll want to make sure the roof catches, though. Or else the fire will eat up the gasoline. The paint on that old poster should burn nicely."

THEY RETURNED TO the mattress, only they didn't sleep.

"We'll make a clean start," Benz said. He thought of the day, years back, that they had aged out of the orphanage without a plan, a home. They had tied themselves to the familiar, the klong that snaked through their neighborhood, and together, they'd followed it to a new place.

The can of gasoline sat in the middle of the workspace, the pool of concrete like a spotlight around it. There was no more rum. Or money. They had spent it. And the generator was running down the last of their fuel.

At dawn Tintin rose. Benz watched as he dragged two theater chairs from the back, their feet scraping through the grime. He braced his leg against the spine of a chair and with a jerk he snapped the wood beneath. He shredded the vinyl cushions, which spilled out pieces of foam. He heaped the splinters and disappeared to get the lacquered sheeting of the old desk. Then he returned with a mess of film reels he threw onto the pile, the shiny black ribbons curling wild.

Tintin settled on the mattress. It was hot enough that Benz could watch the sweat form on his friend's arm. He swiped his finger along Tintin's skin, clearing the beads.

"They say that there are coal veins that have been on fire for years," Tintin said suddenly. "Always raging. When we burn this place down, you know, I hope it stays alight forever. And so looking behind us at night we would see the fire and know that this happened."

He could say things in a way that made Benz believe they would happen. But Benz didn't want a funeral pyre. He picked up the can of gasoline and walked past Tintin's pile to pour whatever they had into the generator.

"What are you doing?" Tintin asked.

Benz began disconnecting the stadium of headlights, one at a time.

"Put on *Rocky* again."

Tintin didn't respond. Each light that disappeared threw new shadows on his face.

"I can do that," he said as Benz reached the final light.

The film felt short and clumsy, the ending now inevitable. But when the reel finished Tintin reloaded it.

And so they went through it again, listening to the arrhythmic murmuring of the fan and waiting for the generator to sputter out, the projector's flare to fade.

Neither of them dubbed the film. They let the images run silent.

Make-Believe

PINKY (2010)

Call me Pinky. Let me guess, you're a sideline? I don't know why Pi Nawa wastes her time on you part-timers. Most of you don't have what it takes. You don't come back after the tour. I know your type. Go on, this is us. The doors swing in.

Classier than you thought, isn't it? Not a blow-job bar. Not a massage parlor. No by-the-hour agreements. We're as upscale as you'll find on this *soi*. As a cheer-beer girl, you'll get a commission on what your tables spend. Get them to buy you tips, "lady drinks." That's the idea anyway. If you want to make real money, you'll need to get them out of here. Men use the bar to window-shop. For us, the real money's in outcalls and what the *farangs* call the "girlfriend experience." Make-believe. They can be so coy.

I mean, until they get you back to their hotel room. Then they're all the same. Then, it's two pops. Most can't, without chemical help, manage more than that in the ninety minutes. It used to be one, but if they blew their load right away, they'd still want the next hour and change and the truth is it's sometimes easier to fuck them than talk to them.

There are cameras in all the corners. The guys can get shifty about being recorded. We tell them it's for their protection. It's not. It's there for us. The hotel rooms are another story. If you get into trouble, call Pi Nawa. You know she bailed me out once after this man took me to dinner at a hi-so French place—I mean *really* French, like *everything* blanketed in cream, the waiters politely looking down on me. Then he went to the bathroom and never came back. On his way, he sent our waiter with a bill. Some sick joke. But even Pi Nawa has her limits. There are bad times, bad men. You show up to a room and it's two instead of one. Or four. That's four times the money. You do what you have to do to get out.

Back here's the staff area. Clock in, clock out. Lockers. Bring your own padlock when you come in. You like that? Lotte has a thing for glittery stickers. He's the main bartender. After Pi Nawa, Lotte's your best friend. Split your tips and he'll look out for you. He'll fill your beer bottle with drinking water, that kind of thing. Can you hold your alcohol? Anyway, you'll learn to backwash.

Bulletin board. This envelope's for business cards. It's mostly the Japanese who leave them. Some of the girls are cold callers, and they'll go through all the cards. I've never seen the appeal. Discount coupons for cosmetics, waxing. This section is for side jobs. Paid weekends in Singapore's nightclubs are a good starting point. Money's good, like *foreign* good. You take home tips and commission. Lodging's included, bunks and toilets, even instant noodles the one time I went. But you've got to pass an interview. They like their girls light-skinned, pretty, no stretch marks. It's a good backdoor into the VIP circles. Local circles, too. Rich kids and their "N-up" drug parties. There's money in that. But also drugs, mostly uppers. You have to know your limits. Or you could end up like that pretty, Babybelle. Poor girl. Now we all know her name. What's your nickname? No, you'll need something more memorable.

Don't be taken in by this quiet daytime street, it looks different by night. You know, this whole strip—from the 7-Eleven that sells out of lube weekly to the grandma omelet place at our end of the *soi*—one family owns it all. Old money. The head of the clan has big hair to match her big name. Owns a classic Benz on suspension so spongy it looks like she's coming around the corner on a parade float when she arrives, mornings of the first Monday, to take rent. Everyone thinks they're above this work but everyone takes a slice. So I say, you're not special. There are the Mae Sai girls, the Phayao girls, the small-timers in your side-*soi* karaoke bars. And then there are the downtown girls, and we're not the same. I had one university girl like you. Looked just like you. Sweet and skinny. Mommy gave her an allowance bigger than most salaries. But she wants a trip to Seoul. She wants SK-II and a Leica. In she comes. There are dabblers. There are part-timers. I could time the swells in you sidelines by the releases of new iPhones.

Don't get me wrong. There are the old-school *ab-op-nuat* places, with their bleacher seats and one-way windows and coffin rooms. There are the girls trafficked from Myanmar, from Cambodia. There's that shit on the border. But right here, the money can be good. "C-suite salaries on the street level," I like to say. And once you're taking the money, you won't be able to imagine working anywhere else. That's the trap. We've come so far. The only time it gets to you is when you're alone, and the tips are down, and the cock is sour. But then you look around for help and . . . See? Nobody is alone here.

With everything going online it's only becoming faster, greater. The men, the money, the want. In the kingdom where from birth the royal decree has been "enough." Take just enough for yourself, we're taught. In Buddhism and song and Isuzu ad. You know what my nickname was, originally? Not Pinky. I was born number twelve of twelve kids and my mother called me Pho—Enough! It isn't.

Like Us for a Whiter You

LARA & NAM (2010)

We're outside Metropole when this native thirty-something in a miniskirt takes Bird's hand and asks him in English, "Mister, my friend, you want sexy massage, mister?"

Stella and I stamp our heels and laugh. It's funny because this woman's so floor-country Thai that she could be Bird's mom. Well, his mom before she married up and into Bangkok, settling in with his Yankee dad like he's a retirement plan. Bird says in easy Thai that he's fine, no thanks, and this woman looks like she's swallowed a straight capful of drink.

"Then I'll give you half off because you're *luk khrueng*," she splutters, recovering. Half off for a half child. Sometimes these natives are even funny.

The club's guard takes IDs but it's the faces he reads. Bird and Stella have to nestle me between them, wash out my muddy color, a fault I lay at my mother's feet.

Inside, it's Bird's table, so Bird's buying. The rum drips out golden and familiar and smelling like metal.

Stella drags her chair next to me, leans my head on her shoulder, and holds up the bottle. "Photo, please." She hands Bird the phone.

I check the image. "Don't post that. I look like a raccoon."

"*That*," she says, tapping the screen, "is why we have face correction."

Even though we're both *luk khrueng,* I'm dark beside her. Hers is a color I know well from the billboards that make a rat maze of our city: Stella modeling this yogurt drink or that instant noodle. Mostly, though, it's whitening creams. Her latest, a Skytrain spread, shows Stella as one of twenty winking women, their portraits cobbled together to form a palette grid. White Peach is the darkest on their skin gradient. Stella's color they call Mascarpone, as if any natives know what the hell that is. Now they think it's a skin tone—just two squares off Porcelain.

Even when it's not Stella up there, it's her I see: showcasing a push-up bra or the latest lace thing from Seoul. Stella's body, you could strum the lines of it.

"Yoga," she always tells me.

Like hell yoga, I don't say. Just like I don't look at the P-stamped pill she slips under her tongue before a meal—what she calls her supplements, and what Bird, during Stella's ten minutes in a toilet stall, calls puke pills. But that's also false, because it all comes out her ass. Picture *that* on your palette.

Bird slaps down his empty glass. He closes his eyes, rolls his head and smiles, his cheeks like waxed apples. He wants to dance. And so Stella and Bird and I come together like old lovers, the moves unambitious but satisfying. We know what not to talk about: the hooks of Stella's hips, say, or Bird's eyes traversing the contours of that man's shoulders, his jawline.

Visiting Metropole is soothing, especially on a night like this. As long as you hit the selfies early, you can dance seams right through your body cream, through your face cake. And tomorrow when your cubicle buddy asks you where you went, and with whom, from over the top of a mirror that's magnifying her brow, you'll have something to show for your night.

"Oh, Metropole," you can say, knowing she'd never get in. Because the club is really a temple, see. It's about ritual, dance, idols. Entering the black box shores up a glossy-magazine worldview; only uppity natives with big-eye contacts, premium-bright whitening

cream, and loose perms are going to manage to steal by the guard. So
what you're looking at—you with a hopeful reflection, you with the
fine-tuning filters, you with an income disposed on cosmetics—is
the fairest in the land.

"IT'S TWO IN the morning," Mom says, discovering me in the kitchen
at barely 1:45, fighting the corkscrew.

The cork pops out and wine sloshes over the white tiles. I steady
my arm to pour a glass, playing sober. "So why are *you* awake?"

Mom says, "It's two on a weeknight."

And I say, "Stop, okay? I'm an adult."

I make an exit with my glass. Mom follows me, turns the lights
out one at a time, chasing me into my room.

Sleeping's hard because I can never keep the day from coursing
through me—echoes of interactions and what I didn't say in them.
Most evenings I need my comedown wine, a habit I inaugurated one
night in a hotel room, an American's (I know, I *know*, but the *farangs*
are easier, most are just passing through, you know?). Unable to sleep
next to this guy, I drank alone in his kitchenette, twirling the compli-
mentary corkscrew, my thigh sticky with his goo. I thought of Dad's
scratchy good-night kisses when I was young. Dad setting down his
leggy wineglass, what always looked to me like a busty woman in red
waiting for him to finish with me. Mom was never that curvy woman,
not even in her next-to-spinster age when she should have been filling out from the middle. Mom will always be severe through and
through. Dad's gone.

I was halfway down the bottle when the American woke up for
the toilet.

"Sorry," he mumbled, running his thumb down my spine. "Jet
lag." He stood with me at the window.

"See those apartment towers there, like a row of graves?" I pointed.
"The second is me and my mom."

"And your dad?" he asked.

"You ever meet a man named Rick on your travels?"

"I guess?" he said, reaching for the bottle.

"Yeah, me neither." I took another swig and left him the tannins.

IN THE MORNING there's a gruesome smile of wine spit on my pil-low.

My morning routine: rubbing cream on my butt. There's a coin-sized spot where, since I was thirteen, I've been blotting whitening Gluta, testing, testing, turning my private part pied. Most women spread this stuff on their faces, but you don't know what the gunk can do to you. It gets rashy sometimes, my spot.

"You're not using it between your legs, are you?" asked my derma-tologist, seeing that my face is the same color it was on my last visit. "Because I have something for that, too."

You know what Gluta is? Some say it's cancer cream. I'm not sure whether that means cause or treatment, but next time you're too fired up to sleep, next time your best friend's over and she complains be-tween swipes that she's, like, bored—*bored!*—try googling glutathi-one injections.

You know the saying: Beautiful by way of the knife. Nowadays: By the needle. By self-induced vomiting and snacking on ice. By sanding down your face. By the belt machines that jiggle cellulite off your hips, like fat sloughing off a spit roast. By acid masks. By sweat-boxes. By the hour on a high stool in the cosmetics section of the mall, the fluorescence spotlighting your every flaw. By hamster-wheeling in the gym. By breaking your cheekbones and trimming your lips, snip, snip, let's restitch that face, doll.

"Fakes," Stella likes to say, with her beautiful-by-birth entitle-ment.

But it's a way of life. It's the way of the "pretties," those second-rate models famous for their car-convention appearances. Pretty as title, as vocation. My question about the profession is: Whose ambi-tion is it to become a car accessory? Also, is there, like, a pretties hierarchy? It's one thing to drape a Maserati—at least that machine has curves—but whose job is it to sexy up the family wagon? I'm just saying, because once, when I was younger, Mom's friend suggested I try it someday.

"You might be dark for a *luk khrueng*, but the fact that you are half white should be enough to land a pretty job."

And if that's how my life had gone? You'd find me in a bar pushing beers by now. "Hey, boys, how about I bring you the BIG bottle?" But that's how those girls live.

Only, yesterday there was a newspaper story about a pretty accidentally injecting Botox into her bloodstream. She died.

You'll understand my caution with the cream.

Mom outside my door, yelling, "Lara, it's seven-thirty already!"

Mom in the driver's seat taking me to my magazine internship. Taking advantage of commuting time, of record-breaking traffic to tell me what I'm doing wrong. It feels like we've stalled forever among anonymous greys and whites, fiberglass encasing other people's lives, shutting in the shit-slinging I know is going on. I suspect Mom planted the traffic here just to shame me.

This is the hour when across Bangkok, on Skytrain platforms and outside police booths, in factories and parking lots and schools, superiors stand with megaphones, imparting daily lessons to those lined up before them. Why should I be any different?

"I know you don't want to listen to me," Mom says, as the light winks from green to red again without our ever moving.

I eat cornflakes from a Winnie-the-Pooh cup and watch motorbikes trickle by. At least someone's getting ahead.

"You remember Bo, Nina's daughter?"

"Mom, you've told me about Bo." I flip down the visor, pretend to retouch my eyeliner. "Also about Inky, Waan, and Joy. You've shown me their graduation photos. I practically know their starting salaries."

I review my reflection, a ritual from my childhood ballet lessons, biweekly exercises in bearing the sight of my body sausaged into a unitard and practicing grace, practicing my plié, my belly an accordion. Also the nauseating rubbing of my thighs. Also the hashed and furrowed flesh. Hell is a hall of mirrors.

"You can't waste your life, okay?" Mom says. "Everyone else has grown up. When are you going to finish university?"

"It's not like I'm a failure or something. It's just taking me longer to figure things out. My career's not exactly a straight line."

"What would your dad say?"

"Fuck Dad."

"He tries to talk to you."

"No, he sends you money—that's not what I'd call trying. He doesn't get to tell me what I should and shouldn't do with my life."

Mom falls quiet. The row of cars, like a belt of luggage, conveys us onward.

A MAN GRINS into his mirror, taps his front teeth as if adjusting the fit of a smile that he's just installed. He tests the effect by walking past a woman, who undulates, goes weak at the knees.

"*That's* how we sell toothpaste," my editor tells me, handing me the storyboard sketch he just acted out.

Not all the *luk khrueng* are modeling, see. Somebody has to write copy.

My manager demonstrates his own grin now. He's why we use sex to sell bottled water.

"He's right, though," Stella says later, when I complain about my day organizing a tooth shoot. "The woman is the measure of the product's success." She points at the stage that's been erected in a shopping mall's foyer. "Hey, here's Bird now." Applause, and Bird emerges uncomfortable, leveling that bow tie.

We're here for the launch of *MRMan* magazine—Modern Renaissance being what it stands for, a lesser *GQ*. *MRMan*'s staff seems to be under the impression that Gatsby-themed events are new.

"Here's Bird," I echo. He stands up there with the MC and looks good, I have to admit. His hair is a polished car hood, his teeth newly minted. He takes his white looks from his white dad. Lucky asshole.

Already I've eaten too much of the finger food borne by pretties displaying matching flapper-girl chignons. My nails raise red tracks on my skin. This is how I handle discomfort, scratching like a child, pretending the problems are skin-deep. I take another flaccid piece of food from a pretty. Her torso is a cigarette.

Stella eats nothing. Her bootheel makes a testy *tap-tap*, impatient with the media team in the corner that has yet to flock to her, to broadcast the word, the who-what-where of her outfit, the oh-this-little-thing? that ornaments her hair. *Tommy Mookjan designed it for me,* she would explain. But tonight nobody asks and up onstage Bird is floundering in Thai.

MRMan's MC is too native to understand Bird's illiteracy—our boy is international-school educated, see, a modern heir to the colonial bootlickers of old, those officers with their clean Queen's English unable to communicate with their own countrymen.

So when the MC gestures a wand at this Thai slogan, at this Thai headline—*Bird, sign here, endorse your voice to this, read it for us, Bird!*—when that happens, the polish rubs off and the petals of his *MRMan* bow tie wilt.

"I forgot how bad Bird's reading is," Stella says.

"*I* didn't." Not me, who had to tutor Bird through a belated Thai education, which is how I know he can't read the letters, that any typeface beyond what might be employed in a picture book is going to be beyond Bird.

And here's Bird onstage and here's something romanized, Thai letters wrought to look like an S, a W. It's what's familiar that unravels him—the shape of his own language.

"Bird?" the MC tries.

And Bird tries. He sweats through his shirt; he reads, sounding out the syllables.

WE STEP OUT of the mall onto the Skytrain platform. Lights play off water fountains, jumbotrons flit through images from a sushi promotion, and poor Bird, caught in the open, is swathed in television hues. Only he's mistaken for that heartthrob from the latest *lakhon* up on YouTube. One teenager's cry rallies the rest. Before Bird even has a chance to deploy his shallow modesty, he's swarmed, the teens at the back whispering, "Who is this anyway?"

"Bird," Stella says afterwards, "how is it you're never mistaken for yourself?"

"Meaning what?" Bird says, knowing well Stella's aptitude for sideswiping a person with her questions. He pretends to be pleased, though of course punctured, smarting in that B-list model way: Does nobody recognize him from the chewing gum commercial? It's enough to spur him to suggest another night at Metropole.

"It's a Thursday?" I say.

"Be an adult, Lara," Stella tells me.

Which is how we come to be at Bird's table at Metropole, where he swallows the pain of the earlier performance and any commentary from Stella on said performance. For me it's my guilt that I gulp down when my phone announces *Mom Mom Mom*. She calls three times, though leaves only one message.

I don't look. I leave that all behind. Lock it away in the house like our fights, like that damaged cassette of me singing Billie Holiday— Mom sliding it into the player again, again saying, "*This* is the gift that you insist on wasting." I tuck it away like the picture of Dad on a bench in quaint New England, his coat collar popped and pointed against the sort of chill we never have in Bangkok.

Bird pours the rum. We ring our glasses together. We drink it down.

"Bird, I have to say, I forgot what your Thai is like," Stella says.

"Shut up, Stella," I say. "You didn't forget."

Bird spins the shot glass and doesn't look up.

"No need to pout," Stella says.

Finding no response, she steps onto a dance floor of Hello Kitty types trying hard not to sweat as they bounce up against a circle of men. The men train their barbed eyes inward, downward, as if around a fishing hole.

They have been waiting for Stella. Ever since she reached puberty, when modeling agencies started bidding on her future: a floodlit stage. All she had to do was show up.

"She didn't fucking forget," Bird says.

"No."

"Stop scratching."

He's right, my arms look like a railway crossing.

"Pour me another?" I ask.

"Maybe you should slow down."

But we're both watching Stella dance and he tops me off just the same.

Stella's dress of wide black ribbons fans out, whips away from her, opens to the eye like a zoetrope.

"She's got something everyone wants," Bird says.

"I can be like that, too," I say, and to prove it before he can laugh at me, I'm up and walking at the *farangs* on the other end of the bar. Not even the world-weary variety of *farang*, those arriving feverish and bug-spotted from aid work on the border. No—these guys here have soft, broad bodies rounded by the mold of a business-class citizenship.

When I catch the eye of one, he's twenty years too old, but tonight I'm reckless. I stand in front of him and cross my legs, present myself like a question mark: yes or no?

"Hi," he says.

"Name?" I ask.

"Adam."

"The first man," I say. "I like that."

Adam gets me a glass of wine that's sour, for one thing, not a quick gulp the way our drink is. He's tall and holds his shoulders behind him like awkward wings. I have to look up to talk. He's here with some trading group. Staying where?

"Oriental House. I wanted to be closer to the nightlife. You know it?"

I nod, yes, yes, everyone knows. Boutique down the street. Rooftop bar. Water feature. Floor-country women prowling. Chuckling, I say, "One woman tried a line on Bird the other night, right here outside Metropole, and I nearly fell laughing so hard."

"Bird?" Adam says like a dull nut.

I wave an arm, gulp the wine and say, "Anyway, those women like it because of all the *farangs* there. Like you."

He says, "*Farang?* Meaning 'fruit' or 'foreigner'?"

He's trying to play along. "Ah," I say, "Adam's practiced his Thai." I push against him, stare up into his eyes, move my thumbs under his belt. "I don't know—you don't look like a guava to me; must be the other kind of *farang* I'm talking about."

"Right." He laughs.

I lean back and survey him. "Then again, I really don't know," I say, leaning in. "Let's peel you and see."

Adam's harmless flirting curdles into forceful desire. "We could go back."

"We *could,* but there's booze here and none out there. You know the corner 7-Elevens are required to stop selling alcohol at midnight? Yeah—welcome to Thailand where we're governed by a fairy godmother."

"How about I get us a bottle of wine to go?"

"What a good idea. Let's," I say.

I see the price of the bottle he orders—he makes sure of it.

"I need to tell the guys I'm leaving, though." A gesture backward.

"Go." But when he leaves, I take the wine with me back to Bird's table.

"Bird," I say. "Bird, can we go? I promised some *farang* I'd go back with him but I'm really not feeling it."

He doesn't hear me. He's watching Stella.

"Bird, look! I got us wine." I hold out the bottle.

"Stella's a mess," he says.

It's true. She's unspooling on the dance floor. It's her go-to drug cocktail, something devastating. We know the results.

"Let her spin out," I say. "It's what she wants, right?"

But Bird has a stake in Stella's public face, and you can't give that away for free. He knows how hard it is to earn. Even with all the baiting he's been doing, the cheap promos he's taken for exposure, nothing moves Bird's numbers like a photo with Stella's arm thrown around him like the slackest life preserver.

He enters the ring of men, their phone cameras spurting flashes at Stella, who snaps around: "Hey! Hey, asshole! I charge for that."

Bird saves Stella to save himself.

OUTSIDE, STELLA AND I climb into an empty police booth shaped like an officer's helmet. Bird goes into a 7-Eleven to buy Stella an electrolyte drink.

Stella gestures at the wine bottle in my hands. "Where'd you get that?"

"I had a man buy it for me."

"Native?"

"*Farang* in a suit."

"You're more resourceful than you look," Stella says.

Bird comes back and hands Stella a bottle. She rubs it on her forehead.

"Drink," he says.

I sweat. I notice all the ways my body folds. The wine's warming in my hands. I get up to buy water from a street vendor. The tin cup stings my lip with its chill.

Back in the police booth, Bird's chiding, holding the bottle for Stella.

"You *have* to drink—look at you, you're sweating and so pale— hell, Stella, always too far . . ."

And her babbling, "Okayokay*okay.*"

The two of them shoulder to shoulder reminding me that even

when I angle Bird to see Ugly Stella, directing him to see her as I see her, he still loves her more.

You'd pick her, too, you know, in a magazine hypothetical: *Which girl would you rather _____?* Yeah, so fuck you, too. Why don't they ever ask which you could *love*? You know? Which could love *you*?

I consider Adam's wine, reconsider Adam's company. Bird suggests a taxi home. I say I've got a boy (a boy—ha!) waiting for me inside.

"Bird, I'm sorry," Stella says, head bopping against his shoulder. "Sorry what I said about your shitty reading."

"That's okay. My reading's shitty, you're right."

"That's right," Stella slurs. "Isn't that right. Mine's not so great either."

But not me. Not the girl who Mom enrolled in "traditional" Thai extracurriculars all the way through her youth. "To cultivate an understanding of where you come from," Mom said, always in stilted, formal Thai, like a court herald announcing my presence: *Here, the mongrel.*

A younger me did try drinking from that well, I should say, staining her knees on their turf, getting a taste for native flavor. I mean, I dated a native boy. What it was like: lovely. Briefly lovely. His eyes two magic mirrors and me shining in them, believing for a spell what he saw in me: slim, glamorous, foreign. Best sex I've had, too; it's always the earnest boys. It was a fairy tale I danced shortly through.

Only you can't stay long with that type. *Not of my world,* I thought, watching the girl in the boy's eyes. But Metropole has taught me the rules of entry and exit. Our mothers' lives, too, serve as cautionary tales. They know the cost of crossing boundaries. The sense of unbelonging has worn Mom down, like it did on those days she spent in Dad's winter country, the absence of sun and humidity changing her, turning her skin into a landscape fissured and coarse.

"Stop scratching," I hear Bird say.

Bird and Stella are steepled against each other.

I say, "Ha—yeah, I forgot my Thai reading, too."

Stella snorts. "Please. We all know you're more native than not."

"The fuck? You're as much Thai as *I* am."

"Chemically." She yawns. "Or biologically or whatever—sure. But, I mean, look at you."

"Look at me what?" I challenge.

"I mean, are you sure your dad is your dad?"

"Hey, calm down," says Bird.

"So sensitive! Sorry." Stella reaches out as if to pet me. I step back. "You think because you're whiter you're better than me."

Stella holds up a hand. "Sweetie, who do you think you're kidding? I've seen the whitening cream you hide in your bathroom."

They watch me expectantly, as if I'm the problem and not Stella. The bottle in my hands is heavy. I hold it out. An offer of alliance. "Here, Bird. You can have it. It's already open."

"I don't want it."

"Okay." I study the bottle, take a sip. This taste is my cue: The night is over. "I'm outta here. Going home."

I walk away from the police booth thinking of Mom waiting in the kitchen, reciting accusations, what she'll tell me about who I am and what I don't understand. And I'll do the same. I'll say, as I've said before, that it was her fault he left us for America. Mom and her gently crooked accent, her limp curtain hair. I've told her this. I've said, "It makes me sick to be half you. It was you, Mom, see? *You* made my dad leave. It was your floor-country dirt skin."

I can see Mom in the kitchen. I can see the fluorescence blanketing our entrance's three steps—too much to climb tonight.

I want to return to an earlier phase of the night. Dial back the moon. Drinking my comedown wine, I walk back to Metropole, the sidewalk now blighted, heaped with garbage bags. A truck blares floor-country music and a man hosing the pavement catches my feet with his spray.

"Closed," the guard tells me. I turn from the lolling doors to the street, walking along the row of shophouses. The wine's half gone and making me sick, anyway. I pass a parked pickup truck, its gleaming hubcaps guarded from strays by rows of water bottles. I set my wine down among the other sentinels and continue down to Oriental House. An eight-story of concrete and recessed windows.

"You're in there, aren't you, Adam?"

Again. "ADAM!"

Nothing. Filmed windows.

"HEY, ADAM. COME ON DOWN!"

Here he comes, bowlegged, stooped and ashamed, my Adam.

"Come back here and talk to me again. I've been waiting for you. All night. All these years. I've been waiting for you."

It's hotel security. This chimp waves me off. Says in Thai, "Go."

"Not *you*." I speak slowly and in English. *"Adam."*

"Go! You can't be making a living around here." He points across the street.

Up at the windows: "ADAM!"

The guard tries to grab me and I lose a heel backing away. "Hey! Don't touch me. Don't!" He seizes my wrist, twists it, and uses my arm to steer us across the street. In Thai: "Okay, stop! I *get* it!" He leaves me on the opposite sidewalk among a line of women facing the hotel.

"You think I'm one of these whores!" I yell at the receding guard.

The crisp hotel lobby swallows him. The image in the glass door ripples like a lake coming to rest. When the door stills, it shows the lineup of women, me among them.

In the taxi home my nails score my arms until the skin, that color of hard earth, blossoms with spots of blood. Skin that I'll later soothe with cool Gluta, smearing it over my body, salving my hurt, thinking, *This! This is how to efface your history.*

"You don't appreciate your heritage," Mom always says.

"I know where I come from," I always tell her, thinking always of the women outside the club, the women outside massage parlors and by-the-hour hotels. Women on the street edge, scrabbling, making work of the sidewalk, making a home of *farang* men. Women on the edge of their marriage beds, crowded out by a man tossing, stretching, throwing his arm across her face in the night. Women making fathers of such men. Fathers who will later tell their daughters, *Hon, you have to understand I never meant to . . .*

What? Make a life here? Make a child here? Die here?

And so back Dad went to a motherland spread wide enough to embrace him (Welcome home, Rick!), condemning two women in Thailand to the outermost fringe of his life. He maintains us from afar through generous greenbacks, complemented by a generous exchange rate. Enough to keep Mom small-stepping around the kitchen, barely lifting her feet, feeling acutely what she calls a "weighing-down force"—not gravity, exactly, but a quieter pull that makes her flesh bag, her knees swell. It is the force that has pinioned her all this time to a distant man but a very close unhappiness. Still, she manages each year to widen her orbit, to pull away. She climbs the stairs for exercise, has strength in her limbs, calls to me, "Look! I'm moving. Moving on. Look how far I've come."

"MOM?" I FIND her slumped at the foot of my bed, asleep, waiting for me with one of my magazines in her hands. It's still bookmarked with the permanent marker I use to leave the models with masks and mustaches, ink bruises. I might etch a Superman torso for fun, or darken an especially bleached woman. There, that's more like it.

I let Mom sleep, close the magazine and uncap the Magic Marker (Writes on Anything!), sitting down before my mirror.

"You see," I tell the face. "There's this Thai saying. 'Beautiful by way of the knife.'" I put the pen to my chin and cut its tip right up the middle of my face, its felt point a lover's tongue. I take my time looking for the telltale *luk khrueng* features. You know what to look for, don't you? We've all been trained to know, to say, "Such dark brows" (I color in the eyebrow on my right side), or "that high bridge of your nose" (I sketch contour lines against my nose's right side), or "that beautiful, Mascarpone skin" (I crosshatch the left half of my face).

I powder my face and neck with talc. Then my hands and forearms, like I'm wearing white evening gloves.

Mom's still asleep. I move beside her.

"Mom?" I touch her. My hand against her hand, white against
skin.

Handsome Red

TINTIN (2011)

I've tried every idol. I'm not proud of it. I've prayed to the colorful faces at the Hindu temple and the stern ones at the Chinese. I've knelt to monks and bowed before big men. I took a bus south to visit that fat asshole with the prophetic doll. My name is carved in a *nang ta-khian* tree. I've fed strays and released sparrows. I even slaughtered a (small, sickly) pig. I've given my time to the temple, my blood to the hospital, my pay to the state lottery. What else, I ask the fortune-teller. He turns over my charts. "More."

If the monks are right, the bad luck precedes this life. And if the monks are wrong, where's that leave me? But while I'm sharing the blame, let me add to my list: Bright, the smarmy whore behind this big idea; and this big idea himself, Handsome Red, rooster of legends, multimillion-baht fighting cock of Ayutthaya. I'll admit that when I saw that chicken, I saw money, too. A White-Tailed Yellow rooster, the breed of the warrior King Naresuan—how could this *not* be a winner? Handsome Red's breeder had started selling his off-spring. Chicks for eight thousand, ring-ready roosters for twenty—more than a month's wages. That's where Bright came in with his "golden fucking eggs."

He pitched it a few days ago, when I was maybe a little drunk at our usual booth, an abandoned police booth outside a 7-Eleven.

Bright nursed a soy milk (oysters, the shits), and I was telling him about my luck.

"Come on, Tintin—lottery's for fools," Bright said. "Why are you still putting money there?"

"I figure with all the money I give away to gambling, I must be building up some good fortune *somewhere*."

"I'll give it to you. I don't know anyone with your bad luck. Maybe it's time to see a witch doctor—"

"I've *seen* a witch doctor. I've seen three. They're in fucking cahoots. My exorcist is holding back. Even the amulet vendors are cheating me. Old Boonmee sold me a dud. I tried to give him back his amulet and, no, *I* was damaged goods. Thing was sapped."

Bright set his empty bottle down behind the seat. He showed me a piece of paper from his wallet. It had some math and a massive number underlined at the bottom.

Handsome Red, the most expensive rooster in the Thai cockfighting circuit, had just retired. Now, his gene pool was on the market for the first time. We could get in early. Go straight for a fighting-age rooster. Ladder up through underground cockpits, just small stuff in the tens of thousands, and then retire him to breeding status by the time everyone caught on and bought themselves their own Red chicks.

"That's your get-rich idea—start a fucking *farm*?"

He flipped the page over. "A hen's got about ten eggs per batch. One year, five batches. Eight years of breeding life. So we're talking four hundred."

"It's a blood sport. I don't like it. Didn't I tell you I was half raised in a Muay Thai gym?"

"Four hundred chicks," Bright continued, like he hadn't heard me. "Even at a cheap thousand each, that's real money, right? Add to that a dozen hens. Like, I know you're stupid, Tintin, but . . . stupid enough to pass up on golden fucking eggs?"

THE NEXT MORNING, Bright picked me up in front of a mall. An old white guy was driving. I climbed in the back seat.

"Hello my fren how are you nice meet you," I said in English.

"No," Bright said. "Russian."

"Yes," said the Russian.

"Hang on, isn't this the *farang* from your beach trip last month?" The foreigner clearly recognized that word, *farang*.

"Dima?" He pointed at his chest and smiled.

"No." Bright told the Russian. To me, "Yeah. Two weeks ago. Retiree visa."

"*Khap rot*," said the Russian clumsily. *Drive.* He drummed his hands on the steering wheel. The man's rental car was why Bright brought him along. Not because the guy loved cockfighting. In fact, as I learned on the car ride, he didn't think the sport was right. He was vegan and just tagging along to convince Bright of its cruelty.

"This mean you're taking long-term customers now?"

Bright turned around in the passenger seat. "Nah. It's my fault. He's sticking around for a good fuck, but I can't get it up."

In the rearview, the Russian's eyes moved between us as if he could follow the conversation. He had one of those ruddy, splotchy faces, like meat marinating in a bag.

"I try to be a professional about it. Watching porn, abstaining and so on. But I think there's damage from last time I hired myself out to a woman. Before we'd even gotten into her bed, she was reaching down my pants to fuck knows where. I was sure she'd come up with my entrails."

"Never a dull night with Bright. Isn't that your tagline?"

I KNEW WE'D reached Ayutthaya by the dust. Nowhere else does the sun bake the earth this dry. It has always looked to me like the end of the world. The rental bumped along until Bright spotted the sign. Hard to believe this shitty farm—low, brown, and bare—had millions in its chickens. We parked and piled out into the welcome building. What I first took to be a shrine to chickens was actually the Handsome Red gift shop. Flags, key chains, stickers, t-shirts.

"The David Beckham of roosters," I said.

The cashier offered us a photo against the farm backdrop, which showed rolling hills and fresh furrows—nothing like the dirt and gravel of the real thing. The breeder was there in a cardboard cutout. Bright put his hand on the cutout's shoulder.

"We're looking for this man."

The breeder, when he came to see us, wore an oversized pink Lacoste polo and sunglasses, exactly what he was wearing in the cardboard copy. He took us on a tour of the facility. Everything he said was "good." Everything was an "opportunity." Opportunity for farmers, for factory workers—hell, for the fucking roosters, too, he'd have us believe.

Did we know anything about raising chickens?

"Tintin grew up in the city." Bright pointed at us in turn. "Me, I hate animals. And the Russian here's vegan."

"Good, good." The breeder nodded. He said he took care of everything. Quality feed, training routine, vitamins, ring experience. He made it sound foolproof. And it all looked the part, the young cocks jumping buckets, doing laps. He popped open a jar of the Handsome Red–branded supplements. Smell? I tried not to. It was like pickled cabbage or yogurt. The breeder listed off the nutritional qualities.

I felt like I was getting a close look at my own upbringing as an overfed sportsman. Growing up, the only sure way to eat well was to become a fighter. At seven I was left by my nothing parents at a boarding Muay Thai gym run by Insee Dam, the famous Black Eagle. The man had boxed at Lumpinee *and* Rajadamnern, but his pro career never took him far enough to earn him the right sponsorships—the kind that set you up for life. In retirement, he'd gone sweet and soft, and started a boarding gym. For almost five years I'd grown up around hard boys with steel calves always engaged in some impossible task: dragging tires, double-skipping rope. Boys who were what the Red Bull ads were selling. Boys who fought, always barefoot, the odds of making it big.

"Not a single rooster leaves through those doors if it doesn't have a fighting spec," the breeder was saying. "All these roosters are Handsome Red offspring, see. This one's sixteen months, 2.9 kilos. Tight, strong beak. Wide nose. Legs tough as cane stalks. Feet shiny as young bamboo. Have a look, huh, have a look!"

"I don't know anything about roosters," I said.

"Put 'em in a ring with those scrawny *gai ban* the bus drivers are fighting with, and he'll clean house. You have my guarantee."

"Or *what*," I said idly.

"Or I'll be eating chicken nuggets."

Nobody laughed. Bright folded his arms. "Show us how he fights."

The breeder shrugged and put the bird into a ring with another rooster.

"The thing about roosters," he said, nudging the two birds into a confrontation, "is they're true. They're honest competitors. You can't call up a bird to tell them to take a dive." He backed up against the padded wall of the ring as the birds launched into a fight. "So what you see is what you get. No deceptions."

The birds had tape covering their spurs, but even with the breeder counting hits it was hard to tell who was winning. Our boy favored high attacks, bowing his head low and then launching into a flying double-kick. Even against the wire-fu standards of the Chinese epics we'd grown up watching, it was impressive.

The Russian mumbled something, shaking his head.

"What's wrong with him?" the breeder said.

"He thinks it's cruel," Bright said.

"Look, see how we wrap the spurs?" the breeder tried to say to the Russian, who couldn't understand a word of it. The breeder tried again, louder. "Our fighters are our *money*! We don't let them *die*."

"Yeah, yeah. I've explained it," Bright said.

"Looks like we're going to need a name for our prize rooster," I said.

"We need a name," Bright told the Russian, who looked dumbly at him. Bright switched to English. "Name!"

The man hesitated. He pointed at his chest. "Dima."

THE ROAD OUT was an ambush of tourist stops. The Russian pulled into a crowded parking lot.

"Hey, what you do?" I said in English.

He parked, rolled down his window, and left the keys in the ignition as he walked into the restaurant. Beside me, the rooster stood up in his cardboard box, which we had belted in, not that this stopped it from swaying the whole time the car was moving. He was watching me through the holes cut in the cardboard.

"Won't he overheat?" I asked.

"Bring it in then."

"Where *are* we?" I looked around. "Like Tarzan's fuckin' hideout."

"If Tarzan was a rich son of a bitch."

The bayan vines were nicely draped around the entrance to what looked like a greenhouse. Inside, it was unnaturally lush. I stopped beside the picture wall, six-by-six of flowers, real flowers, the kind of display my sorry ass had seen only on a job building stages for weddings. I let the sound of gently burbling water lead me to its source, a speaker set in the gift shop. Beside me was a pyramid of melons in individual boxes, nine hundred baht each. I could work a whole day and not afford a melon here.

"Hey, Bright!" I shouted. "Fuck chickens. We should get into the melon business. Are they serious about these prices or did the Russian bring us to some kind of money laundering syndicate?"

"It's an organic farm," the cashier said, coming around the counter in a baby-blue apron. "And I'm afraid you can't bring the animals in here. Put that back in the petting area."

He ushered me out a set of double doors into a canopied garden with low white fences, ferns, flowers, the whole first-world works. A bunny crossed the path in front of us. The cashier took me to a corner of stacked cages with animals inside. I saw a number of roosters and goats, but mostly the creatures here were small and furry.

"Chicken daycare?" I said, but the man just walked away.

I lifted the box to eye level. "All right, don't get up to any trouble now, little Red."

The food was a two-line buffet, Thai on the left, Western on the right. I stood behind the Russian.

"Hey." I nudged him and pointed at the chicken nuggets. "Same same, but different, right?"

He shook his head. "No. *Jay.*"

Bright made a disgusted sound. "He's right. Vegan nuggets. The whole fucking place."

I'd gone vegetarian before, sure, but not out of choice. The green curry was disappointingly bland, more like warm coconut broth. I looked around the hall. That was the problem with the *farangs;* they sapped away everything that was pungent—oil, chili, greasy meat—and left behind kid food, the kind that wouldn't make anybody sweat. What was the point? I tried to communicate this to the Russian, but he was tucking into his orange potatoes, seemingly delighted. To make it worse, they only served that awful red prison rice.

"Bright, *you* know the good life. So explain this to me. When you get rich, you don't eat milled rice anymore?"

"Healthy," said the Russian, who was done eating. He went to peruse the shop, walk the grounds. I sat inside with Bright, thinking about wasted time. The Russian didn't give a shit. He sauntered back in a half hour later with a smug smile, all ease and comfort. I guess that's what money does.

It didn't even end there. The man wanted to detour to Kanchanaburi. He wanted waterfalls and an elephant ride. Me, I wanted to get Little Handsome Red in the ring already.

"Is that what we're calling it?" Bright said.

"Kanchanaburi!" said the Russian.

"Money!" I said loudly.

The Russian counted some bills out of his wallet.

"No, not like that." I looked at Bright for help.

"It's bus fare," Bright said. "I guess you're on your own."

"You're leaving me with the chicken?"

"Hey man, the bird's got a name now. Use it." Bright leaned against the Russian, murmured in his ear, rubbed the man's back like a coach comforting his prize athlete. "I'm on the clock for this. And what do you know, Kanchanaburi's a good two-hour drive away."

BLOOD SPORT. I don't like it, but if everyone else can make a living, why not me? Haven't I put in my time? I did four, five years at the Black Eagle Muay Thai Gym. Hundreds of dawn runs around the reservoir, which was once a shrimp farm but now bred only mosquitoes. Coach cycled ahead of us on his daughter's bicycle, pink tassels trailing from the handles, breakfast from the market in the front basket, leading us with its smell. On days when Coach was feeling like his young self again, he'd take us home the long way, circling around the dump and then the neighborhood, ringing the handlebar bell to herald his parade of hopefuls. All his boys had been re-nicknamed, mostly obvious stuff like Rodtang or Chalam Daeng—Tank, Red Shark. None of the humor of pro-boxer names, with their Earth-Walking-Somtam-Eating Angel and Five-Star Grilled Chicken, among the other champs of Lumpinee Stadium.

Maybe that was it. Coach took it too seriously. His earnest, embarrassing kneeling to bring himself down to our height. His darting focus mitts crossed blue with duct tape because he couldn't afford new equipment. Nightly before dinner he repeated his hope: "I'll feed you boys, and you boys will feed me." Not a bad idea. He kept me around until I was eleven and still showed no promise, only size. Right up to the end he slipped me chicken scraps out of sight of the others. "You know, Tintin, you're bigger than them. You've got all the flavors. Spicy, salty, sweet, sour, savory." He listed them off on his fingers. "But you're *still* missing something. I don't get it."

Among other mistakes, I favored a back-elbow blow, pivoting a full circle on my left foot to land the right elbow. It was a strike I'd learned watching Japanese boxers on TV. Coach called it a graceful, dumbass move—all-or-nothing—because it requires turning your back to the opponent. Why not just kick him instead? I was good in front of the big mirror, but a useless sparring partner. Sundays, Coach would truck us somewhere with rice paddies and it'd be five rounds against kids who made good on their own fierce-hewn nicknames (Steel Heels, Never Give Up). Small and sure-footed, the little rats seemed to take energy from my kicks. They smacked their gloves together and bounced right back in, draining me with every one of my own punches, until I could feel the weight of my gloves, my hands dropping lower and lower. Then, I'd be on my ass, Coach softly dabbing my brow, saying, "Next time, Tintin." Afterwards, he always bought me a meaty dinner anyway.

So I know about blood sport. And one thing I know is you don't go unaided into your first fight. I wanted the best blessing for Little Handsome Red. That's why, on the way to the ring, I stopped at a shrine to King Naresuan, the patron of fighting roosters everywhere. Others had beaten me to him, of course, his shrine lined with rooster figurines, each one a plea heard, a wish fulfilled. "Keep him standing, please. Turn my luck around."

When I got to the ring, I saw I might've been looking for patronage in the wrong place. On all the posters and every wall was the logo of that corporation we all know. Imagine, this wasn't even a sanctioned stadium, only a halfway arena built under an overpass. I should've offered up something to that logo instead. Among other empires under its control, see, is the empire of chicken everything. From chicken feed to chicken farm, they're the big boy in it all. Which is why there are two portraits on the wall behind the ring: Rama IX and (lower) the illustrious Khun D., coal-black hair, sad eyes, sad suit. That man's the reason any of this is legal. Don't trust what they're selling the tourists, that stuff about humane, smiling Thais cradling fighting cocks like firstborns. Okay, so we don't strap razors to cock spurs like our Filipino and Balinese friends, but that's only because Khun D. said no. A sport's got to be clean to be mainstream, right? And while all us groundlings are gambling through cycles of success and debt, wins and losses, there's one house bigger than the betting house that's winning every night. When they say winner takes all, they aren't talking about us.

That didn't keep me from talking up my fighter, though. I egged their bets higher. There was some "staking my life savings on this chicken," and some "you sure that little feather duster's going to survive a round against my guy?" Mostly bus and taxi drivers with a couple food vendors mixed in.

"What's the chicken's name?" I was asked.

"Little Handsome Red." And yes, I meant for my competitors to quake. "Trained by Handsome Red's breeder himself." Not everyone believed me. To back up my claim, I laid down the cost of the rooster in full, twenty thousand, on this first bout. The opponent was some Burmese breed, black tail, mean look. It was meant to be. This was basically our country's founding lore, after all, King Naresuan's victories against the Burmese in old Siam.

The other trainers all had their chickens under their arms, but Red and I didn't yet have that familiarity. I found a stool and set his box beside me. How to gauge his eagerness? He was very still, peering at me with his right eye. I didn't like that look, so I spun the box around. Red turned so his right side faced me again. The dark pupil expanded, appeared to consume the orange iris. I sent Bright a text: *Little is going in.*

I'd seen cockfights before. Seen the darts and feints, the jump attacks and flapping retreats, the roosters with heads low, waiting for the other to initiate. I knew that even with their spurs covered it could get bloody. I'd seen beaks come off. Eyes scratched out. More than anything, it was the sheer exhaustion of the combat, a marathon of eight twenty-minute rounds that gradually ground the birds down,

no matter how fierce or at first triumphant. I knew the Burmese laborers had their tricks, taking mouthfuls of ice water and blowing the
mist over their fighters between bouts. I'd even heard of men who
sucked the blood from their fighter's wounds. And, listen, nothing
prepared me for Red.

Traffic thundered on the bridge overhead. Warm engines hummed
all around. Men cheered and clapped as Red squared up across from
his opponent. And then, just as the umpire called the first round in,
Red fled the ring.

THE BEST WAY to throw a match is to throw yourself into it. I only
fixed a fight once. Coach had told me he was cutting me. He'd done
the decent thing and given me notice, time to put together my next
steps—hilarious, to an eleven-year-old. *What* steps? There was an orphanage waiting for me. "See, Tintin, the thing is it's become hard to
justify keeping you. You're like two meals for every one," Coach said.
"And sorry, kid, but it's either you or two seven-year-olds who still
might make it big for me. For all these boys. It's the gym I'm thinking
of."

Sure, sure. But a little walking money could go a pretty long way.
I used the pay phone at the bus stop to talk to the bookies, see. I was
within watching distance of the gym, the low roof, the bags swinging
lightly on their old chains, as the bookie explained to me not only the
outcome (a dive in the third round), but some spot fixing, too. Sunday came and down I went. Not without a fight. In many ways it was
my best match. I was all elbows, pivoting carelessly, showing the opponent my back, like I had nothing at all to lose. As I laid on the
canvas waiting for the umpire to count me out, I cracked an eye and
looked at Coach. He nodded at me. He knew, I was sure of it. And
still the man let me walk the next morning: "Be good, Tintin." The
bookie paid me. He said it was the worst fucking dive in the history
of worst dives, but Coach hadn't said anything. That walking money
was mine.

———

IT'S NOT ENOUGH to add Red's failure to my catalog of bad luck. The bookies think I fixed the match. But even as a game-fixing cock, he's not exactly convincing. Red was *too* bad. They can't prove anything but incompetence. They can't prove that I know anyone on the counter-betting side. There just isn't any other explanation for the big talk, putting up twenty on a chicken that's never seen a fight. Who does that?

Bright isn't answering his phone, so I call the breeder and open with: "What the fuck." I explain the game-fixing thing to him. "He was *that* bad, okay?"

"You put him in a ring against a Burmese? I told you not to do that."

"The fuck you did! And it's not like he lost. He just cowered against the wall, flapping, like he's never seen a box jump or another rooster, let alone these kung fu Burmese breeds. It was embarrassing, all right? And with *Little Handsome Red* up on the scoreboard like that? I'm telling you the audience will never forget it."

"You called it *what*!"

"Legacy. Isn't that what cockfighting is all about? Little Handsome Red is on the books as we speak. It's your name on the line."

"Listen." The man's voice drops. "I'll buy it back."

I tell him that's all great, but the bird cost twenty and now, with the bad bet, I'm down *forty* and my only fighting chance of ever winning that kind of money is a peace-loving rooster.

"Okay, *forty*. But tell the people it was a mistake. Forget the name Handsome Red. This cock's got nothing to do with him, okay? You go back in there and tell them you made it up. It was all a joke. You've never even seen my farm, got it? I'll give you back the forty."

And just like that, like the first storm of May, the season of my luck actually turns.

"Deal. What about the bird?"

"Get rid of it."

"I'm not killing anything."

"Then bring it up here and *I* will kill it. I'm not having anyone else bad-mouth my farm because of this one bad egg. *Do not* sell him on."

Back to the bus station. Nothing from Bright, so the fare's on me, and I'm tempted to keep the extra twenty, too, if that asshole continues to recuse himself from the work. Bright's always selling ideas. Mostly, the idea of Bright. That works for him because of his pretty face, but the rest of us have to get by with just our hands.

I get my ticket and walk to the market for a meal while I wait. I order (chicken) *krapao*. The *yai* who makes it is square and tough, the kind that might butcher her own fowl. I offer to pay her to do the dirty work, save me the trip north.

"What's this look like, a slaughterhouse?" She, too, buys her meat from that corporation. "I don't kill. Do it yourself." Her cleaver is spun around to me, hilt first, the blade crossed with lines from years of sharpening.

"Can I?"

Like I've got the balls. I pick up the knife, lay the chicken flat on the cutting block, but he stands up instead. I've noticed that he takes to whatever spot I put him down on, this chicken, like the world's his fuckin' plinth. Even I can admire that. His upright comb, his lustrous feathers. Suddenly it feels wrong to take such a regal head off so shortly after having delivered said head into the protection of Naresuan, imploring the stern-eyed statue to never let the bird go down. The last thing I need is another pissed-off deity on my case.

Back to the plastic waiting seats then. I've lost the box somewhere in the day's fray and now I'm just another bird-loving breeder in a bus station, chicken tucked into my armpit, looking like I'm freshly arrived from the fields, like I'm in the big city for *opportunity*. For work in construction, demolition, or hauling. What the man of my imagination hasn't been told yet is there *isn't* any. With Bright's face? Okay. But hands only get you so far. That's why me and every fool in this city are carrying around chickens, amulets, blessed dolls, or lottery tickets. Everyone's looking for opportunity. And along comes a breeder selling golden fucking eggs at some end-of-the-world farm.

"THAT'S NOT ONE of my chickens," the breeder tells me after I've added the bus ticket and a taxi fare to my losses.

"What do you mean, this isn't him?"

"I mean that's not my fucking chicken. Look at it. Does this look like a White-Tailed Yellow?"

And now that he says it, no. The names can be blandly obvious like that.

"This is some pretty bird." He turns the rooster to show me. His voice is smug but also admiring. "Somebody bred these stripes into it. A show bird. They sell these at that expensive house on the corner. You know, the one with all the glass?"

I'm getting Bright on the phone this time. I call relentlessly until: "What?"

"Did you know?"

Bright's a good salesman but not a liar. All right, so the Russian *just* told him. It wasn't malicious, or even premeditated (how, I want to know, does Bright know that Russian word). He just wanted to save the bird, so he switched it with another. A joke, really. He was teaching us a lesson.

"That's forty thousand learned," I say. "Please thank the Russian. Right now, I'm standing at the front of the farm with no taxi in sight and still this chicken, which I'm considering eating. Please tell the Russian I'm a man with nothing else to lose. Who knows what I'll do. Say, are you guys nearby?"

There's muffling, then Bright's voice is closer to the receiver. "Yeah, yeah. I talked to him about that. Listen, to show his good faith in repairing things, and that it was all a big joke, Dima's willing to pay us back."

"Who's Dima?"

"The Russian. He's got one condition."

"I'm not taking any conditions from him."

"Don't kill the chicken."

I set the rooster down. He doesn't have the instinct to run or fight. He just stares up at me. "What am I going to do with a pretty bird? Start a farm?"

"That's the condition. Don't kill the chicken and he'll pay us back the money."

"The whole forty?"

"Fifty," he says.

"Fifty?"

"I told him we bought the bird for fifty."

"You didn't? Ha ha. Bright. Fucking golden eggs, you asshole."

MAYBE THERE'S STILL a couple thousand's worth of luck out there for me. There's always just enough money trickling your way to keep you in. The pro-boxing circuit was, I think, designed by the same people who made the state lottery. Oh, sure, we got the token, side prize money, the tips from drunk aunties, the travel reimbursements. But like the lottery, big success was always what happened next door. It happened to that kid the next gym over. I remember the boy's stardom, sudden and huge, like those spotlights that snapped onto a winner when the judges finally announced their name.

Coach closed the gym eventually. I was back in that neighborhood one day when I spotted his old pickup passing by, the sun bleaching the banners for the Black Eagle Muay Thai Gym back to nothing. From a loudspeaker on the roof, I heard Coach's voice.

I held back. But that day, someone looking over me must have been giving out second chances because the truck circled back around. This time I approached as it rolled past me, enough to catch his voice, like he was calling back from his daughter's bike, listing, as he used to, all the food in the basket that awaited us at the end of the run.

But that wasn't it. I could hear the whole loop of the recording now:

"Construction, demolition, hauling. Hard worker. Good references. Brother-in-law of Khosit Detduang, owner of Det Pochana restaurant. Former coach of the Black Eagle Muay Thai Gym. A one-time featherweight champion, who boxed at Lumpinee and Rajadamnern. Looking for opportunities."

Welcome Me to the Kingdom

LARA & BENZ (2013)

One man, an Argentinian (but of proud European pedigree), had called her Carmen. She had a gypsy's skin, he explained. "Will you leave me, *mi gitanita*? Will you take my money when the wind turns, like your storybook kin?" He hummed the *Habanera* for her. "You know *Carmen*, the opera?" She just nodded, flushed at the time with a fever. They were naked—"What did I tell you, take off your clothes and we will beat your fever together"—his body clasping hers, his teeth like castanets nipping the curl of her ear.

"Love," he sang, and raked his fingers between her legs. "Love is a freed bird."

She said she was cold and slipped back into her jeans, and when he got up for the toilet she unraveled his last joint and carved the right words into the paper with a ballpoint: *Love is a rebellious bird.*

She waited for the weather to change before she ran away, taking the money from his wallet as if to make real the myth. She gambled up the long coast of Argentina, where she was traveling at the time. She understood enough of the card game *Truco* from a previous trip through Andalusia to pick up the basics of the local game. In the Southern Cone they played with a code to communicate strategy with one's partner. It was a language of facial movements and head nods. It kept attention from her accent, but when players finally inquired about the Castilian lisp she had picked up imitating her Language Lovers CDs, she lied about her birthplace.

"Shangri-la," she told the gamblers. "Where is it?" they asked. "East. The Far East." Or "Shambala," she said sometimes. "The Kingdom of Siam." Eventually they would catch on: "Ha! Where else, *muñeca*? Atlantis also?"

Anywhere but Thailand. And she never gave her name. So they made their own names for her. *Chinita,* some called her. Or *Canela en Rama*—Cinnamon Stick, a play on her physique, her skin color, and (or so the rumors went) her spice in bed. *Yanqui,* they called her; in Argentina and Uruguay, *Shanqui.*

"*Shanqui,* looking for someone to be your *papí*?" the men would ask, leaning across wood-board tables. "Need a stake to start you off?"

"Sure," she told them, and beat them at their games, with their money. She blazed through the alleys and scrub of Argentina before crossing into Uruguay, where her *Truco* romp was finally brought up short by a misinterpretation. In Uruguay, apparently, the card game's signals were different. "I couldn't read your face," her partner told her, looking at her body. "Where are you from, anyway?"

IT TOOK A typhoon to bring her back to Thailand: storm clouds roiling like breaking waves tall enough to mire planes in their surf, then toss them up against the brown debris that is Bangkok viewed from the air.

She'd been en route to Macau, but her jet grounded in her home city. So she decided to make a side tour of Bangkok, but in only a week she's lost too much and has stranded herself. She's staying in a guesthouse and hasn't called her mother, who would surely take this opportunity to peg her down to her home turf. Two years she's been gone from this country.

On her bunk she counts cash out of an envelope and sees there still isn't enough for a flight. She has a motorbike taxi take her to another old haunt, a noodle shop, famous for the durability of its fishballs, shaped from cuttlefish with the consistency of tires. Perfect betting chips. The fishballs are a relic from a time when players needed to disguise the gambling. Once caught, the players would have had to bribe the police. In this way, dens like this one used to be a part of the police payroll. Now the corruption is simpler: The police own the dens.

The noodle vendor's boy doesn't recognize her, searches his apron pocket as if wondering how exactly to navigate this transaction with his limited English.

It's the American clothes on local skin, maybe, that muddles him. Skin a middle brown, the color that as a child she had imagined to be the base tone of the earliest people, before the human race had fractured across the world. Not the ivory of the Thai-Chinese and not the rainwater brown of country Thais. It's a color that Bop, her last lover before she fled Thailand, had tried to describe, exhausting himself on the standard comparisons (chocolate, coffee, sandalwood), kissing in a line down from her navel, imbuing each impression with its own pat description.

"Right here is the color of the monsoon season," he said.

"No," she told him.

He tried again, moving downward.

"Here. The mood of an antiques store."

Down again.

"Here. The bruise on a mango."

She had treated it all as child's play, Bop's earnestness and the way she used to sneak into his house on weekends. Once, coming through the maid's kitchen entrance, she had tripped over an old trike wheel and sent a set of pots clattering across the tile.

Bop's mother came in and flicked on the lights. He told her he was looking for books in the old storage room.

"You can come out now," he said.

"Good thing I'm so spritely, right?" She emerged from behind the door, where she had been crouching atop a dusty mattress, willing the springs beneath the fabric not to creak. "How come you've never had to hide in my house's closet?"

"You know my mother likes to check in on me. She'd catch me if I tried to sneak out."

"Right, so you let your ladies do the work. Who wears the pants, anyway?" She punched Bop in the gut. "Hey? You're the Juliet to my Romeo," she mocked.

"I know a handful of girls dying to take your place."

"Yeah? How many of them can scale that wall outside?"

Bop patted the dust from her front.

She smiled. "You just want to touch me."

"Yes."

"So," she said coyly. "Tell me about these girls."

"What girls?"

"The ones looking to die." She brought her lips to Bop's neck, to the sharp Adam's apple she found so attractive, a fruit pit about to grow through the terrain of his neck. And then she nipped him there, catching enough of the skin that Bop flinched.

She had never understood the warning beneath Bop's jokes—a handful of girls dying to take your place—any more than she had his openness. It embarrassed her, the way he could turn to her over a bowl of noodles and tell her that he loved her. "Love is an extra fishball in your bowl," she had responded.

And how many does she have now?

"Six," she says, setting her bowl down at one of the tables at the back of the noodle room. She puts a steaming fishball in the middle bowl.

"Three thousand to play in this group," the table's dealer says. "Cheaper by the entrance." He snaps the cards against the table. "Individual hands."

"Somebody want to advance me some money?"

She likes to play on a loan from another player, even when she doesn't have to. It's okay. She's good for it. She's got the pluck to hit when the count's already high, or to chime in when the bets are raised enough that others reach into their back pockets to make sure their rent money's still there. She wins big.

Every now and then, when she asks for an advance, a man (it is always a man) will ask what she has to give as collateral. Then she will stare at him until his eyes turn to her figure, to the clothing that tells just enough of what might be taken as collateral, what might be held and petted and pushed into. Another player will chuckle, saying, "You'll be backing her hoping she'll lose." It keeps her tame. Even the best players lose.

By rule the dealer himself can't advance a player any money. Of the remaining three, one is a grandfather dropped here by his working sons and daughters, who treat these dens like daycare for the aged, folding enough money into his pocket for him to enjoy the promise of the evening. Although his presence at the table at this hour means he's not only an old man but an old gambler, or that his children have again forgotten him. He pulls out one of the metal folding chairs.

"Sit. Please."

The young man beside her watches from under the rim of his baseball cap, a mawkish homage to American gambling culture. It marks him as a member of a later wave of Bangkok's players.

And then there's a married man across from her, the type she survives on. They come to the table angry at wives, work, children. Mid-forties with a penchant for doing damage, and they will often stake her on that principle, something to be sacked and burned and left by the wayside.

She takes him on directly. "Want to be my betting daddy for the night?" she says with upturned cheek, working the schoolgirl charm.

He considers her openly. A longing look she used to crave, back when she thought it might be her father she'd find at one of these tables. Her father putting down money on her.

"We could *both* win big," she teases.

"I'll back you," he says.

"Let's get on then." The dealer beckons with his chopsticks and drops a fishball into the middle bowl.

"You been playing long?" the young man with the cap asks her.

"Sure, all my life."

"Not long then, yes?" the dealer says. "Ha ha! You're probably Benz's age." He thumps the table in front of the capped man as he moves his hands around. "This one's twenty-plus-plus, yes? His is an ass on a face if ever I saw one, but watch him gamble. Bled me last week."

He takes up his chopsticks and snaps them at Benz. "Yes? I ate rice porridge for days straight to make that up. Almost lost a kilo. Let's order some food over here." He waves the chopsticks at the noodle boy. "Pork, yes?"

Across the room decks are being smacked, stacked, cut. The soup at the noodle cart is boiling over, steaming the room with the aroma of a rich pork broth. There are few women, all of them older.

"I'm Sombhat," the old man says with a nod. "Where did you learn to play? Did you have a gambling father?"

"I don't have a father. Mother taught me everything."

"Did she? I'd like to meet this mother."

"You're missing the round," the dealer says.

Young Benz peels his cards off the table to look at them. "Don't worry," he says to her. "We'll keep you out of Narin's hands. He might look mean, but . . . we're all friends here."

She looks at Narin, the family man, who's watching his own hand.

"Well." Benz turns to her again. "Where did you say you learned to play?"

IT WAS MRS. Anwar who taught her. They would advance on gambling dens masquerading as a mother-daughter team. But Mrs. Anwar never had children. She was already a widow by the time they met. Two Thai women adrift in the United States, one a senior, the other recently dropped out of a graduate program she could no longer afford to work the register at a grocery store.

Mrs. Anwar was nearing seventy. "Too old to learn how to drive," was how she put it when asked whether she needed help carrying the groceries to a car.

"Where are you from?"

This question was Mrs. Anwar's way of orienting a new person on her spectrum of types, which in Mrs. Anwar's mind took the form of a comprehensively thumbtacked world map. She remembered people by place of origin, a practice only her late husband, Mr. Anwar, was spared, and mostly because they were from the same town in central Thailand. Her husband had been her childhood neighbor, their houses separated by a low cinder-block wall over which the eight-year-old Mrs. Anwar had first glimpsed him as a tuft of black hair. His hair never fully greyed, so Mrs. Anwar's relationship with her husband was bookended by twin images of that black mass: at the beginning above the wall, and the last time through the viewing window of the crematory that reduced him to household dust.

Mrs. Anwar: "Where are you from?"

Bangkok.

Mrs. Anwar didn't take it. "Yes, but I know too many people who are Bangkok to me. And look at you, where did you get a color like that? You like to tan or your mother was from a southern province. What, Trang? Farther down. Yala? Tell me."

"Bangkok."

"And your father?"

"I don't really know anymore."

Mrs. Anwar snorted. "What road in Bangkok?"

"Pattanakarn."

"Pattana. A fitting name."

"My name's Lara."

"And Lara speaks Thai—good. Can you drive?"

"I already have work."

"Yes, very lucrative I can see," Mrs. Anwar said. "Grocery-store clerk. I have a car at home but no husband to drive me. And my life is all travel."

"What do you do?"

"I gamble."

The better question was: Where?

She wasn't a local anywhere. The places had to be new.

"Where are we going next?"

Mrs. Anwar's answer, always: "The kingdom!"

It was her little joke. She had been told once that gambling was a man's kingdom. She had beaten the man and claimed his words. "Welcome me to the kingdom of America. A-me-ri-ca," she said, teasing out the syllables. "What a place. Here in America even the poor have flat-screen televisions. Here in America," she said from the passenger seat, observing the light dappling her arms, "the sun doesn't burn my skin."

"No husbands here, either," she continued. "Not anymore."

She called herself a free bird. She had been loosed. And what did that mean? It meant the coast of New England to begin with, the real New England, far up where winter was like a footrace. On the radio: "He beat the snowstorm home" or "It was an old couple. Their wood-stove just couldn't keep up with the cold."

"You ever driven in snow, Lara?"

"No."

"Well, you learn. I need rest. I hear the Filipinos in Maine are playing a new variant of *pusoy*."

She insisted on playing games she didn't know. She was a quick learner.

"In another life I could have been a surgeon," she said once, tapping the brainy place between her eyes. She held out her arm. "Look at this. You don't see it? No? The hand doesn't shake, right? Steady as stones."

It wasn't true. Mrs. Anwar's hands jittered. When she dropped a mug, or her fan of cards, once even her bucket of quarters at a small-time slots casino, she blamed the quality of the objects. "Who makes a mug handle that wouldn't fit even a baby's hand? Made in China," she'd scoff, sitting among Chinese men in a big-two den that fronted as a hot-pot parlor.

She favored the locales tucked away in immigrant enclaves.

"Lara! Take me where the Americans are not American."

Mrs. Anwar found her home among others who didn't belong. But they never settled. On the road, Mrs. Anwar refused the radio, so there was only the *clop-clop* of the tires to accompany them between towns as they drove west across the country: California, the destination.

"It's all about location. California is easier, see. More Asians, closer to home. Our home," Mrs. Anwar said, thumping her breast. "You and me, Lara, and the long dream of the American highway."

"Congratulations." The dealer pushes the last bowl of fishballs across the table at her. She's cleaned him out, effectively ending the game unless anyone else wants to take on his role. "Wait, before you go, let's drink to your success.

"Hey, kid. Bring that wine you're cooking in the back." He turns to the table. "The older brother's been distilling rice wine in the back-kitchen. I can smell it when I take my garbage out to the alley. As a neighbor I think I'm entitled to some."

The vendor's boy brings a clear glass bottle and a cup.

"And for my friends here, too," the dealer says. "What are you thinking? How else will we celebrate? Our girl here has bigger balls than Narin, but how does she drink, hey?"

"Nobody's forcing you." Benz takes off his hat and runs his thumb along the brim.

"I know how to drink," she says.

"Mother teach you that, too?" the dealer asks.

"She didn't need to."

Benz shakes his head. "Don't let them ruin you."

"Ruin her?" the dealer says. "You think she got this way being flighty and soft as a dove? I think she's got her own secrets, her own back-kitchen slop."

She raises her cup in salute.

"*I* have an idea," the dealer says, absently bringing a hand to his chest and cupping a heavy breast through his shirt. "Come back tomorrow and we'll play for double. Maybe not you, Sombhat. He's pushing seventy, and needs to rest."

"That's seventy-*two*."

Lara takes a long draw from her cup, emptying it.

"Well?" the dealer asks.

"You don't have to," Benz says.

"Quiet," Narin says. "She'll play." He levels the ends of his chopsticks on the table and takes a piece of fried pork from the communal food. A point of oil blooms on the plastic tabletop. "That's what you're here for, isn't it, girl?"

TWO SUMMERS AGO, she still had the last year of her graduate degree at an American conservatory ahead of her. Then she would return to Bop. Two years stateside then back to Thailand—that was always the plan—until he told her he wouldn't be there for her.

"I don't understand," she said, already booking a flight to Bangkok in her panic. "Are you there?" she asked the silent line. Her wet breath swelled through the shell of the phone handle. *I'm listening to the sea,* she thought. "Where have you gone?"

"I'm here," he said.

"But soon you won't be?"

"I'll be here," he said.

She tried to understand. "Just . . . not waiting for me?"

"Who's there with you if not me?" she said, when he didn't respond.

She returned anyway to win Bop back from that somebody's-daughter, the sort of Thai girl raised under the parasol of her family name. Pale features. Not chocolate, not sandalwood. Not a shade of skin that needed description in a city where everyone recognized privilege.

She waited for him outside his gate. She pushed the bell again, looked up into Bangkok's night: a grey haze, the color of streetlights on smog. Their nights together—she wanted that back. She wanted the two A.M. taxi rides, shooting down streets sunken into the swamp the city was built on. For a moment, as the car came down a bridge ramp, they were suspended off the seats. Her head hopped from where she had laid it on Bop's lap and she was lifted out of the nod of dreams—dreams that left her eyes compressed and heavy, her cheek warm from the patch of sweat she had made on his thigh. "You always sleep so willfully," he had said then. "Like you're trying to achieve something."

Bop came out finally, closing the gate behind him.

"I can't believe you came back," he said. "Where did you get the money to fly?"

"I took it out of my student loan."

"You're so reckless."

"I thought you liked that," she said. "I thought you liked a girl who could climb walls."

"Why did you come here, Lara?"

"You used to want me around all the time, remember?"

"We were kids playing around."

"Who was playing?" she said. "I wanted forever. Who the hell was playing?"

"You know what's wrong with your world?" Behind Bop the driveway lights flipped on-off. "You live in a foreigner's world, you know? It's like you think you can come and go and it's all the same. You're always going somewhere."

"Stop. You know why I went."

"To find the asshole father that left you? To find out if he even is your father?"

"Fuck you." She couldn't allow him to be right. "To get an American degree."

The garage light went on and off, like someone inside was drumming her impatient fingers on the switch.

"Go back to your American degree."

With that, Bop went inside to that other girl and his family. Lara flew back to her university town, skipped all her classes, practiced at coiling sheets and noosing her limbs to watch how white her flesh could turn.

That's when she met Mrs. Anwar. That's when she learned to play the tables.

ONLY TWO YEARS running has brought her full circle, right back to him. She walked here from the noodle shop, cutting across the city using the canal walkways she memorized in her listless, meandering teenagehood.

Same gate. And, inside, same people. Same happiness. She's come to survey, maybe to take back territory. She starts with the balcony, crawling up over the latticework bannister and into the space among the potted cooking herbs his mother loves so much. Twists one of his mother's shrubs into a laurel, crowns herself, and squats there, masked by the leaves, hidden.

They had established early that she wasn't someone to be seen. "She's dark," Bop's mother had said of her the one time he had invited her over for dinner. "She speaks Thai like a peasant."

It was a casual observation, nothing damning, but Bop's mother hadn't realized that Lara was standing just behind the milky glass door that closed off the kitchen, having lost her way looking for the bathroom, eventually using the maid's one behind the pantry.

"*Who* did you say her people are?"

"I didn't," Bop said. "Father's American. He left them back in the financial collapse. Her mother's from the country."

Like all the other Thais that ran in Bop's circle, his family was Thai-Chinese, although it had already become redundant to say "Thai-Chinese." It was like describing them as new wealth: unnecessary because, as far as any of the children were concerned, they had always been wealthy. Like all the others who had outgrown the language of their parents' generation, Bop had been nursed on the easy power of privilege, giving him a bearing that couldn't be imitated.

She backed away from the glass door that day, and slipped out of the kitchen through the maid's entrance, following the rock garden toward the front door, where she could step back into the house unnoticed. The stones were uneven on her new heels—an attempt to dress up for Bop's parents—and the garden, pitted with dark pools where koi, a Chinese symbol of prosperity, teemed. Whenever the maids threw in a bowl of leftover rice the water's surface churned, turning gold with the bared bellies of so many fish fighting for the grains.

"Let's not do that again," she told Bop afterwards.

He didn't want to show that he was hurt. "Why—did my mother say something to you?"

"No. I just think it's easier."

Hence her familiarity with the climb up the balcony, where she waits now for him to reappear in her life, even as she reappears in his.

She wants a scene that echoes earlier years. The bedroom suddenly lighting up behind the black glass, a play's setting the lovers will stumble into, already kissing, as if life is taking place offstage.

She wants the actors to reenact her love for him. She wants the softness of the Thai language, a language meant for dawn, when husky alcohol evaporates with the dark. She wants this new woman to call his name: *Bebop,* a moniker equal parts affectionate and mocking that she had coined in bed one night to describe the choppy tempo of Bop's lovemaking.

"Speaks to a deeper rhythm," he had said.

"You mean irregular?" she joked.

"There's a tune in there somewhere."

She patted out a beat on his chest, moved her hips with him limp underneath her.

"You're playing for yourself now," he said, slumped back, finished.

"All jazz is masturbatory."

Crouched on the balcony, she studies her reflection, the face a mystery, wild hair dressed in leaves. The glass is close. The play—she can almost reach it, too, touch them, take part in the fun, make it real. Only she doesn't want that. So she doesn't even allow the scene to begin, leaves before they even come in.

OLD SOMBHAT DOESN'T come tonight. Just her and the boys, the boys and their overtures, the dealer pouring round after round, asking, "Whose turn are we on?" while looking only at her.

They all are. What, is it hers? She's sweating. The alcohol is doing that. Rice wine—whatever it is. It's stronger tonight. She can feel it under her arms and where it's warm between her legs. The flush brings beads of sweat to her nose. But the men are sweating, too.

"Hey, girl." Slap of cards on plastic. "Hey."

Her head snaps up. "I know, my turn."

It's hot. She can feel the room watching her, feel her skin that's beginning to show beneath the white t-shirt that she's rolled up above her shoulders.

"What are we playing for?" she asks and the men respond with a parched look, lips licked. There's a rising warmth in her that has nothing to do with drink and more to do with a history of recklessness.

"What are we playing for?" They know and they don't know. She goes for the teacup. The alcohol is cloudy and soft in her mouth.

"Okay." It's Benz this time. "Okay, now. I think you should play out your turn and go home." He has his hand on Narin's shoulder as if to hold the man back, but she wants to say: *Let him come.*

SHE HAD MADE it to California with Mrs. Anwar. But they never reached those Mexican favorites pressed up against the border, where the bars grew out of a hard landscape.

A police car flagged them off the highway as they were making

their way south. They followed the siren lights in the rearview, decided which of them would talk. He wanted to know why they were
driving below the minimum.

"What minimum?" Lara asked.

"Right—the minimum speed? Why are you driving so slow? Is
there something wrong with the car?"

They'd always been careful with that upper limit. They existed
under the radar.

"What a backward place," Mrs. Anwar muttered in Thai, "where
they can stop you for driving safely."

"What'd she say?"

"Nothing. My mother said nothing."

Mrs. Anwar bumbled in English: "Oh! So sorry. So sorry."

The policeman turned to her. "Speak English! This isn't Korea.
What are you doing here?"

Just two tourists from the East. They didn't know where else to
go, and the desert was killing Mrs. Anwar.

"The air is so dry. Like breathing sand," she said that evening. Her
lungs were shredded. "Just like my husband. Such sounds at night.
Then he was dead. I need air."

They drove to a strip of the coast where the wind blew in long
pulls, taking huffs at Mrs. Anwar's tumbleweed hair. The land opened
onto the Pacific. A splintered fence kept the sand at bay.

Mrs. Anwar stood out by the ocean, shaking her head.

"Where next?"

"Next!" Mrs. Anwar said. "What is next? Next I will be dead, I
suppose. Full stop." Mrs. Anwar pressed her fingers to her sternum,
beneath which there was clearly something wrong; they could hear it,
a whispering like long grass. "You need to learn to stop, too."

"Weren't you the one who taught me to work the tables, run the
circuit?"

"I taught you how to live on the move. *You* move to live. Where
next—ha! You think you can run forever? Bad lover, bad father. Two
bad men and already you're running. What do you think you'll be

like when as old as me?" Mrs. Anwar asked, her voice high above the throaty waves.

"Maybe I'll be happy." She stretched out on the sand and closed her eyes, opened her mouth to the sea spray.

"What's this?" Mrs. Anwar kicked sand on her. "Wake up! You think you can run to the promised kingdom? We live here. In this. It's a desert! And they cannot even tell Korean from Thai."

"So I'll go elsewhere."

"Go, then. Find that you cannot go forever."

SHE LEFT MRS. Anwar in a hospice and spent the summer at a half-built hostel up in Oregon. In exchange for lodging, she tended the house's vegetable garden. She was briefly happy with a broad Mid-western boy named Danny. Danny put up walls for a living. She told him that he was built to break earth, that is, to lug a plow, and that they should start a farm together. She wanted to run down crop rows. Eat radishes fresh from the ground, with the soil still hugging their roots. They could pretend to be frontiersmen, claiming land in far-away places. She had heard that volcanic soil was especially fertile. But by the autumn of that year, with the last of the summer crop harvested, she was already gone, leaving empty pockets in the ground where the vegetables had been pulled.

She traveled when she had money, lingered when she didn't, stay-ing with men who thought they had won her. What she finally learned from Mrs. Anwar was how not to be like her. She took to the tables as the old woman's negative, a nullifying space.

"You're a tough one to read, honey," the men told her. Leering men, they saw something at stake and she wanted to see it, too—a worth.

"A real puzzle," they said. "How do you do it?" She was no one. "What did you say your name was?" She never did.

"Why are you being so reckless?" asks Benz.

The dealer and Narin, they keep their knees still. Their eyes, lips, breath—everything held.

"Do you want to lose?" Benz says.

"I know what I'm doing," she says, three chips away from losing the game. She's come back from this before.

"Stop and leave." Benz wants to force her hand but she resists. "Just give the fishballs to me and leave, okay?" He holds out his hand. "Here."

"You don't understand," she says. She needs to play. She needs the reckless bile on her tongue, which she savors along with the flavor of a fishball that she puts in her mouth, chewing it to demonstrate to Benz: "Sometimes you need to feel you can lose." She bets the last of her fishballs, the two pieces that might keep Narin's fingers at bay, already anticipating those nubs pressing into her as men have always insisted on pressing.

"Women are meant to be soft," they tell her, searching.

She should have told them that she was all bone, picked over by teeth that had been there already, consumed by men at tables like this one, her body laid out, nipples gnawed on, fingers sucked, the cartilage of her ear bitten into. Each time, she feels like less, comes closer to nothing.

The men are waiting for her.

"Who's still playing? Show your hands, then." She twists her fan of cards to show the dealer. "Go on, show me."

But still Benz's hand is held out to her.

"Here."

Risk makes her rub her elbows, brings out the scars that cross her forearms. It makes her recall a blackjack game in a reservation casino where the dealer had asked, "Are you and your father playing together?" And before she turned to see the Chinese man beside her, before the easy laugh they shared, before "No. No, we don't know each other," her lungs had seized as if responding to the shock of cold water. Her spine, ribs, knees had cradled toward a point at her navel, as if to protect what is vital. Not the machinery of flesh. Not the plumbing, the engine. But to preserve the organ of memory, the part still able to communicate pain, so that she'd always be able to evoke those nights with Bop at a street-side food stall when they were two drunk students with knees crowded under the folding table, the wet sound of noodles slapping about the metal basket as the vendor soaked, drained, and tipped their food into blue bowls.

"I want it here," she said, cupping her hands for the broth. She wanted to eat out of her own fingers, to lick soup from the creases of her palms.

"You want to burn your skin off?" Bop took her hands in his, kneading with his thumb in a detached way he considered affectionate but that always reminded her of a doctor's probing. "Bones, bones, broken bones?" Bop joked, when she told him about feeling medically examined. His hands quested up her arm, shoulder, collarbone. "Ah—" finding a breast between the buttons of her blouse. "Here."

She would always be able to evoke her first time in a redwood grove, Mrs. Anwar holding her arm, neck craned, disbelieving. "Lara, in this kingdom of America, even the trees are high rollers."

And sitting with Mrs. Anwar in a parked car somewhere on the Great Plains: "Here, there's only sky." A breeze played the long grass like a rattle, rolled through the open windows and floated the women's clothes around their bodies. "Freed birds," Mrs. Anwar said.

"HERE." BENZ'S HAND a question held open. "Why are you being so reckless?"

Once, she wants to tell him, someone had loved that about her.

City of Brass

JIMMY & PING (2016)

The generals were in power. There was drought, also flooding, and a rock musician was running across the country to raise money for the poor. That was everything Jimmy knew about the kingdom, he told Ping, when she picked him up at the airport. Did she have anything to contribute?

"You want to know if I'm seeing someone," Ping said.

"I didn't say that."

"Good. So don't ask," she said. "That's the rule."

Except for this initial indiscretion, Ping humored Jimmy's new-arrival fancies. He bought a Thai iced tea at the airport, the cup sweating messily over the taxi seat. Then he wanted to stop at a death-themed café that had opened in Ping's neighborhood. He'd found the place on a list of Bangkok's niche attractions, a category that encompassed a cosplay sex club and a cultist temple.

The city looked different to Jimmy, more glass towers interrupting the skyline, more brown highways laid over the streets like dark belts constricting what might otherwise have been beautiful: the wooden houses along the klong, the determined clusters of greenery that reclaimed empty land plots. The neighborhood where the taxi dropped them felt upwind of the glossy downtown, uncontaminated by that perfumed mall life, but nonetheless expensive. Down the street was a Mercedes dealership, just a few steps from an alley of food vendors. And the death café was likely the darling project of some idly rich kid, scion of one of the neighborhood's dynasties.

The entrance was a black corridor. The sun slit through the ceiling at intervals, tastefully illuminating the hanging signs that Jimmy translated from Thai as they passed beneath them.

"'Does anyone really understand you?'" he read.

"I've got work due tonight, Jimmy."

"'Is there anyone waiting for you?'"

"You really don't have to show off your Thai to me."

"'Are you human?'" He read the final sign. "I heard this is what they ask men before they can become monks."

Ping looked at the sign, humoring him. "It's from a folktale. A *naga* disguised itself as a human so it could seek enlightenment."

"Yeah? And did the *naga* make it?"

"Of course not. They caught it."

At the end of the tunnel was the Buddhist learning center that housed the café. Instead of walls, columns of black fabric hung from the roof, billowing in the crosscurrents made by fans standing like attendant waiters beside each table. Ethereal, classical music drifted down from speakers. A skeleton reclined on a beanbag, its arms currently encircling two teenage girls angling for the perfect selfie. Beside the beanbag stood an obliteration box, a blackout room with roaring white noise that drowned out everything—another approximation of death.

"It's a shrine to the lords of goth or Muji," Ping said.

"Why not both?"

Jimmy toed an arrow painted on the floor. It pointed to the final attraction, a white coffin on a plinth.

"The website said ten percent off a drink if you get in for three minutes." He stepped onto the platform and lifted the coffin lid. "Don't you Thais cremate your dead?"

Jimmy climbed in when it was clear she wasn't going to. It was deep enough to turn the classical music tinny and small, like an elevator tune.

"They don't exactly invest much in comfort. I can feel the wood right through the satin."

"Lie flat," she said, pushing him down.

JIMMY HAD LIVED in Bangkok before. His father had been stationed here as an investigative reporter for Voice of America, which even in the nineties was an unconvincing cover for the CIA. What his dad actually did in those years, he'd never know. Jimmy was busy living a nostalgically American childhood. He ran the diamond on the baseball field, guzzled imported Kool-Aid, and celebrated Halloween in the only neighborhood that fed hungry ghosts on the holiday. He only broke the mirage to take Thai lessons after school. Jimmy was the white kid among local peers who, at the international school, had never learned Thai. The language left outside the school, lost to the many cul-de-sacs of their earnestly American compound. Otherwise, he lived so fiercely in suburban nineties America that by the time Dad brought them back to New York City in the new millennium, Jimmy experienced the culture shock of having been moved in time. It took until grad school to catch up with the American present. And having arrived, he'd intended to stay.

But a contemporary American life was never Ping's plan. She and Jimmy had met in grad school and been dating five years before she finished her PhD and was enticed back to Bangkok with a new job. They sat down and talked marriage. It was a decision they had let roll ahead of them like a coin flashing down the slope of their relationship, which, with Ping's new job, had dropped into the unknown. Ping was hopeful; Jimmy listened for the bottom.

HE WOKE AND grasped for the walls of the coffin. But he was in the condo, a smothering blanket thrown over him like that first shovel of earth. His nap had been interrupted by a countdown outside, a broadcast of beeps that he recognized as the prelude to the national anthem. As a kid he had loved this moment. He stepped onto the balcony and watched as every person within earshot of the anthem slowed, like components in a clock winding down. The people below came to a complete stop. The song issued from an army complex, where the flag was coming down for the night.

"Jimmy, get ready!" called Ping.

He stepped back inside. She was changing. Or she had changed, the soft parts sloughed off under a sun dialed to a different range. A magazine body, he thought boyishly, with its modish angles, which he should have wanted to hold, but the new sharpness felt like a warning more than an invitation. She put on a white linen top and cropped navy pants, all of it starched stiff, and she wore it like armor.

Dinner with her friends was walking distance. She said they were going in shallow, before she introduced him to the city proper, spoken as if he didn't know the real Bangkok.

Her friends were regulars at the restaurant. The owner came over, a wiry man who held out a hand inked with geometric tattoos.

"I'm Jom. You're new."

Jimmy pointed across the table at Ping and, aiming for charming self-deprecation, said in Thai, "I'm just her boyfriend."

"Boyfriend." Jom smiled and held his hand too long. "Are you half Thai?"

"I grew up here. I mean, no."

"But you speak it a little?" Jom said in English. "I love you UN people." Jom pointed at each of their group in turn. "South Africa, Netherlands, Italy, Canada, Japan, Thailand. And"—he paused significantly on Jimmy, wiggling two uncertain fingers—"America with Thai flavor."

Jimmy tried to see them as Jom did. The image didn't hold. To Jimmy, they were just seven millennials with graduate degrees speaking English. Big deal. Even the office clothes the others wore looked cut from the same catalog.

Across the table from Jimmy sat Ping and Cesare, whose name was pronounced the bombastic, Italian way. Cesare's dark hair was tightly curled, and he had that perfect Mediterranean stubble; Jimmy's hair, still lank and damp, was plastered to his head like a brown skull cap. He had to stop himself from rubbing his own splotchy, airplane whiskers, instead studying the stud in Cesare's right ear, which when Jimmy was a kid had meant something but now he wasn't sure. Ping was leaning into the attention. Wasn't hard to understand. The man's sex appeal was undeniable. Overpowering. The best course was to surrender to it. Which isn't to say Jimmy wouldn't use this moment against her later. When they had sex, he'd want to see her as Cesare saw her. Ping knew he did this kind of thing.

Jimmy let the jet lag take him. The conversation, anyway, was full of names he didn't recognize. And bad managers were the same the world over. So Jimmy didn't realize he was being spoken to until Ping tapped his hand.

"Jimmy tried the coffin," she was saying.

"And?" Cesare said.

"Did it create an appreciation for death?" Ping prompted.

"I don't know." Jimmy knew how to catch up. "I mean, I like the idea: If you can make it proximate, you make it familiar, and what's familiar isn't feared." He wasn't sure he believed this, but it sounded like what one said at such a restaurant.

Cesare disagreed. So much of what he feared, he said, was familiar, even intimate. "Don't you think?" He turned from Ping to Jimmy, unblinking.

Ping often said she didn't have the patience for this type. A man who used conversation to create opportunities, to open mouths wide enough that he could ram his own opinions down your throat—at least, that was how Ping often described Jimmy's own tactlessness.

"I mean, no, not really," Jimmy said. "This is a little off the deep end, but I've got a relevant example."

Ping said, "Jimmy . . ." in a way he knew was meant to stop him.

"It's a good story, I promise. See, my father is seventy-six with late-stage dementia—he needs help. So my fifty-year-old mother chooses a special sort of nursing home for him. The place has been outfitted by a film-set designer. It looks like Main Street in a quiet American town circa, like, 1955. It's a specific Hollywood skill, you know, to make it look real from the outside. The buildings are three-quarter size, like the shop fronts at Disney World. Mom loved it. The whitewashed, wholesome backdrop." He listed off his fingers. "Malt shop, jukebox, overbearing wallpaper, and an American flag with twisted rods along its lengths to keep it unfurled. The hallways are wall-to-wall carpet the green of spring lawns." Ping faced him with her eyes fully closed; she was communicating the group's interest in the story, apparently none. "All right, anyway, my dad's former, doddering uncertainty was lifted. The hesitation and the guessing . . . Gone. The fear . . . Gone. So maybe, for those living with dementia, what's familiar is comforting? Now—"

"Jimmy!" Ping interrupted.

"What?" It was an anecdote he'd successfully delivered at other dinners. Mostly, it went over well in the way of a semi-divisive, big-table topic. Inevitably there were comparisons to the films *The Truman Show* and *Good Bye Lenin!* Once it even kicked off a debate about benign authoritarianism, a hypothetical state that used a monopoly over force and truth to gently herd its citizens along, say, the serene pastures of their better memories.

"Jimmy, that's not even how it happened." Ping's features were taut with her effort to hold them still. He'd upset her.

"Okay, fine." He spread his hands. "I like a happy ending. The *truth* is that my father cried when we brought him there. He cried and rocked himself right out of his wheelchair. Maybe he felt helpless, an adult trapped in childhood. Or *maybe* the false memory registered as madness. Either way, my mother forfeited her deposit. She moved him to an ordinary home, where the hallways are just hallways."

He checked his audience. The Japanese woman was scrolling on her phone in an obvious, I'm-looking-away-from-your-shame way. Ping stared beyond him at the table of Thais as if searching for help. Cesare, though, studied Jimmy curiously.

"It's an unusual place," Ping said, finally, about the death café, presumably. *Fair enough,* Jimmy thought, *digression over.* He could roll with it.

"Bangkok has many unusual gems," Cesare offered.

The fusion salmon carpaccio was served with chopsticks. "Does this look, like, suspiciously pink to anyone?" Jimmy asked.

The Italian turned a piece over and put it in his mouth as the others took over the conversation again, filling, Jimmy felt, the absence left by his inadequacies. He still wanted to charm them, for Ping's sake, and waited for an opening.

"Last week I uncovered a jazz venue," Cesare said. "It's in a person's living room. The players are local graduate students. Excellent music taste, but the wine, from Khao Yai, was like vinegar."

Jimmy tried again: "You know we like jazz as well. Speaking of which, did Ping ever say how we met?"

Ping set her beer down with an odd degree of force, sloshing it onto the table. "No," she said flatly.

"What? It's relevant! I mean not *met,* but . . . our first date, you know? We went to an open mic at a pop-up jazz bar in Queens. Ping hadn't sung in years, but we'd made the trip happen. I put her name on the sign-up sheet and by the time we got down the list we'd had like a half handle of whiskey and I thought she'd never get through 'Lullaby of Birdland'—"

"Ella Fitzgerald." Cesare nodded.

"Only, Ping's a fan of the Sarah Vaughan version. More unpredictable, right? But anyway," Jimmy continued. He didn't face Ping because he was seeing another person just then, a Ping he remembered on that low stage, turned toward the drummer for her cue. Only, somehow a story that had taken a whole evening to live came up short in the telling. He was done before the main course even arrived.

"I didn't know you sing," Cesare said.

"I don't really. Just that one time," Ping said quietly.

"Saranya!" said the Canadian. "Have you heard of Michael Bublé?"

"WHY ARE YOU Saranya?" Jimmy asked in bed. It had thrown him at dinner, as if they were talking about someone he didn't know. Ping never used her full name. She had been Poongping as a kid, and Ping by the time Jimmy met her.

"Why are you Jimmy?" she countered.

"And not Cesare?"

"Has the competition intimidated you?"

"He's the real thing, I guess. None of this Italian-American, spaghetti-and-meatballs bullshit. Is he gay?"

"Cesare? No."

"Not even a little? I mean, it's unusual for a man to be so put together."

"I'm sure."

She was deliberately goading him. Don't ask, that was the rule, right? There were other rules to the relationship, but only this one required Ping's enforcement. The open thing was her idea, a corrective to a problem that predated him. Her first boyfriend had cheated on her repeatedly. Repeatedly, she and Jimmy had revisited that relationship, so that Jimmy knew its every crag and break, knew how the boyfriend was hewn from harder stuff, brittle and cold—what she'd once mistaken for masculinity. Instead of being a bad example, however, that first love had become the unhealthy archetype. He stood for all men, and all men, said Ping, would cheat given the opportunity. The only way out, then, was to change the terms entirely, to standardize cheating and thereby rob it of its potency.

"What do you think?" she had asked, a week before she left for Bangkok.

"What? You mean like an open relationship?"

"*God*, no. That sounds so juvenile. Just, I don't know, the assumption that the other person is seeing other people, and that's okay. Right? No questions?"

"Which is, like, a *bad* open relationship." Sex, even with someone

Jimmy knew, was too often a test he didn't pass. He preferred porn, where the guilt was self-inflicted. They'd managed for years, hadn't they? Only, New York City was familiar, Ping said—her routines had allowed her to tamp down the anxiety. But in a new place, new anxiety.

"Say yes, Jimmy. Okay? That's what I need from you right now."

HE THOUGHT SHE'D fallen asleep when she suddenly spoke into the darkness: "You didn't tell it right. The singing story."

"Yeah, it was terrible. *I* am terrible. And jet-lagged, to be fair." He was trying to hide his real disappointment. He had embarrassed her.

"Just—I don't know. Stick to normal stuff. People don't know what to say when you tell your stories."

"They didn't even know you sing, though. I mean, how can your friends not *know* that about you?"

"I don't, though. That was just this fantasy I had."

"See, you're doing it again. Talking like it's behind you."

When they had first met, Ping told him she'd wanted to be a jazz singer but had been required by her university scholarship to study economics. In another life, presented with other doors, she was sure she'd have been a singer. Nowadays, she didn't sing much at all. Jimmy had diagnosed this as fear—that she was afraid of not living up to herself, to her one drunken night at that jazz place. Jimmy saw himself as the sponsor of her success that night: He'd given her what she always wanted. But the morning after her performance, she'd woken up with a hangover and revealed to him that no, she couldn't remember the details. Not the lullaby, or the bourbon, or the husky singers who drew her in, claiming her as one of their own. Ping was a sober-playing drunk, but her blackout threshold was unsparingly low.

And so he'd told her the story, which, that spontaneous first time, came out perfect, as if told through him rather than by him. He felt like Sarah Vaughan himself, finding the notes of the story as he told it. Every subsequent attempt smacked of stale reiteration. How to re-create the original to make it seem new?

Ping often said he was stuck because of his training as a journalist, the obsession with a scoop, the need for novelty.

Maybe. But what he really thought was that somewhere along the way he'd been ruined, he'd just lost the skill. The likely culprit was his three years working at a call center, mechanically reiterating his approved scripts. Only odd Abe, a bodybuilder, had thrived in that place. Abe, cradling the earpiece familiarly, practically cooing as he described snow-globe saltshakers and steel-bowl salad spinners that would "literally change your life."

A silver lining to the cold-call experience was the dwindling number of landlines available for invasion. Also, the arrival of machines that could maintain the superhuman levels of charm ("With feeling!" yelled his boss daily) through hundreds of calls.

One respondent was a woman who referred to herself in the third person. Lotta—nothing resembling the name on file.

"Talk to Lotta," she'd said. "Lotta's dying. She wants her last words heard. Can you stay on the line?"

He told her there were numbers for this kind of call. He didn't know that for a fact, but believed in the market system, its canny distributing mechanisms—the proverbial hand moving him, like a steel peg on a production line, to the required place. Which, he supposed, could be the other end of this call with Lotta. Perhaps this *was* that kind of call. A call for help.

He resolved to try. He told Lotta what he'd read about Japan, where many seniors were dying alone in their apartments. In Japan, the enterprising old persons had their own system: two people at their windows at nine A.M., waving. *I'm still here,* said the wave. "If you think about it," he told Lotta, "it's not a method of checking if a person is dead, but rather, whether they're still living."

Such meanderings failed to soothe her. "Can you stay on the line?" she insisted, which felt like a test of his humanity. But he

couldn't—old man Rodríguez was on his ass about his call load. He
was underperforming.

"Sorry, Ms. Lotta. I actually can't do that."

Still, he had continued to think about her—half of what she
must've wanted from him—her words held and revisited. Now, of
course, he wished he had asked her. What would Lotta have said if
she thought theirs was the final conversation? Maybe nothing more.
"Stay," she had already said. "Please," she'd said. "Is there anyone on
the other side?"

A YEAR BACK they had run out of things to talk about at dinner. Not
absolutely, but the meal had become repetitive, and this was Jimmy's
fault, he knew. As a corrective, he had suggested a new evening tradition: They would read to each other from *One Thousand and One
Nights,* which, he told Ping, was a textbook in making something out
of nothing. Each story held other stories, navigated by the masterful
Scheherazade, whose labyrinthine storytelling had, like the best tales,
the tenor of desperation, of Theseus fleeing the Minotaur, of a miller's
daughter trying to spin straw into gold.

For their first dinner in the condo, he picked up food from the
street, combining regional cuisines haphazardly. Ping pointed this
out. He said he was a foreigner; he had a claim to ignorance.

He hefted the tome he had brought over. "Tonight is 'The Story
of the City of Brass.'"

They took turns reading. In the tale, a caliph sends a band of men
to recover brass bottles from a faraway land. The journey takes the
men to the City of Brass, which is a city of the dead. Dead are the
guards in their garrisons, swords drawn and bows strung, their spears
tipped expectantly toward the gates. At the cloth market, the mer-
chants recline dead against their bolts of silk, their skin dried to
parchment. Dead are the perfumers, amid a wealth of musk and
camphor. Also the jewelers, with their pearls, jacinth, and precious

minerals strewn across the path like a welcoming carpet. The walls are marble inlaid with lapis lazuli. The men find gold and ivory. They find a tablet telling a story of drought and sickness. "Long time they ate and drank," it read. "But now, after pleasant eating, they themselves have been eaten." In the palace, encircled by treasure, is a princess garlanded with gemstones and embalmed with quicksilver behind her eyes, an approximation of life, for when the men look upon her, they mistake her for the living.

THEY WENT TO IKEA. In the kitchens, the tables were laid for four. The couches were over-sampled, the cushions sagging as if under a ghost weight. The beds, though, were sturdy, their blankets drawn back expectantly. They skipped the children's section. They bought furniture and a fake plant.

The next day, while Ping was at work, Jimmy flipped through local TV channels and assembled the furniture. One channel showed the fundraising rock star, Toon Bodyslam, running along a highway with an entourage fanned out behind him, everyone in black. The camera followed his progress all day. A kilometer counter and a fundraising counter rose in tandem. Long and dark and relentless. *Why am I Jimmy,* Jimmy thought, *and not Toon Bodyslam?*

A man rang up—he was here to install the water filter. When Jimmy went downstairs, he found the man's daughter and wife were in his truck with him, the windows rolled down and their phones out.

"They can come up, if they want," Jimmy said, with what he hoped was a sense of easy consideration. "It's air-conditioned."

After insisting, Jimmy had the whole family upstairs. It was almost six, and he took the little girl to the window.

"Watch." He pointed at the roof of the nearby military building, which he had discovered was the Territorial Defense Headquarters. The roof had been painted green, but along the perimeter was a trail where the coating had been worn down, like a path trodden through a field. A man was running this elevated trail.

The man stopped as the anthem countdown began, then he charged across the roof, approaching the edge at full pelt. The girl gasped as the man suddenly stopped short, turning his body sideways in a violent halt.

Standing at the edge, he then raised his arms and flounced his hands like he was conducting the music.

When the anthem ended, the girl marched around the one-bedroom like an inspecting field marshal. She stopped beside the incomplete IKEA dresser, which was on its side with legs extended, a collapsed animal.

"Do you want help?" she asked.

Her father told her not to bother their customer, but Jimmy said he did, in fact, need someone to hand him the tools, which she did now with martial determination.

"What do you do?" she asked, holding out the screwdriver.

"Me? I make furniture. What do *you* do?"

"I'm your boss."

WHEN THEY WERE planning the move, he had considered taking a job teaching English. Seeing the pay, Ping had laughed. It wasn't even the difference between her last salary and the one with this new promotion. "Honey," she'd said touching Jimmy's cheek. "Just do the writing thing, huh? Seriously, take the time. We don't need that money."

They'd met at an age when dating was still about potential, when they imagined their careers would be laid out before them like feasts. He would get into long-form journalism and she would go into international development. Sure enough, soon after, she was with the UN. Jimmy, though, was faced with either adjunct non-pay or temping. And so he worked down his student debt in the call center, while at night producing overworked essays that came back from editors with onomatopoeic adjectives: glum, plodding, dense.

To fill his newly empty days here in Bangkok, Ping had recommended a Thai teacher, a cheery law student who met Jimmy at the death café. He told her he didn't really need her help; mainly he just wanted to modernize his Thai. She asked him what he did for work. Was he with the UN as well?

"Didn't Ping tell you?"

No, Ping hadn't said anything about him. This was his cue to tell her he worked in narrative marketing. His current assignment was revitalizing the maligned robusta, a coffee species. Arabica, he said, was a marketing gimmick, like organic produce, which required three times as much land to produce an equivalent yield. How were they going to feed everybody? Robusta, on the other hand, was resilient and could grow at lower altitudes. It was the snobs that had to be reeducated, and Jimmy had been hired to create a story about a sustainable coffee future. Thailand was his field research.

When he told the Thai teacher that he worked in marketing, like when he said to the hairdresser that he was a freelance video-game designer, and when he left large tips everywhere, he wasn't lying about himself, exactly, but simply alluding to other selves, aspirational shapes he might press himself into. The lies were doorways, as in Wonderland, where the person changed to fit the door.

Or the doorway in a story they read in the *Nights,* a week later:

A poor man steps through a forbidden doorway. It takes him to another, abundant land, where he marries the queen and lives in luxury. The only condition to his new position is that he never use another, similarly forbidden door. Only, having learned from his first success in breaking rules, he tries the door and is promptly returned to his original, derelict state.

"When we say doors," Ping remarked, "we mean marriage."

"I don't follow."

"Marriage is the door, not the end," she said.

"The door to happiness?"

Ping's look told him he didn't understand at all. "That's not what he found."

"THINGS ARE FINE," he told his mother, who was now living as if newly single in North Carolina, not far from Dad's drab facility. He turned on his camera and showed her the view from their glossy condo. His social media profile was an image of him rising from a coffin, eyes rolled back as if still dead. He posted pictures of himself at the odd places he went to during the day, while Ping was at work. Photos taken by servers or tourists.

He even reached out to friends from the international-school days. The only ones still in Bangkok were the Thais who came from families wealthy enough to make the country's annual *Forbes* list. They went out to an overpriced sushi restaurant that looked like it had taken a design cue from purgatory.

"Back from the dead!" Champ slapped Jimmy's back more exuberantly maybe than the friendship called for.

"You look old," Jimmy said. "Like the family work is taking a toll, maybe?"

"What work?" said Fiat, rising to hug Jimmy. "His only work is playing the budding entrepreneur in *Tatler* photo shoots."

"More like indulging midlevel Chinese businessmen," Champ said.

"Golf isn't so bad," Jimmy said.

"If it were only golf. Come out with me on a corporate-tab night and I'll show you what it's like."

"Don't do it," Fiat warned. The clubs, the company, even the drugs were B-list. Last time they'd snorted something that had kept her awake for two days.

"What was it?" Jimmy asked.

"Babe." Fiat laid a hand on his arm. "I know what it was *not*."

This ground-up prescription stuff, Fiat said, laced all of Southeast Asia's high society. She knew this from her consulting job at a company that advanced her through the region's major cities. Through countries whose checkered histories (colonized or not, and, if so, by whom) showed in the varying disparities of poor, while the rich were always the same: international schools, university abroad. "We're in a region where an English accent passes as pedigree."

"Anyway," said Champ, whose entire male line finished from Eton. "What are you doing these days, Jimmy?"

He had become a photo illustrator, he told them. Back in New York City, his specialty was staged shots of upscale gift baskets around the big American holidays: Easter, Thanksgiving, Christmas—photos alluding to better, bucolic places for the city-bound clientele. With the move to Bangkok, he wanted to make a smartphone game premised on staged photographs strewn with clues.

"I'll use the photos to make up a story, and you have to piece together clues to move forward. I'll shoot it all on one of these VR cameras, so you can roam at will. You have to figure out what's the game, and what's just life debris."

"Like a VR escape room," Champ said. "Sounds like a fun job. And *I* have to sit around sex clubs with balding Chinese men for a living."

"That's spot the difference," Fiat said.

"What?"

"Spot the difference. It's a game. I mean, yours is more elaborate, but do you remember those machines in the malls when we were young? You'd drop in a coin and have to find the differences between two photos. We used to play for hours."

"Oh," said Jimmy. "I don't remember that."

WEDNESDAY, OUTSIDE A pizza place that was somehow French, Ping took Jimmy aside.

"I know you like to tell a story, Jimmy. But sometimes you need to be here in the world. It's just—when you get going, you don't stop."

He did his best to explain to her that the story told *him*.

"Yeah, okay, but so just—don't *let* it. Okay? Give everyone else a bit of room to talk."

"This *is* talk. This is how I talk."

"No, Jimmy. You make shit up. And, for the sake of a halfway decent conversation, don't."

Fine. He was happy to sit out on office gossip, anyway, or when her friends set about diagnosing the country's problems: corruption, bureaucracy, price discrimination, sexpats, and, of course, the myriad things from back home that were maddeningly unavailable here. With Thailand exhausted, the group went global, talking as if above the fray yet entirely able to get the lay of the land and assess the approaching trouble. It spoke to an older world order, this perspective. Even the use of "missions" to describe their air-drop consultancies at the country offices had something of a colonial ring to it. Peacebuilding practiced on a dinner-table scale, policy finesse the reliable accompaniment to the meals, though there was no system to the pairings. Rohingya and sushi. Shrimp-farm slavery and kebabs. Syria and pizza.

Ping's friends brought their hierarchies out with them, Jimmy learned, since their employer's transparent system meant everyone knew what everyone else was paid. The South African was talking right now, but he had the largest salary so this was okay. Whereas when the Japanese woman contributed—a couple pay grades below—they quietly turned their attention away, if not outright contradicting her.

As Cesare spoke, Jimmy was reminded of the detached, revolving vantage of a drone. Ping watched Cesare, not so much with carnal interest as performative, like a singer waiting on the drummer for her cue. It would have been easier to see naked desire, some impetus to confront her, but this subtler intimacy utterly undid any accusations before Jimmy ever articulated them.

At the end of the meal, each person converted the bill to a more familiar currency. They hadn't learned to gauge the worth of a transaction without holding it against something at home. Against money that sounded roundly opulent: dollar, euro, pound.

And then, drinks.

Thursday night, they went to a club styled like an opium den. Jimmy stood at the bar and took photos of Ping dancing, trying to capture this new self of hers in the right light.

"Jimmy." Ping was breathless and drunk. She braced herself on his arm. "Stop with the photos. Just, you know, *talk* to people. Shit, flirt if you *have* to. But, like, be a person in a club. Not this sad-sack Andy Warhol."

THE NEXT EVENING, he was making *penne al forno,* the *forno* here being a toaster oven. He sent Ping a text. What time was she coming back?

There was Friday happy hour, she said, and then they were going out clubbing. A drinks promotion somewhere. He was welcome, of course, but either way it'd be late before she was back.

He didn't want to spend the evening alone in the condo, wondering if it was possible to mortally wound himself kicking IKEA furniture. The pain thus far suggested yes.

He called Champ. Was it a good time? By which he meant, was it a corporate-tab night?

The routine, Champ explained, leading Jimmy into the club, was always the same: steak followed by an upscale men's club. The Chinese clients were already inside.

"They love this place. I call it the Belt and Rope Initiative, get it? It caters to the more obvious fetishes, which is enough to enthrall middle management." He brought Jimmy over to the booth and waved lazily for an introduction. The place was dark and red, and onstage women were contorted. One was being tied to a pulley. The club's suffocating noise meant Champ didn't need to field questions in his patchwork Mandarin. He leaned closer to Jimmy, mouth first, as if for resuscitation. He complained about the turns his life had taken, its course meandering, any destination at once random and predictable. Then death. What kind of life was this? It was like the imaginative power of his attendant soothsayers was as limited as that of the men surrounding them, who now had their eyes fixed upon a woman suspended from the ceiling. The men's hands unconsciously loosened their ties.

"And then the noose comes for us," Champ said, turning his gaze up as ropes slowly drew apart the woman's legs.

It got elaborate and Jimmy was embarrassed by his low threshold for shame. He didn't want to look anymore. At some point, he realized, he'd gotten drunk, the bottle of Black Label—between, what, six of them?—not even half gone.

"How is this not empty?" Jimmy said.

"Oh, they replace the bottle before it's out," Champ said, reassuringly. "So my clients never notice. Bottomless Black."

"Surely this kind of place can't be good for business."

"Actually, it's excellent. The Chinese see Bangkok as the place to go for a little life. For a reminder that they're living, which we always think of in terms of the obvious—the joy, say, the lust, the anger. We think adrenaline, right? But why not *shame*? The type of shame you're forced to acknowledge, to say, you know, 'I see you.'" Champ's hand went from waving to almost a caressing stroke. "And you let it lead you." Then, with sudden speed, he snatched at a passing hostess's lace girdle. She froze. Champ kept his eyes on Jimmy. "The shame works, though. You should try it. It brings you closer." He yanked the hostess back toward them, stretching the lace. "Like sharing a secret." Champ's fingers relaxed now, as if he were releasing a fish back to its element. The hostess didn't move.

"If you buy her a lady drink she'll stay." Champ still hadn't looked at the woman.

"A lady drink?"

"Not a real drink, mind you. A tip. The fee for her fine company.

Here." Champ flipped open his wallet, took out some big bills, and folded them into Jimmy's hand. "Go on. Have one on me. Take your time. Like feeding fish at the temple, right?"

Jimmy glanced at the woman. Her outfit was twisted where Champ had grabbed her. She turned to stand with her body in appealing profile.

"Sorry, Champ. I don't think my politics allow *that* kind of shame."

"I mean, sure, be a feminist. But not a hypocrite. You know? Look, we all watch the same porn."

The woman watched all of this with evident impatience. "I'm sorry," Jimmy said in Thai. "*What's* your name?" He used the question as cover for handing her the money.

"Oh, you speak Thai?" she said. "I keep losing out to the other girls because my Chinese sucks."

Champ waved a hand at her. "Take him into the back, okay? A VIP room. Tell that slob Pradit that this is my very good friend."

The doorway to the back rooms was curtained in black velvet. The sign above the threshold read, in English:

ABANDON ALL INHIBITION

And below:

by invitation only

The VIP room was a glorified karaoke booth. A couch ran the whole wall. The hostess gestured casually at the kiddie pool, a passing novelty, a bit of kitsch. "Bubbles are only for groups. You're not paying enough."

She stopped at a light panel and clicked through the color spectrum.

"What mood do you want? Blue? Red?"

"What do they usually pick?"

"Red, then."

It was better. What he had seen of her body only reminded him of the morgue, the pallid flesh, the coldness. The red, at least, was suggestive, and Jimmy was willing to be persuaded.

She tapped his belt. "Off."

"How embarrassing. For us both, I mean. You should know I'm drunk—just in case I embarrass myself." He blinked at her. She had silver contacts that lent her eyes a flat affect. "I'm so drunk I'm talking to dolls," he murmured. "What's your name?"

"Call me Pinky."

He hadn't moved to undress. She yanked his belt buckle impatiently.

"No, that's okay. You really don't have to touch me." Jimmy took a few steps backward and sat down heavily beside the pool. "Just, like, stay over there, right? That's good. Like we're on the phone. See? Hello! Is there anybody on the other side!"

She stared at him blankly.

Determined to make his point, he made his fist into a phone and waved it at her. "A harmless phone call. Go on."

"I've done kinky," she said, "but never *this*." She held a hand to her ear.

"That's good. All I need is for you to stay on the line." In his drunkenness his words had slurred into English. "I want these words heard. And remember, no questions. That's the rule. I like a happy ending. But you know what the truth about the jazz story is?"

"What are you talking about?"

"It's not even true. I made the whole thing up. You know what? Ping never even made it onto that stage."

ON THE STAGE are three saxophones in stands, their brass oxidizing green in places, making the collection look like sunken treasure against the navy curtain backdrop. There's a keyboard and a drum set. But no other decoration.

"You've got some underground authenticity going on here," Jimmy says at the sign-up table.

The woman hands him a clipboard. "Open mic. You performing?"

"She's singing." He gestures at Ping, behind him.

Addressing Ping over his shoulder, the woman asks, "What will you sing, dear?"

"Jazz!" Jimmy says.

"What was that?"

"I can do 'Lullaby of Birdland,'" Ping says.

"That's good. I'll let the band know. Now, you're last on the lineup, but we've got some drinks here. It's five for a cup of wine. Boxed wine, but you know." She shrugged. "Take a table. Make yourself at home."

"What is this place?" Ping asks.

"It's my family's. We're between tenants and we like jazz. It's a temporary thing."

Jimmy pays for sodas and tops them off with whiskey glugged conspicuously from the bottle in Ping's bag. The whiskey was her one condition, flirting on campus, to agreeing to sing at this open mic. A handle of whiskey. He delivered, but now he's sure he's set her up for failure. She checks the lyrics on her phone. It's the scatting, she explains, that's so hard without practice.

Everyone else is having a picnic. The white tops of the folding tables are laid with a casserole tray, a container of fried rice, an order of pizza, tortilla chips, two-liter Cokes, even a spread of checkered tablecloth. The abundance of a summer picnic, Jimmy thinks, on this gloomy Thursday evening. The place brightens as the sun goes down, the change like warning lights at the theater: *Get to your seats.* The audience shushing as the first performers clop onto the stage to a beat of silence, then hearty applause.

"Shit," says Ping. "I don't know if I can. I'm shaking. Look. Take my hand."

He takes her hand. The two young boys in front of them clap and holler throughout, like they're learning how to, as they are learning to listen for the ends of solos. The night's already over by the time Ping gets onstage. She's dead last.

"I'm Ping." She nods to the band. "And this is 'Lullaby of Birdland.'" The drummer counts her in.

Ping begins. Her right hand makes circular motions, the voice a shy, retreating talent that has to be coaxed from her. When it does arrive, it's with force, and the rest of the band nods smugly at one another, like they've pulled the best number from a hat. She doesn't get the improvisation completely right, but it doesn't matter because her voice is clearly made for something classical, the sound larger than this brief room. And there's no clear predictability in Ping's scat singing. No, Jimmy thinks, it's about the uncertainty. It is song made purely in the moment. Each note not recalled, rather, found.

English!

PEA & NAM (1974)

Pea jams a match under the burner. (In English: "Ignite!") He holds on until the flame licks his nail. A cook's fingers. He feels nothing! Left hand: one spoon of oil into the wok. Two spoons ("For health," he whispers in Thai). The sheen catches the noon sun.

Right hand: salt, garlic (peeled in the night, before he rubbed down Yai's feet, her heel-skin cracked and flaking like old garlic bulbs, toes purple from sleeping upright in the wheelchair), bird's-eye chilies, pork fat thumbed from a jar—all into the clay mortar. Thumps it into a paste with a wooden pestle. The metal food stall rattles. The oil smokes. He scrapes a spoon around the mortar and tosses the paste into the pan. It spits. The first smell: garlic. Then the bite of chili.

Nam, watching beside Pea, coughs like a newborn. Pea's right foot (right toes!) finds the dial for the fan. Twists to *High Power* (Pea practices English by labeling things). Fumes pour out into the street, away from the shophouse where Pea, Yai, and Ba live. Only Ba's been gone for a month.

Pea's left hand, slick with oil the way Ba taught him, scoops pork bits into the hot mix. The spatula rings against the metal, scrapes and folds. Oil spills. A tongue of flame flutters about the lip of the wok. Nam steps back but Pea doesn't flinch. Both hands ("Twelve is too young to lift the wok with one arm," Ba always said. But soon!) jerk the wok's handle, sending pork leaping off the blackened bowl. Pea catches it. Most of it. One piece leaves a trail of gristle across the metal counter.

"Pea, careful, careful," Pea imagines Ba saying.

But no! The lunch hour looms. From the street is a motorbike growl. Pea reaches behind. He doesn't even look. Hands find the dark soy sauce, the light soy sauce. One shot from the left bottle, three from the right. Sugar from the bowl. Stock from yesterday. He takes a handful of holy basil leaves out of the stall's glass cabinet.

Nam ladles the rice herself. She knows to find the cooker tucked beside the gas tank. As Pea breaks an egg (one hand, but he's been doing that since he was nine) into a second pan, he pauses to notice Nam opening the rice cooker. The steam lifts into her hair.

The egg is done. Crinkled brown corners, a cloudy yellow yolk (Yai's eyes in the morning). Nam offers her foam container. Pea nestles the pork beside the rice, tipping the last of it with a quick heave of the wok. Too quick. The stool beneath him rocks. Nam has to steady him with a hand to his waist. She keeps her hand there.

IN THE MONTH since Ba left on a bus for some mountain temple, Pea and Yai have lost the regulars. Each day, Nam comes to buy lunch for her father, but the shophouse is otherwise empty. Pea has stacked the plastic stools and metal tables in a corner. There is no kitchen; everything is cooked on the food stall parked at the entrance, at the top of a ramp leading to the sidewalk. The stall is an open metal counter with two burners, four bicycle wheels, and a glass cabinet that houses vegetables. Across the stall's front a hand-drawn sign reads: *Pad Krapao!* Below that, in English: *Stir-Fry with Holy Basil!*

Service is from eleven through seven. Pea takes orders and Yai takes money, tucks it into the kangaroo pouch on her soiled orange apron. She wears a hairnet, too, though Pea doesn't understand why. She can't cook because she's sick. And anyway, she hardly has any hair left, just a few feathers of grey that sprout through holes in the netting. Sometimes Pea hates her for those tufts, and for the sour smell he has to wash from her clothing. It's difficult to lift Yai without Ba, too, so Pea doesn't change her as often. The mother of Pea's mother, Yai is part of what's left of Mama, and now she's dying.

"Pea, don't hammer the pork like that. That is not an axe." Yai has a basket of holy basil in her lap. She plucks the leaves from their stalks and drops them into the bowl by her feet. She occasionally puts a stalk in her mouth.

"I'm not hammering." Pea sinks the blade into the cutting block. "I'm chopping."

"Pea!"

"Fine," he says. "Crone," he adds in English. He's been waiting to use that.

"What did you say?"

"Nothing."

"You are as bad as your father, speaking English," Yai says. "If I could stand, I'd take the clothes hanger to you. All your hammering and oil splashing and English words will scare the regulars away." But there are no customers left to scare away.

Nam, though, always returns. Her father, an English teacher, likes their *krapao*. It's understood that the fried egg (an extra, typically) is given in exchange for the occasional English lesson. But mostly Pea manages with an illustrated English dictionary, which Ba bought him a couple of years back. Yesterday's new word: "bludgeon." Nam had used it to describe Pea's wooden pestle.

"Policemen have them for clubbing people into mush," she said. "The way you do with papaya." Only Pea doesn't cook with papaya. Doesn't like the texture.

Pea likes to label things in English. They looked up "bludgeon," but the illustration was not quite right, the pestle studded with spikes. The dictionary offered "baton," as well, and "blackjack." He settled for a label written in pencil, now taped around the handle of his pestle. Pea's almost finished labeling his utensil set, all that is left unnamed as yet: tamarind-wood chopping block, metal spatula, wok (*not* a "frying pan"). As for the scent of cooked rice, he doubts he'll ever find an English word.

Ba always said that English is the language of a better place. During his drinking nights Ba yelled in the scraps of English he'd learned as a child serving pork skewers to American soldiers on leave from Vietnam. English, Ba said, is how he became so successful, although, as Pea pointed out, no one in Udon speaks it.

"It doesn't matter. They know," Ba said. And so he always used words like "ketchup" instead of tomato sauce.

"What is this 'chup chup'?" Yai would respond. "Speak Thai!"

"People like the English," Ba said.

"Who likes it?"

"My friends."

"Don't worry about friends—customers."

"Go crazy," Ba said in English, smiling at Pea.

Yai clapped her teeth at him. "It is your food that they like."

It's true. Ba's was the best *pad krapao* on this side of Thaharn Road. In the late morning, Ba attached his stall to the motorbike and they went to the market. Pea went, too, riding between Ba's arms, clutching the mirrors, hair fanned out so he arrived looking like a pop star. They set up shop on the corner.

"Have you ever seen anyone cook *krapao* this fast?" Ba would prompt the newcomers. On two burners, with just his own two hands, Ba could manage three servings in five minutes. With Pea around: *five* servings. Two scoops of rice per foam container, two containers per plastic bag. Hold the containers by the edge, or risk breaking the egg yolk. If they ask, give more rice (unless it's Nam, for whom Pea always spooned extra to begin with). So Pea didn't make it to school every day, but the market is also a classroom, Ba would say. "Right, Pea?"

For instance: "What new did you learn about rice today?"

"If the crop is too fresh, the rice is sticky. It requires less water."

"And the rice today?" Ba said.

"Too sticky."

Ba nodded. "Good rice should be like brothers, close, but not *too* close."

With Pea at school, there would be nobody to run home for another bag of holy basil, a handful of chilies, or to force Yai to take her mud-colored pills ("No, I'm ready to die"). Nobody to lug the steaming container against his leg, thinking, *This is how Ba grew so strong.*

Pea would peel, mince, mash, but Ba didn't want to teach Pea to cook. Once, as Pea reached over a frying egg, some oil spat onto his wrist and left a purple splotch. He looked at Ba's forearms, stained silver with burns.

"Look, I'll grow up to be like you," Pea said, laying his arm alongside Ba's.

Ba hit him on the back of the head, hard enough for Pea to drop his rice spoon.

"Don't say that." He picked up the spoon and handed it to Pea. "You don't want to spend your life cooking in this stall."

But one morning, a few months ago, Pea (always too small) came down to find a stool in front of the burners. Ba's eyes were still red from whiskey.

"We're not going to the market?" Pea asked.

"Not today. Let me see your fingers." Every night Pea coated his fingertips in the hot wax of the spirit house candles. Ba ran a thumb over the shiny skin. He nodded.

"A cook's fingers."

SINCE BA LEFT, Pea has walked down the entrance ramp every evening to look at the motorbike, with its single eye-shaped headlight. Under its neck is an engine that looks like fish gills. It was all blue once, before the paint began flaking into scales. Now it looks more like a relic from a war. The motorbike is too tall for Pea, but, then, so were the burners until Ba found Pea a stool. Now, with customers draining away like water in a basket, Pea knows he has to take the stall to the market to bring food to Ba's buyers. He has to drive the motorbike. Pea rubs the purple scar on his leg from his only attempt to ride the motorbike alone. He remembers how the skin came away sticky where it had touched the exhaust pipe.

Nam returns to their shophouse at dusk, unfolds a table beside the food stall, and does her homework while Pea cooks. Pea and Nam played together as kids, and now Teacher has asked Nam to share her notes with Pea. So Nam tells Pea what he's been missing at school. She takes her notebook out of the plastic bag she's wrapped it up in and writes out all the English words in red.

"Who are you cooking for?" She takes in the empty room.

"Ba says that if you cook, people will come." Pea washes the holy basil in a bowl of water.

When Nam works her shoulder-length hair falls around her. She brushes it behind her ear each time she turns the page. Pea waits for this. The curtain that hides her face, the hand that pulls it away, then the gradual enshrouding as the strands fall back into place.

"Did you know that the largest organ in the body is actually just the skin?" Nam says.

Pea doesn't respond.

Nam flips to the back of her notebook. "The English word of the day is 'stormy,'" she says. "Like a monsoon."

But Pea prefers the funny-sounding ones, words that coo like a dove, like "goon." Or "oyster!" (To Pea, an exclamation of pain.)

Nam sets a bag of fruit on the counter. She takes one out. It's covered in green hairs but the skin itself is a deep red. It's ripe.

"Rambutan. That's the English for it. My father told me."

"Rambutan?" Pea repeats.

"Yes."

Pea loves it: rambutan! Glorious. Sounds like a country, a war cry—nothing like the *ngoh* that Nam and Pea know it as. He digs his nail under the skin and tears it apart. White flesh. Nam bites, chewing around the seed. She hands it to him. There are teeth shapes in the fruit, in the "rambutan." What a language.

A couple comes up from the street to order. The seats are stacked away, so Pea tells them to wait on the bench at the bottom of the ramp. He fires up the burners and Nam leans against the stall to watch.

"You've seen this a hundred times," Pea says.

"Teacher says that people learn through repetition. In school we're doing the same words over again, which means I'm learning a lot. My father says that someday I'll be an English teacher like him." She points at an ant journeying along the rim of the sugar jar. Pea catches it and smears it against his shirt.

"When are you coming back to school?"

Pea slows the pounding in his mortar. "I can learn English by myself. I don't need a teacher." He holds up the pestle, red paste crusting the tip. "Bludgeon." They both laugh.

"Look." Pea lays his utensils out on the counter. Nam touches the labels one at a time, saying the English words aloud ("Spoon. Fork. Cleaver.") until she's standing in front of the burners ("Ignite!"). She grasps the bamboo handle of the wok. Taller than Pea, she doesn't need to use the stool.

He spoons the paste into the oil. She moves out of his way.

"No. Stay." He climbs on the stool. Now they're the same height.

"Let me see those fingers." He hands her the spatula. She grips it at the top, farthest from the heat, like she's holding a skewer.

"Don't be afraid of the fire," he says, repeating what Ba has taught him.

Pea helps her, guiding the spatula with his hand below hers.

"Push, pull, scrape, and fold," Ba had told him. Now he tells Nam.

"It's easier if you say it."

Nam laughs. They repeat it: "Push, pull, scrape, and fold."

"You can smell the garlic," he says.

"Wait for the chili. You'll know its scent in your throat, not your nose," Ba had said, but instead Pea had smelled the whiskey caught in Ba's teeth.

"I smell it," she says.

"Make sure the paste is cooked through," Ba always emphasized. "The paste is everything."

"Now the pork. Wait!" Pea dips two fingers into the oil and presses them into Nam's palm, kneading in an outward circle. He imagines that her skin is smooth, but actually he feels nothing. She grabs a handful of pork and drops it in the wok.

The hiss of frying meat draws Yai from the back room.

"Good evening, Yai." Nam lifts her hands to greet Yai with a *wai*.

"Teacher's daughter," Yai replies curtly. She points at the two people waiting outside. "Have they paid?"

Pea pretends he doesn't hear her.

Yai wheels closer and drums her hand against the counter. "Pea, have they paid?"

"Not yet."

Yai always collects the money when customers take their seats inside, but this couple is waiting beyond the ramp, and Yai's arms are too weak to slow her chair on the decline. Pea wants to see her roll into the street, dash herself against the pavement, wants her to ask for help, as she never does.

"My feet are sore," Yai usually says. "This blouse, it's getting scratchy."

Then she waits until Pea kneels to knead her bunions, young hands on old skin, both callused. Pea has noticed that parts of his own body are aging faster than others. Around his fingernails the flesh is bunched from years of dishwashing with hard yellow soap. Patches of hair are missing on his forearm where he has reached over an open burner. His palms are potato skins: pitted, coarse.

But Pea's skin is nothing like Yai's, he realizes, whenever he peels the blouse from her as she leans up from the wheelchair. Moles pepper her breasts. When Pea changes her cotton pants, he has to work one side at a time, losing his thumbs in the folds at her waist, tugging the elastic away from bruised flesh, down to her thigh on one side, and then the other, towing the fabric in diagonals until he has it at her ankles. Then he takes a hot towel to her, scraping the beads of dirt from under her arms and breasts, from her neck, from the folds of her knees. The bucket of water turning darker as it cools. Yai stares ahead as though none of this has anything to do with her. Not her body, not his hands. She doesn't speak. Pea never touches her underwear; Yai does that herself. When they are finished she wheels herself backward, out of his reach.

Yai glances from Pea to the customers outside.

"I can get the money from them," Nam offers.

Yai ignores Nam. She always does. This is how she handles Nam's relative prosperity.

"Pea, don't forget to take the money," Yai says as she rolls through the shredded plastic curtain into the back room.

Pea and Nam listen to the pork crackle. He lets it sit even though the meat is overcooking by now. He's reminded that Nam doesn't need to be here, that she doesn't *need* to earn her lunch. The red plastic box under the counter holds the shop's money, and it's emptying faster than Pea can fill it. Soon he won't be able to buy fresh pork. Already he has started on the emergency stash of frozen meat.

Nam prepares two containers of rice.

"Did you know that they don't actually eat American fried rice in America?" She holds out the foam boxes. "Teacher said it was invented here, for the soldiers in Vietnam who missed home. That's why they put tomato sauce and hot dog in it."

"I already know that," Pea snaps. "Ba told me before Teacher told you."

"Okay." Nam puts the containers on the counter. "Anyway, I'm going home. It's late."

"Fine."

Pea takes the food down to the couple. Juice from the pork has soaked into the rice.

The man looks at his girlfriend and says something about it being soggy again.

"MY FATHER FOUND one for you," Nam says when she arrives at eleven the next day. "'Smoking hot.' It means really hot. Like your burner. 'Smoking hot.' Isn't that funny?"

Pea writes it down in the back of his order log. He sketches a flame, a wok, the exhaust on a motorbike. His columns of foreign words are stained with pork grease and the smudge of chili.

"You're late, though, I already made it." Pea hands her a container fastened with a rubber band. She isn't actually late; Pea just started the food early, worried that Nam might notice the dwindling portions.

When Pea opened the cooler in the morning, there were only three packets of frozen meat. He thawed one, leaving it out in a bucket on the ramp, like an offering to the morning sun. He watched the bundled lump unfreeze, imagining it as a curled-up animal, eyes squeezed, slowly unfurling in the sun's warmth.

There's enough meat left in the cooler for a day at the market, if Pea can make it there. He'll try tomorrow.

"Too much," Pea says when Nam hands him a bill. The red money box is empty and there's a mere fistful of coins like dregs at the bottom of Yai's apron pouch. "I don't have anything for change."

"Keep it," she says.

"No," Pea says, angrier than he means it to be. "It's not my money."

"Make me two then," Nam says. "I'll wait."

"Who's going to eat it?"

"It doesn't matter."

"It matters." Pea moves away from her. He begins preparing a paste.

"Where's Yai?" Nam asks.

"In the back, sleeping. She's sick." Yai didn't sleep well, made painful noises (*oy, oy, oy*) in the night. But Pea pretended he was asleep. He didn't want to rub balm into her back.

Nam unties the bag of rambutan on the counter. She rips the skin off one and squeezes the whole piece into her mouth.

"It's not even English," Pea says.

"What's not?"

"Rambutan. *Webster's* says the word is Indonesian. It doesn't actually mean anything in English."

"My father says it's English." Nam spits the seed into her palm. "Maybe *Webster's* is wrong."

Pea stares out at the street. Two things are certain: Ba's cooking and *Webster's*.

"It's never wrong."

Only he's not watching the pestle, and it strikes the mortar's edge, cracking the clay. A wedge splits from the bowl and the red paste spills onto the counter.

Pea and Nam stare at the mortar. Pea picks up the piece and slides it into place. He almost can't see the crack, but the clay falls out. He tries again. The broken piece clinks against the metal counter each time.

"It's broken, leave it alone."

"It's not." Pea jams the wedge into place and holds it there. He needs it to stay.

"Just buy a new one," Nam says.

"The paste is everything."

Nam tries to take the piece, but Pea jerks away. He wipes at his eyes and walks to the back room.

"Yai, we need a new one," he cries. "I broke it and now we need a new one. I need money to buy it."

But Pea knows what she'll say; he's heard it before.

"WHAT MONEY? YOU drink away all the money."

"This is the last time," Ba had said.

"You want money, you go and work at the market," Yai told Ba. "There's no money here."

Ba had opened the cabinet. The whiskey was gone (hidden underneath the dictionary in Pea's bedside crate).

"Where is it?" Ba yelled, coming at Yai. "Where did you put it?"

He took the wheelchair by the arms. He leaned over her.

"You drunk. Get away." Yai clutched her bird arms to the pouch on her chest.

Ba grabbed the apron and pulled it. Yai was tugged into a bowing position, the apron's knot dragging the skin of her neck into her hair.

"Let go!"

Ba slammed Yai's wheelchair into the wall. Yai jerked backward and crumpled into her seat.

In the doorway was Pea, watching, the whiskey bottle in his arms.

Ba noticed Pea and took the whiskey away. Yai made gurgling, baby noises. Then Ba struck Pea with the bottle.

PEA'S STANDING IN the doorway clutching the triangle of mortar. He sees Yai slumped over the armrest of her chair.

"Yai!" She's limp as meat when Pea tries to lift her upright.

"Yai, get up, please," he says. "Get up."

He puts his body into her. The skin pulls but Yai hardly moves. Her hairnet slips off, exposing bare patches of skull.

Nam, in a whisper behind him: "I'll call my father. He'll know what to do." Her voice jerks Pea to his feet.

"Father," he mumbles in English. Yai's hairnet is in his fist. He rubs the coarse fabric against his eyes. He backs away from Yai.

"Where are you going?" Nam says, her voice rising. "Pea? Stay here."

But there is no time for the ambulance. It's the lunch hour. Time to fire up the motorbike (ignite!). Pea's going to the market. That's right: Cook and they will come back.

Pea bulls through the curtain. He won't cry. He feels nothing! He kicks the bricks from under the stall's wheels. It rolls at him. Pea throws his weight against it (always too small, too young—not today!). He'll show them.

"I'm sorry, Pea. It's my fault," Ba will say again, like he did that last morning before he disappeared. "I'm so sorry."

Ba had woken to find Pea pinned under the motorbike at 11:15 ("Ba, we're late for the market"), the hot exhaust against his leg, Pea's eye still shut where Ba's bottle had landed the night before.

"I'm sorry."

"Pea, what are you doing?" Nam shouts.

"I need to go." But Ba never said how long.

The stall lumbers onto the ramp. Pea, trailing, sets his heels, slows it. Not enough. A wheel squeaks. He smells hot rubber. The stall is too fast. It bowls down the ramp. Pea runs. His right hand loses hold. The stall drums against the sidewalk, jumps the gutter, leaps off the curb. The utensils leap with it. The mortar strikes the pavement as a hundred brown shells; the wok, caught under a wheel, folds into a crescent as the round chopping block rolls out into the street traffic. Pea catches the pestle. Bludgeon—he waves it. His throat: a rasping, like the bite of chili. The air: wet pork, sugar suspended and shimmering, the bag of fruit exploding beautifully against the glass cabinet. His ears: a foreign language, his own voice yelling.

He's trying but he's too small. Twelve is still too small.

The Tum-Boon Brigade

BENZ, TINTIN & LARA (2014)

The call comes through in a static jabber: "Two trucks. Two dead. Bang Kapi."

The other side of Bangkok, not their territory. Benz lets it go. He holds the radio up to the truck's cabin light. Music squeals as he dials it across frequencies. He beckons the new kid.

"Bring your head over here."

Tintin, slumped in the back seat, lifts a finger in the direction of the radio. "You've got to sing with it." The big man reaches for a high C, raising his hand up with the note and striking an imaginary bell when he hits it. "Only way to tune the red radio."

Another feed comes through, this time of a hostel blaze near Khao San, that dead end of Thai tourism. No reports of casualties yet. Backpackers from neighboring hostels have flocked to photograph the flames. A fire truck is on the street and asking for assistance to keep the crowd back.

The kid asks, "Are we responding?"

"Let one of the other groups take that," Benz says.

Tourists are dangerous; they clog up accident scenes, get run over. They try to help. Also, Benz shies away from fires; burn victims are too delicate. A responder doesn't know where to lay his hands without a shriek, without flesh rubbing off like ripe-fruit peel.

"Good ole Benz," Tintin teases. "Cautious Benz."

Benz lets the kid fiddle with the dial. Occasionally the old box picks up on a signal outside of the volunteer network, a taxi dispatcher maybe, or a crackling *luk thung* song. Once they even caught a sex line. "Guess where my hand is now?" the voice invited, and Tintin shook the back seat with his *hu-hu-hu* laugh.

The kid comes across a temple broadcast and they listen to a spoon-fed monk telling the city what he knows of good, hard work. "*Tum boon,*" the monk tells them. Do good. Earn merit. Karmic rewards carry over into rebirth. Nothing the brigade doesn't know, but Tintin sits up and reframes it for the kid anyway.

"Hear what he said there? See, with our work? Next life I'll be born onto a bed of pearls."

Volunteers, they call themselves, but it's understood among the bookkeepers on high that karmic merit is their pay. They're saving up by saving people. And so it's for this—for the promise of a future reward, either in the afterlife or another life—that the team is parked under a highway, poised around the radio, waiting on misfortune.

The voices drop out. What's left is residue, airwaves recently strummed, distant night chatter.

"How come nobody's calling in?" the kid asks.

Tintin unzips his uniform to the waist. "This isn't *Batman,* kid. Sometimes there's nobody to save." He shrugs his torso out of the yellow jumpsuit. "Heat's making me crazy. Fuckin' mosquitoes in this damn cocoon outfit."

Another dispatch of a double motorbike collision. Two dead and one injured.

"That's us." Benz starts the pickup truck.

Tintin takes the radio and calls in the team's location. He gives the siren a good *whoop* even though theirs is the only vehicle on the street.

THE LAST MAN dies before the team even arrives. Not much to do, then, but hammock the bodies in cotton and haul them on out. A policeman writes the accident report as the rains begin.

Benz herds a group of onlookers off the scene. He's lining up orange cones when he's presented a baby—a pink bundle in her mother's arms—for his obligatory caress and blessing.

When he touches the girl she takes hold of his finger, brings him down to her level. "Hello there," he says. In response she pats him between the eyes—there, there—and Benz steps backward onto the wet road, washed red and blue by siren lights, feeling like he's been cleansed. He's reminded that even his first real lover, a country-raised girl nursed on ghost lore, turned away from his touch on the nights he'd handled the dead. It didn't matter that he was doing a good thing. "It's the bad that carries through." That lover had gestured then at his fingertips. "It comes through touch."

In the beginning collection and cremation had been their only function, but after watching accident victims die waiting for ambulances, the volunteers started trucking the injured to hospitals themselves, earning a small commission and no small credibility among the families of survivors. Mothers no longer warned their children away from yellow-and-green uniforms. Volunteers could make a living wage just off donations.

For four years Benz has worked the circuit, stood shoulder to shoulder with the bereaved, helping identify those who'd been lost. "Did he have these chest tattoos?" or "Do you recognize this ring?" After four years, Benz has stopped revisiting the wrecks in his sleep, stopped counting the unclaimed (slum orphans, migrant laborers, gutter drunks). Still, he recalls his first night as a volunteer, how a street boy had watched him load a gunshot victim into the pickup. The boy raised his finger like a pistol trained on Benz. "You'll put someone's eye out with that," Benz joked. The boy leaned his head to sight along his arm: "Bang."

Benz swings down the pickup's tailgate and lifts the hatch door. The truck has an enclosed bed, like a hearse, windows splotchy where the film has peeled.

"Kid, help Tintin out." Benz gestures at a corpse.

The kid takes the foot end.

Benz finds the man who called in the crash, a motorbike taxi driver in an orange vest. The volunteers rely on the public to call in accidents over the red radio network.

The man's eyes are unresponsive. He pulls a radio from his vest pocket, presses and releases the call button. "That's the third I've seen in a month. Does that mean I'm unlucky, or lucky it's not me?"

"Next time you call me directly, okay?" Benz holds out a phone number and some money, but the man's gaze drags back up the road to where other taxi drivers are taking charge. They reroute traffic, heap motorcycle debris, and sluice soapy water over the road. Benz walks through the suds to his truck. It's riding low. He tests the tire pressure with his boot. Tintin's sitting on the supplies cooler, explaining to the kid, "We all have things that sustain us." The boy stares as Tintin crumbles a morphine pill over sweet green custard spooned from a tub. Tintin stands to put the tub back in the cooler behind the rubbing alcohol.

Tintin licks the spoon clean. "The thing you'll find, a few months, maybe a year in, is that you need to pick your addiction. You could be a karma junkie." Tintin points his spoon at a taxi driver bowing his head, collecting donations for the victims' families. The Buddha pendants clustered at the man's throat swing and clatter. "Or maybe you're like Benz here, superhero syndrome," he says. "Death addict."

"And you are . . ." the kid says, glancing back at the spoon.

Tintin wipes crusted custard from the corner of his mouth. He grins. "Fuckin' high."

AT TWO IN the morning the clubs spit up drunks, who take to the wet roads. The team is parked at the end of a queue of taxis. The downpour chases people under street awnings, sends them home early, turns this party night sleepy.

The taxi driver ahead of them taps his impatience on a brake pedal, pulsing that red glow right into their cabin, where it strikes

Tintin's blinking, haggard face. Five years as a volunteer has actually worn the big man thin. From the back seat comes the sleepy knock of the kid's head against a window. Benz is in the driver's seat looking at his phone.

"What time do we finish?" the kid asks, shifting in the back.

Benz looks at him in the rearview. "Right now."

"So what are we waiting for?"

The question sits between them. "Lara," Tintin says. "The last rescue call. The one that only goes out to Benz."

"Who's that?"

"Someone he found playing cards," Tintin says.

Lara had been in the habit of gambling herself deep. Benz saved her.

"Saved me?" Lara had laughed. "Saved me for yourself."

"Looks like your *farang* fling isn't calling tonight," Tintin says.

Benz checks his phone again. "We'll give it another ten."

Once a week Lara calls Benz to find her, inevitably red with alcohol, leaving a nightclub with a man, telling him, "Your apartment can come afterwards. First, though: Dancing makes me hungry, huh?" And so she sits him at a noodle stall. She's a sloppy eater, which looks to some men like the promise of easy sex. Drugs make her teeth gnash, mill the rice noodle. She sends her location to Benz: *Find me.* He's there before the broth turns cold, taking her away in the pickup. The siren at least deters men from chasing her, its bleat carrying the pitch of madness.

"Look at your chewed lips," he'll tell her. Always, Benz asks her what she's been taking.

"Oh, I don't know, a little thing, a half holiday." She'll chase this with a full laugh. "Or maybe it was more."

"Answer me properly." But when Benz gets angry Lara climbs into the back, takes turns at the spoon and custard with Tintin. On those nights, she's blue by the time they're back in his apartment. But what can he do, draw out the poison with his lips? He puts her to bed, hates the smell of alcohol, sleeps on the floor.

"Home time, okay?" Tintin says, squeezing Benz's shoulder. "Give it up."

Benz drives the crew to their apartments and then parks at his place. He brings a can of cold coffee into the shower and takes the bristle brush to his fingernails, a habit from his construction days.

On the toilet tank the red radio is giving out a low drone, the expectant humming of Bangkok at night. He opens the shower window. Where does it come from, the city's grey music? He once thought it was the echoes of thrumming air conditioners, or truck thunder from the highways, though it seems now to come from the emptiness itself.

MOST VOLUNTEERS HAVE day jobs. For years Benz cut hair, easy work he floated in and out on until Tintin lured him into the brigade. They were once boys together, running small crimes to pay off the orphanage that raised them and the corrupt police from a local outfit. And while they'd long since been released from those debts, Benz still felt an obligation to his old friend, the need to keep an eye on him. Tintin has never been in it for the distant karmic payout; he wants the hit now.

It's late afternoon when Benz arrives at the Catholic church listed in the funeral announcement. Hearing the requiem, he's drawn to the open doors, where a Filipino man says something in English. When Benz doesn't respond, the man tries again in Thai.

"Were you a friend?"

No, but Benz had been the one to carry the body from a wreck.

The casket is closed. As he enters, the music changes and the mourners start to sing. It must be a Christian song, nothing Benz has heard in those crowded, low Chinese temples, where the air is dark and choked with incense. Here the eaves catch the music, not a lament so much as a marching tune, as if to establish a pace for life after death. Still, grief undresses the faces around him. He tries to feel the loss of the man in the box as the song rises to swallow the sobbing that has burst from a woman in the front pew.

As he leaves the church the brigade's mantra comes to him. *You can't save them all.* But Benz believes in sheer willpower, and it's by will that he keeps Lara close, staving off the fear that she'll leave him. That she'll be taken from him. He can't sleep. He's taken to keeping the red radio clipped on his belt, and when a week goes by that he doesn't hear from her, he'll spend the morning trolling frequencies, wondering if the next body dredged up will be hers.

Rama IV Road. One woman.

He's seen them all. Motorbike deaths. Gunshot. He's seen falls and jumps. People choke; they poison themselves. He knows heart failure. He's seen bloated corpses blue with drugs. And when his imagination has been stretched to its boundaries, he's drawn across town to a familiar metal door painted sea green.

Palm on the green door, Benz checks his watch. Still hours until the brigade's starting time. The door opens to a tin-can elevator. Inside, a fan sputters in its ceiling and through its walls Benz can hear the big band tuning up. The elevator door slides open again and he steps into the middle of a rehearsal.

"There aren't many respectable jobs for singers in this country," Lara had told him. She was raised singing jazz standards, her father's favorites, until he left for a life back in his American hometown. She started a marketing degree at a university in Bangkok, but a childhood as a songbird had spoiled her. She was meant to be a star. Which is how she ended up in graduate school at an American conservatory, where her mother sent her to be classically trained. By the time Benz met her, Lara had dropped out of that, too, and returned to Bangkok. A mezzo singing background in hotel lobbies. The big band, her only chance to be loud.

The band practices in an abandoned office space, too small for all that brass, but they seem to have achieved a sort of harmony, the instruments aligned to fit the space. They have given up telling Benz that he's not welcome. And so he edges around the wall to the front of the building and slides open a filmed window. Outside, on the cement ledge, Lara is studying a score.

"You can't be here, all right?" Lara says without looking up. "I told you to stop coming here."

"I wanted to make sure you're all right."

"Why *wouldn't* I be? I'm fine."

She has to climb past him to get back in. Her dress crawls up her leg.

"I used to see you more." He squats beside her stool and lays his hand on her knee. She tenses. He takes the hand back.

"What are you guys playing today?" He reads the title. "I don't know it."

"Of course not."

The pleasantly discordant warm-up begins with the solemn trombones, which are soon joined by the showier trumpets and saxophones. By the time the two clarinetists start up, Benz can hardly hear Lara. She has to repeat herself.

"I need you to leave before my part, okay?" She looks at him. "Please."

He has heard her sing only once, that first time he brought her to his apartment, her eyes washed out from moonshine. She'd slid off her clothes while watching him, amused, and it was he who'd felt undressed as she gave him a demonstration—feet together, hands together—standing at the foot of his mattress, which might have been a concert hall for the way she sang before it.

Seeing his surprise, she climbed back into bed. "This," she said, patting her voice box. "Nobody expects this. I mostly keep it to myself."

He had touched her throat, imagined a warm engine winding down.

"You're not like the boys I've known," she said.

"No."

"It wasn't a question."

"WE USED TO be ashamed of wearing the yellow." Tintin leans on the locker-room door as he talks to the kid. "To most people, we were worse than corpses. You know? Cursed. But when we started carrying survivors instead, the stories became about the living. And now look at us."

The kid stands before a mirror straightening the collar on his new uniform. Beside him Tintin spritzes on cologne.

"Here." Tintin dabs two fingers behind the kid's uniform collar. "Spray there."

They leave the changing rooms by the entrance to the volunteer headquarters, passing the shrine where laypeople come to take their share of the karmic merit.

"Good work and bad work," Benz says as they pass the people waiting to donate money for coffins for the unclaimed. "*Boon*, that's all you take with you when you die. So you better hope it measures up."

Tintin pats the truck's rickety hood for luck. He sighs.

Once they had American-fire-truck dreams—red and roaring. Not the trundle of their own wagon, a beat-up blue Toyota passed on to them by a grateful family. It used to be that the team set aside some of their donation money, paid it back to the pickup. They bought stretchers and neck braces, fitted two side benches along the enclosed bed. They mounted a siren and lights on the roof. But that team had been younger. Of the original troupe only Benz and Tintin remain, and they both feel they've given too much to this work already. The truck's a long haul from healthy by now. They can hear that it's failing: the death rattle of fluids leaking from old drum brakes, the ignition's persistent cough.

Now, in the middle of traffic, the siren and lights wink out.

"Junk. Fucking junk." Tintin punches the roof. "Who wired this? Oh, *I* did—ha! It's like steering fuckin' scrap metal." He switches to the horn but the cars close in on what little room they'd given the emergency vehicle.

By the time they arrive at the accident the dispatchers have gone quiet. Around an overturned minivan is a stadium of volunteers from a rival organization. A camera's flash hits the scene, shimmers on the tongue of windshield that's being wrenched from the van's face.

Beyond is the other team's ambulance, a white machine with blue stripes across the side.

Tintin tries to break through the crowd, but the volunteers push him away.

"Back off. This one's ours."

He bulls through, though, on his second try, and Benz has to follow. Two men with headlamps are sawing the last victim out of the driver's seat, the man's legs pinned under shredded metal and engine. He's unconscious, blood like a spray of feathers covering his shirt. The volunteers hold flashlights; one of them siphons the van's gasoline.

The man with the pump looks up at Tintin—"Get out of here"— and when Tintin doesn't move the man turns the hose and jets a stream of gasoline right onto Tintin's shoes. The others laugh.

Tintin stares down at his feet, at the men surrounding them.

"Tintin," Benz warns.

The man with the hose stops pumping now and straightens. "Do the smart thing, asshole. Get back in your spit cup over there and drive on home."

Benz takes Tintin's arm, has to remind him why they're here. "The work's basically done."

The scream of a hacksaw against metal follows them to the pickup. Tintin kicks off his soaked shoes and stuffs his socks into them. He starts the engine but lets the truck roll past the rival team.

"Hold the wheel."

Before Benz can respond Tintin has set fire to his shoes. Heat and the stink of gasoline flare in the cabin and Tintin hurls the shoes against the side of the white ambulance. The flaming bundle splatters the van's door.

Jerking the truck around emergency cones, Tintin steers them into oncoming traffic.

"Easy!" Benz says.

"Fuck off." Tintin clicks the turn signals back and forth, snaps the high beams on a jittery Volkswagen, and accelerates through a red light.

Benz looks out the back window. "Calm down. You're freaking the kid out back there. They're not even chasing us. Just pull over and park somewhere."

They stop beside some food vendors and Benz and the kid climb out, leaving Tintin in the driver's seat.

"You okay?" Benz says. He orders the kid some skewers and they sit down on the curb to eat.

"See, nobody pays us to bring in bodies," Benz explains. "But this new government insurance will pay patient bills, so hospitals will pay for patients. That's what gets Tintin fired up. It's commission. Building *boon* requires—"

"Building *boon*," Tintin says, joining them, "would've scored us a fucking castle by now but for all these new kids in our territory." The big man has cushioned his mood with a fix. "Six. Right there. Six *alive*."

"Enough." Benz places a pork skewer in Tintin's hand.

Tintin points at the kid with his skewer. "How old are you?"

"Seventeen."

"Yeah, keep eating. We could use young ones like you. How'd you end up in this, anyway?"

"My mother. I never did well around religion. When I was ten I got burned by someone carrying their incense sticks low. Stuck me in the cheek, right?" He turns his face to display a scatter of scars Benz had assumed was acne. "Then last year she tried monkhood on me."

"Oh yeah, I know that monkhood racket." Tintin's fingers run imaginary clippers over his head.

"She wanted me to take the three months as a novice—you know, for her. So she'd be okay in heaven. But I couldn't make it work. Just couldn't sit still. Missed the city, I don't know . . . So now this."

"If I've learned anything about our job," Benz says, "it's that it accepts all who are willing to give themselves."

"Even movie stars are volunteering," Tintin says. "But murderers or motherfuckers, it really doesn't matter. All that matters is to do good work. That's where the *boon* comes from."

Tintin tosses his skewer into a drain, adjusts the badge on his uniform, and stands to pay the vendor. The vendor tells Tintin that today the food's on him. No problem.

Tintin shrugs and takes another skewer from the grill. "Here, kid. Better than being a monk, right? Free food *and* you can touch a woman."

A SUNDAY EVENING. He sends her a text. *Do you want to ride with us tonight?* It's all she's asked him these last weeks and he's said no until tonight.

Immediately: *A night with the brigade?*
That's right.
Cool, come find me.

HEADLIGHTS PASS THE accident—another motorbike, another boy—but seem to bask upon Lara, crouched in black tights beside the body.

"Put your fingers here. Behind the jaw. Feel the pulse?"

"He's dead," Lara says. When Benz confirms it, she draws back, crosses her arms and lets Benz wrap the body.

"I've never touched a corpse before," she says.

"But you wanted to, didn't you? We pretend we don't keep it into adulthood. That child's curiosity. We all resist it. But . . ."

She surprises him with a kiss he doesn't return, the sensation of a cooling body still haunting the fingertips he used to check for a pulse.

"Disgusting." Tintin comes around the truck with the custard tub cradled in his arm. He points the spoon at Lara. "You shouldn't be here," he slurs. "Isn't there a rule against this, Benz?"

"What rule?" Benz says.

"I wanted to experience it," Lara says. "What you guys do."

Tintin's smile is sleepy but conspiratorial. "So you can go back and tell your people how fun it was? A night ride with the corpse carriers."

"What's wrong with *that*?"

"Chase thrills too long," Benz says, "and you'll end up like Tintin, who thinks only about today. Doesn't see consequences." Benz pinches the end of the spoon and pulls until the big man's arm is fully stretched out. Tintin doesn't let go. "See? Look at his arm shake. And the color in his skin. You want to be like him?"

"Fuck off." Tintin lets his arm drop. "We're taking her home."

"Like hell you are," she says with that brash American confidence passed down through her father. "I'm just getting started, all right? I'm running with the *tum-boon* brigade tonight. I was promised three years of merit accumulation."

Benz tries again to take the spoon from Tintin, who contemplates the scar on his clenched fist, as if the hand belongs to someone else. Tintin slowly releases his grip on the spoon. He turns to Lara and laughs. "You're right, Benz. She *is* like me."

A WOMAN IS hunched against a guardrail clutching the broken post of a highway marker. The marker's reflective strip catches their headlights and she flinches.

"My husband's under the car," she tells them, gesturing at the wreck up the road. "No—the front one, up there."

"Kid," Benz says, "get Tintin and the stretcher over there."

"Tintin's asleep," the kid says, and jogs up to the front car to search for the victims.

"The tire blew and he'd just pulled over to fix it." The woman puzzles over the wooden post in her hands, drops it. "Then the other car hit us. The other people are alive. I checked."

When Benz asks her if she's hurt she gestures at her side, from which is protruding a splinter of wood painted white as bone.

"I fell on a post."

"Oh, fuck," Lara says.

"Okay, don't move that," Benz says.

"I'm fine." The woman rests her hand on the splinter. "See, I'm fine. I'm going to sit in your truck. Girl, help me up, would you?"

Lara and Benz help her into the back of the pickup, get her sitting on the bench with a bandage holding the wood in place before Benz goes to wake Tintin.

Benz opens the passenger door and shakes Tintin by the shoulder. "Hey, we need your help with the stretcher. Hey? Tintin?"

Tintin grasps the driver's seat and hauls himself upright. "Helluva night, huh? Where's Lara? She having fun?"

"We need your help," Benz says.

"Sure. I can do that," Tintin says. He pats Benz's hand and lays back down.

Benz leaves Tintin and takes the stretcher over to the wreck.

"These two are alive," the kid says, gesturing at the men he's dragged out from the crash and laid side by side.

"What about her husband?" Benz asks. He can see the man still trapped beneath a car.

"Dead."

They carry one of the men back, securing the stretcher to the truck bed with clips.

"You." The woman pats the man familiarly. His face ruined, bones breaking the skin. "I told you, didn't I?"

"That's not your husband," Lara tells her.

"You hear me? I *told* you not to drive this car into the city. We should have waited for Mogh to bring the good car home."

Lara says once more, louder this time, "That's not your husband."

Headlights cut through the window.

"Police?" the kid asks.

"No. Another team. There's still a man out on the road," Benz says, and immediately Tintin sits up.

"Out of my way," he bellows, clambering out of the back seat.

Benz takes the driver's seat and starts the engine. "Leave him to them!" he shouts to Tintin. "Close it up. Let's go."

"Mogh will be home tomorrow," the woman is saying. "Just stay here."

The other team pulls parallel with the accident. The kid and Lara climb inside the pickup, but Tintin still holds the passenger door wide.

"It's that same goddamn team. From the other night. Little shits."

"Let's go, Tintin, all right? Leave it."

Tintin reaches across Benz, switches on the siren, and pumps the horn as if to frighten a pack of strays. He crouches to feel under the passenger seat. When he straightens, he's holding a gun.

Nobody speaks.

"Benz." Tintin points down the road at the remaining injured man. "That man is *ours*."

Benz switches off the engine. Behind the night's grey sound he can already hear the accident report: *Gunshot wounds. Three volunteers shot dead.*

"What's gonna happen next time that group catches up with us?" Benz says. "Huh? You're not thinking here."

"I'm protecting our territory is what."

"You're putting us in *danger*." Benz turns to look at the kid and Lara, who's got blood streaking her forearms. "Look, everyone's terrified, okay?"

Tintin squints at the two in the back.

Lara nods at Tintin's hand. "That's, like, an awfully real gun."

The cabin is black and hot. Tintin claps the weapon between his palms. "It's just to scare them off."

Benz tightens his hold on the wheel. "We're leaving."

"Yeah, well—without me, then." Tintin steps out, leaving the door wide. He walks unsteadily along the yellow highway line back to the crash.

Lara leans forward from the back seat: "Should we try and help him?"

Benz looks through the windshield as if at a television screen. He rolls up his window. But even through the glass he can hear Tintin confronting the men. They have the remaining victim on a stretcher now, which they release to form a circle around the big man accosting them.

Tintin looks back at Benz in the truck. He takes the pistol from his pocket, levels it at one of the men and gestures for them all to move back to the van.

"Oh shit," Lara whispers.

Benz watches Tintin raise the gun and fire a shot above the men's heads, reigniting the woman's chattering behind him.

Crack.

"You hear me?" the woman cries, slapping the unconscious man. *Crack.* Benz closes his eyes and imagines—*crack-crack-crack*—the smack of shredded tire rubber against the road as the husband slowed toward the shoulder. Impact. *Crack.* The blast of glass and metal as the second car struck theirs.

When Benz opens his eyes, Tintin has the gun pointed at the withdrawing red lights of the other team's van. Benz starts the engine.

"You can't just leave him out here," Lara says.

"He has to learn." Benz drives them right past Tintin, who stands beside the man on the stretcher and watches them leave.

Benz turns the siren on, and in the back the woman's head snaps up.

"You!" she cries. "This is all *your* fault."

I'T'S TWO WEEKS later when Benz parks across from a nightclub.
Benz didn't tell the kid what he's known those past two weeks. Not
after each night's shift, as they waited in empty wards while their
commission was counted out; or when they hosed down the truck
bed, flushing the night's stains back onto the streets; or when the kid
fumbled his last goodbye *wai* tonight, walking backward from the
truck.

But Benz wasn't surprised when the call came for him last night.
Over the red radio: one of ours.

He arrived first to the old apartment building, lights still blown
out after a power surge. Led into a dark back room by Tintin's roommates, each bearing a flashlight, he stopped for a moment on the
threshold, headlamp roving, eyes adjusting, desperately wanting to
believe that he was not about to find a body.

And although Benz knew as soon as he touched Tintin, he never-
theless took out the stethoscope, ignoring an instinct that comes
from years of handling the dead (*it comes through touch*). He moved
the stethoscope from wrist to chest to neck. The housemates already
knew what Benz would not announce and turned off their own
lights, prematurely veiling the body, leaving only Benz's headlamp
drawing a white circle on Tintin's chest, the point Benz drove his
hands into. He broke his friend's ribs before the sternum yielded to
his compressions. The heart, though, never did.

What Benz has known these past two weeks he says alone now in
the truck cabin: "I let him die." An electric fan clipped to the rearview blows the chemical sweat off his skin. He has a bottle clamped
between his boots. He drinks and coughs up the rum.

He's parked across from the club, and his impulse when Lara finally steps through the doors is to go to her. He notices the trail of
cigarette smoke. She's promised to quit—it ages her voice.

Why has he come? A need to see the wreck he's made? When he
looks out again Lara's eyes meet his. She separates from the group and

crosses over to him, the motorbikes on the street making way. He feels the collision of her presence before she even reaches him.

She knocks on the window. He rolls it down. "I'd recognize this junker anywhere. You were parked outside my house on Tuesday, too, huh?"

He turns off the engine. "I came to find you."

"Where are your boys?"

"Gone."

She looks past him at the empty seats. "What do you want?"

He says he wants to take her home. And why is she out on a Thursday anyway? Shouldn't she be studying for the conservatory entrance exam? She promised she would apply.

"You always know what's good for me don't you, Mercedes Benz?" Lara says. "Your parents sure had big ambitions with that nickname, didn't they? But I know you. Eager to watch, slow to live. Benz. Should've gone for something more like Tuk-Tuk. *That,* you could have lived up to that."

"I want to take you home," he says, reaching for the door, but she leans her weight against it.

"No, don't get out. You stay in there."

Trapped in his deep seat, Benz feels like a child. "Stand back," he says.

"No, all right? Look, I didn't call you. And why are you spying on me?"

"I was driving through. I don't know—I just wanted to see if you needed me."

She thumps the truck. "*Stop* it. Okay? I'm not gonna be another casualty on your roll call."

He opens the door.

She takes a step back, watches him step out, dares him to come after her.

Another step backward. She hesitates. "Are you drunk?"

"No."

"Like hell. You can't even stand. What the hell happened?"

A man comes toward them, one of her friends, Benz realizes, seeing the others watching from the sidewalk. He doesn't need to turn to the battered pickup to know that he's embarrassing her.

The man says something to Lara. She shakes her head, and in a voice loud enough that all her friends can hear, says to Benz, "Why are you here?"

Already she's turning from him.

He picks at his badge. "You used to call me for help, remember?"

THE KID DOESN'T answer his calls. Benz has to go alone to see his friend fired up in the crematorium. The ceremony has nothing on a Filipino funeral, no rising voices, and it is Lara, not Tintin, that Benz thinks of as smoke funnels out through the smokestack. He leaves before the ashes even come out. Doesn't want it marking his hands.

He goes to the sea-green door, its elevator beyond, and stands there jamming the button, wanting to rise, even as he knows he won't find Lara up there. He looks into the ceiling fan, its shape the same as the one at the crematory, and he thinks that the only difference between Tintin and himself is now and later: Everyone dies, right? But will every soul rise to the same place? As if responding to the question, the elevator shudders to life and the big band's music descends and envelops Benz, who, sleepless and coming down from the morphine tablet he chewed during the cremation, hears Tintin's brassy voice lifting to the call of the radio. *You've got to sing with it.*

Benz takes the transceiver from his belt. He presses the call button and opens the volunteer airwaves to a eulogy worthy of Tintin: music delivered through an elevator quivering on a frayed cable, resonating in a way only an instrument on its last string can. To this requiem, Benz pictures Tintin on the brink—black room, white powder, a flame playing along the needle.

Lara may be listening, and if she is, she'll know he is reaching out.

Volunteers across the city will be tuning in—others like him, briga-
diers, first responders, clustered around radios under highways, on
street corners, in parking lots, finally able to hear what's behind the
static: a confirmation of their toil, the ovation they have been listening for. This is their rallying anthem, Tintin's eulogy, and it calls them
to work. *Tum boon,* it sings. *Do good. Save yourselves.*

Acknowledgments

Rob McQuilkin and Max Moorhead.

Marie Pantojan, Jocelyn Kiker, and the Random House team.

Art Omi, the Bread Loaf Writers' Conference, Kundiman, MacDowell, and the Tin House Summer Workshop.

Meakin Armstrong, Claire Boyle, Tobias Carroll, Lucy Diver, Brian Lin, David Lynn, Megha Majumdar, Rebecca Markovits, Ladette Randolph, and Alexandra Watson.

Robert Cohen, Deborah Eisenberg, and Kathryn Kramer.

C. Pam Zhang.

Jesse Bennett, Anna Chitman, Andrew Chong, Enda Eames, Denise Hartwig, Meng Jin, Drew Johnson, Sanaë Lemoine, Josh Mak, Aseem Mulji, Ploi Pirapokin, Belal Rafiq, Kartik Raju, Nat Rudarakanchana, Kevin Tien, Madura Watanagase, and James Yu.

Mailee Osten-Tan.

Suze, Mom, and Dad.

ABOUT THE AUTHOR

MAI NARDONE is a Thai and American writer whose work has appeared in *American Short Fiction, Granta, McSweeney's Quarterly, Ploughshares,* and elsewhere. He lives in Bangkok. *Welcome Me to the Kingdom* is his first book.

ABOUT THE TYPE

This book was set in Garamond, a typeface originally designed by the Parisian type cutter Claude Garamond (c. 1500–61). This version of Garamond was modeled on a 1592 specimen sheet from the Egenolff-Berner foundry, which was produced from types assumed to have been brought to Frankfurt by the punch cutter Jacques Sabon (c. 1520–80).

Claude Garamond's distinguished romans and italics first appeared in *Opera Ciceronis* in 1543–44. The Garamond types are clear, open, and elegant.